MAIGRET HESITATES

and

MAIGRET TAKES THE WATERS

Also by
SIMENON

★

MAIGRET HESITATES

and

MAIGRET TAKES THE WATERS

*

SIMENON

THE
COMPANION BOOK CLUB
LONDON AND SYDNEY

This edition, published in 1971 by
The Hamlyn Publishing Group Ltd.,
is issued by arrangement with
Hamish Hamilton Ltd.

*Made and printed in Great Britain
for the Companion Book Club
by Odhams (Watford) Ltd.*
SBN/S. 600771342
SBN/D. 600871347
6.71

CONTENTS

*

MAIGRET
HESITATES

★

*Translated
from the French by*
LYN MOIR

CHAPTER ONE

'HELLO, JANVIER.'

'Good morning, chief.'

'Good morning, Lucas. Good morning, Lapointe . . .'

Maigret couldn't keep back a smile as he reached the latter. Not only because young Lapointe was wearing a slim-fitting new suit, pale grey with tiny flecks of red. Everyone was smiling that morning, in the streets, in the buses, in the shops.

The day before had been a grey and windy Sunday, with wintry squalls of rain, and suddenly, although it was only March 4, they had wakened to find it was spring.

The sun was still a bit sharp, certainly, and the blue sky brittle, but there was a gaiety in the air, in the eyes of the passers-by, a sort of complicity in the *joie de vivre* and in recognizing anew the delicious smells of Paris in the morning.

Maigret had come out without a coat and had walked a good part of the way. As soon as he had entered the office he had opened the window. The Seine had changed colour too, the red lines on the funnels of the tugs were brighter, the barges like new again.

He had opened the door of the inspectors' office.

'Are you coming in, boys?'

It was what they called the 'little briefing,' in contrast to the real briefing which got all the divisional superintendents together with the big chief. Maigret called his closest associates together.

'Did you have a good day yesterday?' he asked Janvier.

'We took the children to my mother-in-law's, at Vaucresson.'

Lapointe, uncomfortable in his new suit which was a little too summery, kept in the background.

9

Maigret sat down at his desk, filled a pipe and began to go through his mail.

'That's for you, Lucas. It's about the Lebourg case.'

He held some other papers out to Lapointe.

'Take these to the Public Prosecutor's Office.'

You couldn't say there was foliage yet, but there was just a touch of pale green on the trees along the quay.

There was no big case on at the moment, none of those cases which filled the corridors of the Police Judiciaire with journalists and photographers and which provoked peremptory telephone calls from high places. Only ordinary things. Cases to be followed up. . . .

'A madman, or a madwoman,' he pronounced as he picked up an envelope on which his name and the address of the Quai des Orfèvres were written in block capitals.

The envelope was white, of good quality. The stamp was franked with the postmark of the post office in the Rue de Miromesnil. What struck the Superintendent first, on pulling the letter out, was the paper, a thick, crackly vellum of an unusual shape. Someone must have cut off an engraved letterhead, and this task had been done with care, using a ruler and a very sharp knife.

The text of the letter, like the address, was in very regular block capitals.

'Perhaps not such a madman,' he growled.

'I do not know you personally, but what I have read of your investigations and of your attitude to criminals gives me confidence. This letter will astonish you. Do not throw it into the waste-paper basket too quickly. It is not a joke, nor is it the work of a maniac.

'You know better than I do that the truth is not always credible. A murder will be committed shortly, certainly within a few days. Perhaps by someone known to me, perhaps by me myself.

'I am not writing to you so that the murder will not take place. It is in a way inevitable. But when it happens I would like you to know.

'If you take me seriously, please put the following advertisement in the personal column of the *Figaro* or the *Monde*: "K.R. I am waiting for a second letter."

'I do not know if I shall write it. I am very worried. Certain decisions are hard to take.

'I may perhaps see you one day, in your office, but then we shall be on opposite sides of the fence.

'Yours faithfully.'

He wasn't smiling any more. Frowning, he let his glance pass over the sheet of paper, then looked at his associates.

'No, I don't think it's a madman,' he repeated. 'Listen.'

He read it to them, slowly, emphasising certain words. He had had letters of this kind before, but most of the time the language was less well-chosen and usually had certain phrases underlined. They were often written in red or green ink and many of them had spelling mistakes.

The hand had not trembled here. The strokes were firm, with no flourishes or erasures.

He held the paper up to the light and read the watermark: Morvan Vellum.

He got hundreds of anonymous letters every year. With very rare exceptions, they were written on cheap paper sold at any corner store, and sometimes the words were cut out of newspapers.

'No specific threat . . .' he murmured. 'A sense of hopeless distress . . . *Le Figaro* and *Le Monde*, two daily papers read largely by the intellectual bourgeoisie . . .'

He looked at all three men again.

'Will you see to it, Lapointe? The first thing to do is to get in touch with the paper manufacturer, who must be somewhere in the Morvan.'

'Right, chief.'

That was the beginning of a case which was going to give Maigret more worries than many front-page crimes.

'Put the advertisement in.'

'In the *Figaro*?'

'In both papers.'

A bell rang for the briefing, the real one, and Maigret, file in hand, went to the director's office. Here too the open window was letting the sounds of the city steal in. One of the superintendents was sporting a sprig of mimosa in his button-hole and he felt obliged to explain:

'They're selling them in the street for some charity. . . .'

Maigret did not mention the letter. His pipe was good. He watched the faces of his colleagues lazily as they set out the details of their cases in turn, and he made a mental calculation of the number of times he had been present at the same ceremony. Thousands.

But many more times than that he had envied the divisional superintendent who had been his chief, as he went every morning to the holy of holies. Mustn't it be wonderful to be Chief of the Crime Squad? He hadn't dared to dream of that then, no more than Lapointe or Janvier or even Lucas did now.

It had happened all the same and, after so many years, he didn't even think about it any more, except on a morning like this, when the air smelled sweet and when, instead of swearing at the roar of the buses, people smiled.

When he got back to office half an hour later, he was surprised to find Lapointe there, standing in front of the window. His fashionable suit made him look thinner, taller, much younger. Twenty years before, a detective-inspector wouldn't have been allowed to dress like that.

'That was almost too easy, chief.'

'You found who makes the paper?'

'Géron and Sons, who have had the Morvan Paper Mills at Autun for three or four generations. It's not a factory—it's all done by craftsmen. The paper is hand-made, whether it's for de luxe editions, usually books of poems, it seems, or for writing paper. The Gérons have no more than ten people working there. From what I was told, there are still a few paper-mills like that in the region.'

'Did you get the name of their agent in Paris?'

'They don't have an agent. They work directly with art publishers and with two stationers, one in the Rue du

Faubourg-Saint-Honoré, the other in the Avenue de l'Opera.'

'Isn't that right at the top of the Rue du Faubourg-Saint-Honoré, on the left?'

'I think so, from the address. . . . The Papeterie Roman.'

Maigret knew it because he had often stopped in front of the window. There were invitations there, and visiting cards, and one could read names there that one doesn't usually come across:

> The Comte and Comtesse de Vaudry
> have the honour to . . .
> The Baronne de Grand-Lussac
> has pleasure in announcing . . .

Princes and dukes, real or not—one wondered if such people still existed. They invited each other to dinner, to shoots, to bridge parties, they announced the marriage of their daughters or the birth of a child, all on sumptuous paper.

In the other window one could admire desk-blotters with armorial bearings, engagement books bound in morocco.

'You'd better go and see them.'

'Roman?'

'I think it's the more likely district.'

The shop in the Avenue de l'Opéra had a quality trade, but it also sold fountain pens and ordinary stationery.

'On my way, chief.'

Lucky man! Maigret watched him go like a schoolboy watching one of his friends sent on an errand by the teacher. He had only the usual drudgery to do, paperwork, always paperwork, quite devoid of interest, for a magistrate who would file it without reading it because the case was closed.

The smoke from his pipe began to turn the air blue and a light breeze came in off the Seine, making the papers flutter. By eleven o'clock Lapointe, full of high spirits, bursting with life, came into the office.

'It's still too easy.'

'What do you mean?'

'Anyone would think he'd chosen that paper on purpose. By the way, the Papeterie Roman isn't owned by Monsieur Roman any more—he died ten years ago—but by a Madame

13

Laubier, a widow in her fifties. She would hardly let me come away. . . . She hasn't ordered any paper of that quality for five years—no one was buying it. It's not only too expensive, it doesn't take typing well.

'She still had three customers for it. One of them died last year, a count with a château in Normandy and a racing-stable. His widow lives in Cannes and has never ordered any writing paper. There was also an embassy, but when the ambassador was recalled, the new one ordered a different paper. . . .'

'There's still one customer?'

'There's still one customer, and that's why I say it's too easy. It's a Monsieur Emile Parendon, a lawyer in the Avenue Marigny. He has been using this paper for more than fifteen years and won't have any other. Does that name mean anything to you?'

'I've never heard it. Has he ordered any recently?'

'The last time was last October.'

'Headed?'

'Yes, very tastefully. Always a thousand sheets and a thousand envelopes.'

Maigret picked up the telephone.

'Get me Maître Bouvier, please.'

A lawyer he had known for more than twenty years, whose son also was a barrister.

'Hello, Bouvier? Maigret here. You're not too busy?'

'Never too busy to speak to you.'

'I'd like some information.'

'Confidential, of course.'

'Just between the two of us, that's right. Do you know a colleague of yours called Emile Parendon?'

Bouvier seemed surprised.

'What in heaven's name can the Police Judiciaire have against Parendon?'

'I don't know. Probably nothing.'

'That's very likely. I haven't met Parendon more than five or six times in my life. He hardly sets foot in the Palais and then only for civil cases. . . .'

'How old is he?'

'Hard to tell. He might just as easily be forty as fifty.'

He must have turned to his secretary.

'Look up Parendon's date of birth in the Bar Yearbook, dear . . . Emile. . . . There's only one, anyway.'

Then, to Maigret:

'You must have heard of his father, who's still alive or if he's dead it was only recently. . . . Professor Parendon, the surgeon at Laënnec. . . . A member of the Academy of Medicine, of the Academy of Moral and Physical Sciences, etc., etc. . . . A character. When I see you next I'll tell you about him. He came to Paris very young, with the hay still in his ears. He was short and stocky and looked like a bull . . . and he didn't just look like one. . . .'

'What about his son?'

'He's a jurist, really. He specializes in International Law, particularly in Maritime Law. They say he's unbeatable there. People come from all over the world to consult him and he's often asked to arbitrate in delicate cases where big business interests are at stake.'

'What kind of a man is he?'

'Insignificant. I don't know that I'd recognize him in the street.'

'Is he married?'

'Thank you, dear. . . . There . . . I have his age here. Forty-six. Is he married? I was going to say I didn't know, but it's coming back to me. He certainly is married—very well married, too! He married one of the daughters of Gassin de Beaulieu. . . . You know. . . . He was one of the most ferocious prosecutors at the time of the Liberation. Then he was appointed First President of the Supreme Court of Appeal. He must have retired to his château in the Vendée now. The family is very rich. . . .'

'Don't you know anything else?'

'What else would I know? I've never had to defend them in a summary court or at the Assizes. . . .'

'Do they go out a lot?'

'The Parendons? Not in my circles, anyway.'

'Thanks a lot.'

'You can do the same for me sometime.'

Maigret re-read the letter which Lapointe had laid on his desk. He re-read it twice, three times, and each time his brow grew darker.

'Do you know what all this means?'

'Yes, chief. Muck-raking. Excuse the word, but . . .'

'It's probably too mild. A noted surgeon, a First President, a specialist in Maritime Law who lives in the Avenue Marigny and uses the most expensive writing paper. . . .'

The type of trouble Maigret feared most. He already had the feeling that he was walking on eggs.

'Do you think he wrote that . . . ?'

'He or someone in his household. Someone who had access to his writing paper, in any case.'

'It's odd, isn't it?'

Maigret, who was looking out of the window, didn't answer. As a rule, people who write anonymous letters don't make a habit of using their own writing paper, particularly when it's a rather rare kind.

'Too bad. I'll have to go and see him.'

He looked up the telephone number in the directory and put the call through on the outside line. A woman's voice answered.

'Maître Parendon's secretary speaking.'

'Good morning, Mademoiselle. This is Superintendent Maigret of the Police Judiciaire. Would it be possible for me to speak to Maître Parendon? I don't want to interrupt him.'

'Just a moment, please. I'll find out.'

It was the easiest thing in the world. Almost immediately a man's voice said:

'Parendon here.'

There was a questioning note in his voice.

'I wanted to ask you, Maître . . .'

'Who is that speaking? My secretary didn't quite catch your name.'

'Superintendent Maigret.'

'I can understand her surprise now. She must have heard properly, but she didn't imagine it was really you who . . . I'm delighted to be speaking to you, Monsieur Maigret . . . I've often thought of you . . . I've even been on the point of writing to you to ask your opinion on certain matters . . . I haven't dared, knowing you to be such a busy man. . . .'

Parendon had a timid voice, yet it was Maigret who was the more embarrassed of the two. He felt ridiculous now, with his meaningless letter.

'Now I'm the one who is disturbing you. And for a mere trifle, into the bargain. I would prefer to speak to you in person, as I have a document I would like to show you.'

'When would you like?'

'Have you a free moment sometime this afternoon?'

'Would three-thirty be convenient? I must confess that I usually take a short siesta and I feel terrible if I don't have it.'

'Three-thirty will be fine. I'll come to your house. Thank you for your kind co-operation.'

When Maigret put down the receiver he looked at Lapointe as if he were waking up from a dream.

'Didn't he seem surprised?'

'Not in the least. He didn't ask any questions. He says he's quite looking forward to meeting me. There's one thing that intrigues me. He says he has been on the point of writing to me for an opinion more than once. Now, he doesn't plead in the criminal courts, only in the civil courts. His speciality is Maritime Law, about which I don't know a thing. What does he want my opinion on?'

Maigret told a small lie that day. He telephoned his wife and told her that he was held up at work. He wanted to celebrate the spring sunshine by having lunch at the Brasserie Dauphine, where he even treated himself to a *pastis* at the bar.

If there was muck-raking to be done, as Lapointe had said, at least it was beginning pleasantly.

Maigret had taken the bus to the Rond-Point and in the hundred yards he walked along the Avenue Marigny he saw at least three faces he thought he recognized. He had forgotten that he was walking alongside the gardens of the Elysée Palace and that the area was heavily guarded day and night.

The guardian angels recognized him too and gave him a discreet and respectful salute.

The building where Parendon had his flat was vast and solid, built to defy the passage of time. The gateway was flanked by bronze candelabra. From the entrance one could see that the concierge did not have the usual little room, but a veritable drawing room, with a table covered with green velvet, as if it were in a Ministry.

The superintendent found a familiar face here, too, a man called Lamule or Lamure who had worked in the Rue de Saussaies for many years. He was wearing a grey uniform with silver buttons and he seemed surprised to see Maigret looming up in front of him.

'Who have you come to see, chief?'

'Maître Parendon.'

'Take the lift or the staircase on the left. It's on the first floor.'

Behind the house there was a courtyard with cars, garages and low buildings which must once have been stables. Maigret emptied his pipe mechanically, tapping it on his heel before he started to climb the marble staircase.

When he rang at the only door, a butler in a white jacket opened it as if he had been waiting for him.

'I have an appointment with Maître Parendon.'

'This way, Superintendent.'

He took Maigret's hat with an air of authority and showed him into a library the like of which the superintendent had never seen before. The room was long, with a very high ceiling, and books lined the walls from floor to ceiling except where there was a marble fireplace with a bust of an oldish man on the mantelpiece. All the books were bound in leather, most of them red leather. The only pieces of furniture were a long table, two chairs and an armchair.

He would have liked to examine the titles of the books, but a young secretary wearing glasses was already approaching him.

'Will you come this way, Divisional Superintendent?'

The sun was pouring in through windows more than nine

feet tall and playing on the carpets, on the furniture, on the pictures. For, from the corridor on, the place was filled with antique pier-tables, stylish suites, busts and paintings of gentlemen in the costumes of every age.

The girl opened a light oak door, and a man who had been sitting at his desk got up and stepped forward to greet Maigret. He too wore glasses, with very thick lenses.

'Thank you, Mademoiselle Vague.'

He had to walk a long way, since the room was as big as a state apartment. Here too the walls were lined with books, there were portraits, and the sun broke up the whole into diamond patterns.

'If you only knew how happy I am to see you, Monsieur Maigret. . . .'

He held out his hand, a little white hand which felt boneless to the touch. In contrast to the décor the man seemed even smaller than what must be his real size—small and frail and curiously light. And yet he wasn't thin. His outlines were quite rounded, but the whole effect was of weightlessness, of insubstantiality.

'Come this way, please. Let's see. . . . Where would you prefer to sit?'

He pointed to a tawny leather armchair, near the desk.

'I think you would be most comfortable here. I am a little deaf. . . .'

Maigret's friend Bouvier had been right in saying that the man was ageless. He still had an almost childish expression in his face and his blue eyes, and he looked at the superintendent with a kind of wonder.

'You can't imagine the number of times I've thought of you. When you are on a case I devour several newspapers a day so that I don't miss a detail—I might almost say that I wait to see what your reactions are. . . .'

Maigret felt awkward. He had grown accustomed to the curiosity of the public, but the enthusiasm of a man like Parendon put him in an embarrassing position.

'Well, my reactions are just the same as those the average man might have in my place.'

19

'The average man, maybe. But there is no such thing as the "average man". . . . That's a myth. What isn't a myth is the Penal Code, the judges, the juries. . . . And the juries who were "average men" the day before become different people the minute they enter the court-room.'

He was wearing a dark grey suit and the desk he was leaning on was much too big for him. But he didn't look ridiculous. Perhaps that wasn't naïveté either, shining in the eyes behind the thick lenses of his glasses.

As a schoolboy he had perhaps had to put up with being called 'half-pint,' but he had resigned himself to the inevitable and he gave the impression of a benevolent gnome who had to keep his high spirits in check.

'May I ask you a rather personal question? How old were you when you began to understand men? I mean to understand the men we call criminals?'

Maigret reddened and stammered:

'I don't know. I'm not sure that I do understand them. . . .'

'Oh yes, you do! And they know it very well. That's one of the reasons why they are almost relieved to confess.'

'It's the same with my colleagues.'

'I could prove the contrary by mentioning several cases, but that would only bore you. You studied medicine, didn't you?'

'Only for two years.'

'If what I've read is true, your father died, and since you were unable to continue your studies you joined the police.'

Maigret's position was growing more and more delicate, almost ridiculous. He had come to ask questions and he was the one being interviewed.

'I don't see in that change a change of vocation, but a different way of expressing the same character. . . . Excuse me . . . I have literally thrown myself at you since you came in. I was waiting your arrival impatiently. I would have opened the door myself when you rang, but my wife wouldn't have liked that—she insists on a certain decorum. . . .'

His voice had lowered several tones on speaking these last words and, pointing to an immense painting depicting, almost full-length, a judge dressed in ermine, he whispered:

'My father-in-law.'

'First President Gassin de Beaulieu?'

'Do you know him?'

During the last few minutes Parendon had looked so like a little boy that Maigret felt he had to admit:

'I did my homework before I came.'

'Did anyone say anything against him?'

'It seems that he's a great judge.'

'There you are! . . . A great judge! . . . Do you know the works of Henri Ey?'

'I've read his textbook on psychiatry.'

'Sengès? Levy-Valensi? Maxwell?'

He pointed to a section of the bookshelves where the books bore these names. But they were all psychiatrists who had never taken any interest in Maritime Law. Maigret recognized other names as he glanced at them. He had seen some of them quoted in the journals of the International Society of Criminology, and he had in fact read the works of others: Lagache, Ruyssen, Genil-Perrin.

'Aren't you smoking?' his host suddenly asked him, astonished. 'I thought you always had a pipe in your mouth.'

'No, I won't, thank you.'

'What can I offer you? The cognac isn't particularly good, but I have a forty-year-old armagnac. . . .'

He trotted over to a wall where a section of panelling between the rows of books hid a liqueur cabinet with some twenty bottles and glasses of all sizes.

'Just a little, please.'

'My wife only lets me have a drop on special occasions. She says I have a weak liver. According to her I'm weak all over and I haven't a single healthy organ in me.'

That amused him. He spoke without bitterness.

'Your health! If I have been asking these personal questions, it is because I am passionately interested in Article 64 of the Penal Code, which you must know better than I do.'

Indeed, Maigret knew it by heart. He had gone over it again and again, many times, in his mind:

'There is no crime or misdemeanour if the accused was in a

21

state of dementia at the time of the act, or if he was driven to it by an irresistible impulse.'

'What do you think of it?' asked the gnome, leaning towards him.

'I am glad I'm not a judge. That way, I don't have to pass judgment.'

'That's the kind of thing I like to hear you say. This is the kind of thing I want to know—sitting in your office in front of a guilty man, or a man who is presumed guilty, are you capable of determining how far he is responsible?'

'Rarely. . . . The psychiatrists, afterwards . . .'

'This library is full of psychiatrists. The older generation, for the most part, answered "responsible," and went on their way with a clear conscience. But read Henri Ey again, for example. . . .'

'I know.'

'Do you speak English?'

'Very badly.'

'Do you know what they mean by a hobby?'

'Yes. A pastime, something one does without payment, a craze, a mania. . . .'

'Well, my dear Monsieur Maigret, my hobby, my mania, as some people say, is Article 64. I'm not the only one. And that celebrated article isn't only found in the French Penal Code —in more or less identical terms it is found in the United States, in England, in Germany, in Italy. . . .'

He grew animated. His face, which had been rather pale, grew pink and he gesticulated with surprising energy.

'There are thousands of us all over the world, no, tens of thousands, who have made it our goal to change this shameful Article 64, which is a relic of the past. It's not a secret society. There are official organisations in most countries, magazines, journals. . . . Did you know what answer they give us?'

And, as if to make the 'they' more personal, he glanced at the portrait of his father-in-law.

'They tell us:

' "The Penal Code is a whole. If you change one stone, the whole edifice is in danger of falling."

22

'They also object:

' "If one did as you wish, the doctor and not the judge would have the task of judging."

'I could talk to you about it for hours. I have written many articles on the subject and I will get my secretary to send you some of them, which may seem presumptuous on my part. You know criminals, if I may say so, at first hand. As far as a judge is concerned, they are creatures who fit almost automatically into this compartment or that. Do you understand?'

'Yes.'

'Your good health.'

He drew his breath, seeming to be surprised, himself, at having got so involved.

'There aren't many people I can talk to so openly. I hope I haven't shocked you?'

'Not at all.'

'In fact, I haven't even asked you why you wanted to see me. I have been so thrilled at this chance that it never even occurred to me. . . .'

And, with a touch of irony:

'I hope it's nothing to do with Maritime Law.'

Maigret had taken the letter out of his pocket.

'I received this letter in this morning's mail. It has no signature. I am not at all certain that it came from this house. I would just like you to look at it.'

Oddly enough, the lawyer began by feeling the paper, as if his sense of touch was the most strongly developed of his senses.

'It could be mine. . . . It's not easily come by. The last time, my engraver had to order it from the manufacturer.'

'That's exactly what brought me here.'

Parendon had put on a different pair of glasses, crossed his short legs and was moving his lips as he read, saying a few phrases in a low voice.

'A murder will be committed shortly. . . . Perhaps by someone known to me, perhaps by me myself.'

He re-read the paragraph carefully.

'I would say that each word had been carefully chosen, wouldn't you?'

'That is the impression I got from the letter.'

' "It is, in a way, inevitable." '

'I don't like that sentence so well. There's something unnecessary about it.'

Then, holding the paper out to Maigret and changing his glasses again:

'Strange . . .'

He wasn't the man for long words, for emphasis. His commentary was restricted to that one word.

'One detail struck me,' Maigret explained. 'The person who wrote this letter does not address me as Superintendent, as most people do, but by my official title, Divisional Superintendent.'

'I thought of that too. Have you put the advertisement in?'

'It will appear in *Le Monde* this evening and in tomorrow morning's *Figaro*.'

The oddest thing was that Parendon was not surprised or, if he was, he didn't show it. He was looking out of the window at the gnarled trunk of a chestnut tree when his attention was caught by a slight noise.

He was not surprised by that either. Turning his head, he murmured:

'Come in, my dear.'

And, getting up:

'Let me introduce Superintendent Maigret in person.'

The woman, who was about forty, elegant, very vivacious, with extremely restless eyes, took only a few seconds to examine the superintendent from head to toe. She would doubtless have noticed if he had had a tiny speck of mud on his left shoe.

'How do you do, Superintendent? I hope you haven't come to arrest my husband. With his poor health you would have to put him in the prison infirmary.'

Her tone was not biting. She did not say that with any ill-will, but she did say it, though, with the gayest of smiles.

'I expect it's about one of our domestics.'

'I have had no complaint about any of them. That would be a matter for the local police.'

She was dying to know why he was there. Her husband knew that as well as Maigret did, but neither of them made the slightest allusion to it, as if they were playing a game.

'What do you think of our armagnac?'

She had removed the glasses.

'I hope you only had a drop, dear?'

She was wearing a light-coloured suit, a spring style although the season had only just begun.

'Oh well, gentlemen, I'll leave you to your own affairs. . . . I was going to tell you that I won't be back before eight, dear. You can always join me at Hortense's, after seven, if you like. . . .'

She did not leave immediately, but managed, while the two men remained standing silent, to make a tour of the room, changing the position of an ashtray on a pedestal table, putting a book into line with the rest.

'Goodbye, Monsieur Maigret. I am very pleased indeed to have met you. You are an extremely interesting man. . . .'

The door closed behind her. Parendon sat down again. He waited a moment longer, as if he expected the door to open again. Finally he laughed, a child-like laugh.

'Did you get that?'

Maigret didn't know what to say.

' "You are an extremely interesting man." She is furious that you didn't say anything to her. Not only does she not know why you are here, you didn't comment on her dress or, more important, on how young she is. Nothing would have given her greater pleasure than for you to have taken her for my daughter.'

'Have you a daughter?'

'Yes, she's eighteen. She has passed her *baccalauréat* and is taking some classes in archaeology—I don't know how long that will last. Last year she wanted to be a lab assistant. I don't see a lot of her except at mealtimes, when she deigns to eat with us. . . . I have a son, too, Jacques. He's fifteen and in the third form at the Lycée Racine. . . . They are all the family we have.'

He spoke lightly, as if the words had no importance or as if he were laughing at himself.

'In fact, I'm wasting your time and we ought to get back to your letter. Wait a moment. . . . Here's a sheet of my writing paper. Your experts will tell you if it's really the same paper, but I am already certain that it is.'

He rang a bell and waited, his head turned towards the door.

'Mademoiselle Vague, would you be so good as to bring me one of the envelopes we use for the tradesmen?'

He explained:

'We pay the tradespeople by cheque at the end of the month. It would be pretentious to use our engraved envelopes to pay their bills. So we have ordinary white envelopes.'

The girl brought one.

'You can compare them too. If the envelopes and the paper are both the same, you can be almost certain that the letter came from here.'

That did not appear to upset him unduly.

'Can you think of any reason why someone might have been inspired to write this letter?'

He looked at Maigret, first rather bewildered, then with a more disillusioned look.

'Reasons? I wasn't expecting that word, Monsieur Maigret. I realize you must ask the question. But why reasons? Undoubtedly everyone has some, consciously or not. . . .'

'Do many people live in this flat?'

'Living in, not very many. My wife and I, of course. . . .'

'Do you sleep in separate bedrooms?'

He gave Maigret a swift look, as if he had scored a point.

'How did you guess?'

'I don't know. . . . I asked the question without thinking.'

'It's quite true, we do sleep in separate rooms. My wife likes to go to bed late and stay in bed in the mornings, and I am an early bird. . . . In any case, you are free to go through all the rooms whenever you like. I may as well say at once

26

that I did not choose the flat, nor have anything to do with furnishing it.

'When my father-in-law'—a glance at the First President—'retired and went to live in the Vendée, there was a sort of family council. There are four daughters, all married. They more or less divided up their inheritance before time and my wife got this flat with all its contents, including the portrait and the busts.'

He neither laughed nor smiled. It was more subtle than that.

'One of the sisters will inherit the country seat in the Vendée in the Forest of Vouvant, and the other two will share the titles. The Gassin de Beaulieus are a very wealthy old family, so there's enough for everyone.

'So I am not quite in my own home, but rather in my father-in-law's, and only the books and furniture in my bedroom and this study belong to me.'

'Your father is still alive, isn't he?'

'He lives almost opposite, in the Rue de Miromesnil, in a flat he furnished for his retirement. He has been a widower for thirty years. He was a surgeon . . .'

'A famous surgeon.'

'Yes. You know that too. Then you must know that his passion was not Article 64, but women. . . . We have a flat just as big as this one, but more modern, in the Rue d'Aguesseau. My brother and his wife live there. He's a neurologist.

'Now the family. . . . I have already told you about my daughter Paule and her brother Jacques. If you want to get on well with her, you had better know that my daughter calls herself Bambi and insists on calling her brother Gus. I suppose that will pass. And even if it doesn't, it's not very important. . . .

'As for the domestics, as my wife would say, you have already seen Ferdinand, the butler. His surname is Fauchois. He comes from Berry, like my family. He's a bachelor. His room is on the other side of the courtyard, over the garages. Lise, the maid, sleeps in the flat, and there is a Madame Marchand who comes in daily to do the cleaning. . . . I was forgetting the cook, Madame Vauquin—her husband is a pastrycook and she has to go home at night.

'Aren't you taking any notes?'

Maigret just smiled, then he got up and went over to a large ash-tray where he emptied his pipe.

'Now, my side of the household, if I may call it that. . . . You have met Mademoiselle Vague. . . . That's her real name and she doesn't find it at all ridiculous. I have always called my secretaries by their surnames. She never speaks of her private life and I would have to consult my records to find her address.

'All I know about her is that she goes home by Métro and that she will do evening work without complaining. She must be about twenty-four or twenty-five and she is rarely in a bad temper.

'To help me in my chambers I have an ambitious clerk, René Tortu. His office is at the end of the corridor.

'Finally there is what we call the scribe, a boy of about twenty who has just come from Switzerland. I think he has ambitions to be a playwright. He does everything. A sort of office-boy.

'When I am handed a case it's almost always a big one, a matter of millions, if not hundreds of millions, and then I have to work day and night for a week or more. After that we fall back on routine and I have time to . . .'

He blushed and smiled.

'. . . to pay attention to our Article 64, Monsieur Maigret. One day you must tell me what you think of it. In the meantime, I shall give everyone instructions to let you wander round the flat at will, and to answer all your questions truthfully.'

Maigret looked at him, a bit worried. He was not sure if he was looking at a very astute actor, or, on the other hand, a poor, sickly man whose only consolation was a subtle sense of humour.

'I shall probably come in tomorrow, sometime in the morning, but I shan't disturb you.'

'In that case I shall probably disturb you.'

They shook hands and the hand that the superintendent held in his own was almost that of a child.

'Thank you for receiving me so kindly, Monsieur Parendon.'

'Thank you for your visit Monsieur Maigret.'

The lawyer trotted behind him as far as the lift.

CHAPTER TWO

ONCE OUTSIDE he found the sun again, and the scent of the first fine days of the year. There was already a faint smell of dust. The guardian angels of the Elysée Palace walked along nonchalantly and made him discreet signs of recognition.

At the corner of the Rond-Point, an old woman was selling lilacs which smelled like suburban gardens, and Maigret resisted the impulse to buy some. What would he have looked like arriving at the Quai des Orfèvres carrying a huge bunch of flowers?

He felt light-headed—an odd sort of light-headedness. He had just left a hitherto unknown world where he had found himself more like a fish out of water than he would ever have believed. As he walked along the pavements, among the jostling crowds, he could visualize the solemn flat presided over by the shade of the great judge. He must have given formal receptions there.

From the start Parendon, as if to put him at his ease, had given him a sort of wink that said:

'Don't get it wrong. All this is only a décor. Even the Maritime Law is only a game, only make-believe. . . .'

And he had brought out a toy, his Article 64 which interested him more than anything else in the world.

Unless Parendon were a deep one? In any case, Maigret felt attracted to the skipping gnome who devoured him with his eyes as if he had never before seen a superintendent of the Police Judiciaire.

He took advantage of the good weather to walk down the Champs-Elysées as far as the Place de la Concorde, where he finally took a bus. He couldn't get one with a platform, so he had to put out his pipe and sit inside.

When he got back to his office it was time to sign his mail, and he took twenty minutes to get through the letters. His wife was surprised to see him come in at six o'clock, looking gay.

'What's for dinner?'

'I thought I'd make . . .'

'Don't make anything. We're going to eat out.'

It didn't matter where, just as long as they could eat outside. It was no ordinary day, and he wanted it to stay special right to the end.

The days were growing longer. They found a restaurant in the Quartier Latin with a glassed-in terrace pleasantly warmed by a charcoal heater. The speciality of the house was *fruits de mer*, and Maigret sampled almost every kind, even some sea-urchins flown in that very day from the Midi.

She looked at him, smiling.

'You've had a good day, haven't you?'

'I saw a very odd man. . . . A very odd house, too, and some very odd people.'

'A crime?'

'I don't know. . . . It hasn't been committed yet, but it could happen at any time. And when it does, I'll find myself in a very awkward situation.'

He rarely talked to her about cases under way, and she usually learned more about them from the newspapers and the wireless than from her husband. This time, he gave in to the urge to show her the letter.

'Read that.'

They had reached the dessert. They had drunk a bottle of Pouilly Fumé with their grilled red mullet, and its aroma still surrounded them. Madame Maigret gave her husband a rather surprised look as she handed back the letter.

'Was it written by a child?' she asked.

'There is in fact a child in the house. I haven't seen him yet. But there are such things as childlike men. And childlike women too, when they get to a certain age.'

'Is that what you think?'

'Somebody wanted me to go into that house. If he hadn't, he wouldn't have used writing paper which is only sold these days by two stationers in Paris.'

'If he is planning to commit a crime . . .'

'He doesn't say that he is going to commit a crime. He is telling me there is going to be one, and he doesn't seem to be too sure who is going to commit it.'

For once she didn't take him seriously.

'It's just a joke, you'll see.'

He paid the bill. It was so warm that they strolled home, making a detour to walk through the Ile Saint-Louis.

He found lilacs in the Rue Saint-Antoine, so there were some in the flat that night, after all.

The next morning the sun was just as bright, the air just as clear, but already one took less notice of it. He found Lucas, Janvier and Lapointe there for the little briefing and he looked straightaway for the letter in the pile of mail.

He was not sure that it would be there, for the advertisement in *Le Monde* had not appeared until the middle of the previous evening, and the *Figaro* had only just come out.

'There it is!' he cried, brandishing it in the air.

The same envelope, the same carefully-written block letters, the same writing paper with the heading cut off.

The writer didn't call him Divisional Superintendent any more, and the tone had changed.

'You made a mistake, Monsieur Maigret, in coming before receiving my second letter. Now they all have a flea in their ear and that means things being speeded up. From now on, the crime may be committed at any moment, and that will be partly your fault.

'I thought you were more patient, more reflective. Do you really think that you are capable of discovering the secrets of a whole household in one afternoon?

'You are more credulous, and perhaps more vain, than I had thought. I cannot help you any more. My only advice to you is to continue your investigation without believing what anyone tells you.

'With regards. In spite of everything I retain my admiration for you.'

The three men standing facing him realized that he was

embarrassed, and he handed them the sheet of paper with some reluctance. They were even more embarrassed than he was at the off-handed way the anonymous correspondent was treating their chief.

'Don't you think it's a kid having fun?'

'That's what my wife said yesterday evening.'

'What do you think?'

'No. . . .'

No, he didn't think that it was a joke in poor taste. Besides, there was nothing dramatic in the air in the Avenue Marigny. In that flat everything was clear and well-ordered. The butler had received him with calm dignity. The secretary with the funny name was lively and pleasant. As for Maître Parendon, he had shown himself to be a most charming host in spite of his strange appearance.

The idea that it might be a joke had not occurred to Parendon either. He had made no protest against this intrusion into his private life. He had talked a lot about many subjects, particularly about Article 64, but, after all, hadn't he seemed to have an undercurrent of unhappiness all the time?

Maigret did not mention it at the big briefing. He realized that his colleagues would shrug their shoulders if they knew he was involving himself in such an incredible affair.

'Anything new with your lot, Maigret?'

'Janvier is just on the point of arresting the man who killed the postmistress. We are almost sure, but we'd better wait a bit and see if he had an accomplice. . . . He's living with a young girl and she's pregnant. . . .'

Ordinary things. Banal things. Everyday things. One hour later he left the everyday world as he went into the building in the Avenue Marigny. The uniformed concierge waved to him through the glass door of the lodge.

Ferdinand, the butler, took his hat and asked:

'Do you wish me to announce your arrival to Monsieur?'

'No. Take me to the secretary's office.'

Mademoiselle Vague! That was it! He had remembered her name.

She worked in a small room with green-painted filing

cabinets around the walls, and she was typing on the latest model of electric typewriter.

'Did you want to see me?' she asked, not at all upset.

She got up, looked around her and pointed to a chair near the window which looked on to the courtyard.

'I'm sorry I haven't got an armchair for you. If you'd rather, we could go to the library or the drawing-room . . .'

'I'd prefer to stay here.'

He could hear a vacuum cleaner running somewhere in the flat. Another typewriter was clacking away in one of the offices. A man's voice, not Parendon's, was speaking on the telephone:

'Yes, yes. . . . I understand you perfectly, my dear chap, but the law is the law, even if it sometimes runs counter to commonsense. . . . I have spoken to him about it, of course. . . . No, he can't see you today or tomorrow, and that wouldn't help anyway. . . .'

'Monsieur Tortu?' Maigret asked.

She nodded. The clerk was speaking in the next room. Mademoiselle Vague went over and shut the door, cutting off the sound just as if she had turned off the wireless. The window was open a little and a chauffeur in a blue boiler-suit was hosing down a Rolls-Royce.

'Does that belong to Monsieur Parendon?'

'No, to the tenants on the second floor. They're Peruvians.'

'Does Monsieur Parendon have a chauffeur?'

'He has to, because his eyesight is too bad to let him drive.'

'What kind of car does he have?'

'A Cadillac. Madame uses it more often than he does, although she has a little English car of her own. Does the noise disturb you? Are you sure you wouldn't like me to shut the window?'

No. The jet of water was part of the atmosphere, of spring, of a house like the one he found himself in.

'Do you know why I am here?'

'I only know that we are all at your service and that we are to answer all your questions even if we think they are indiscreet.'

He took the first letter out of his pocket again. He would

have a photocopy made of it when he got back to the Quai, otherwise it would end up in shreds.

While she was reading it, he examined her face, which her round tortoiseshell spectacles managed not to make ugly. She was not beautiful in the usual sense, but she had a pleasant face. Her mouth in particular held the eye, full, smiling, its corners turned up.

'Yes? . . .' she said, handing back the paper.

'What do you think of it?'

'What does Monsieur Parendon think?'

'The same as you do.'

'What do you mean?'

'That he was no more surprised than you are.'

She forced herself to smile, but he could tell that the shot had gone home.

'Should I have reacted in any special way?'

'When someone announces that a murder is going to be committed in a house . . .'

'That could happen in any house, couldn't it? Before the moment when a man becomes a criminal, I suppose that he acts like any other man, that he is like any other man, otherwise . . .'

'Otherwise we would arrest future criminals in advance. That's true enough.'

The strange thing was that she had thought of that, for few people in the course of Maigret's long career had given him that simple piece of reasoning.

'I put the advertisement in. This morning I had a second letter.'

He held it out to her and she read it with the same attention, but this time with a certain anxiety too.

'I'm beginning to understand,' she murmured.

'What?'

'Why you are worried and why you are taking on the investigation yourself.'

'May I smoke?'

'Please do. I am allowed to smoke in here, which isn't the case in most offices.'

She lit a cigarette with simple, unaffected gestures, unlike so many women. She smoked in order to relax. She leaned back a little in her articulated typing chair. The office did not look at all like a commercial office. Although the typewriter table was metal, an extremely beautiful Louis XIII table stood beside it.

'Is the Parendon boy a practical joker?'

'Gus? He's quite the opposite. He is intelligent, but reserved. He is always at the top of his class at the lycée, though he never does any work.'

'What is he most interested in?'

'Music and electronics. He has built a complete hi-fi system in his bedroom, and he subscribes to I don't know how many scientific magazines. . . . Look, here's one which came in this morning's post. I'm the one who puts them in his room.'

Electronics of Tomorrow.

'Does he go out a lot?'

'I'm not here in the evenings. I don't think so.'

'Has he any friends?'

'Sometimes a friend comes to listen to records or to do experiments with him.'

'How does he get on with his father?'

She seemed surprised by the question. She thought for a moment, and smiled to excuse herself.

'I don't know what to say. I have been working for Monsieur Parendon for five years. It's only my second job in Paris.'

'Where was the first?'

'In a business in the Rue Réaumur. I wasn't happy, because the work didn't interest me.'

'Who got you this post?'

'René. I mean Monsieur Tortu. He told me about this job.'

'Did you know him well?'

'We used to have our evening meal at the same restaurant in the Rue Caulaincourt.'

'Do you live in Montmartre?'

'In the Place Constantin-Pecqueur.'

'Was Tortu your . . . *petit-ami?*'

'First of all, he's not so little—almost six foot three. Anyway, except for one time, there hasn't been anything between us.'

'Except for one time?'

'I've been told to be absolutely frank, haven't I? . . . One evening, not long before I came here, we went to the pictures together in the Place Clichy, after we left "Chez Maurice"— "Chez Maurice", that's the restaurant in the Rue Caulaincourt. . . .'

'Do you still eat there?'

'Almost every evening. I'm part of the furniture.'

'And he?'

'Not so often now that he's engaged.'

'So, after the pictures . . .'

'He asked me if he could come up and have a drink at my flat. We'd already had a few drinks and I was a little bit drunk. I said no, because I hate the idea of a man coming into my room. . . . It's something physical. . . . I said I'd go with him to his flat in the Rue de Saules. . . .'

'Why didn't it happen again?'

'Because it didn't work out, we both realized that. . . . Just one of those things, in fact. . . . We're still good friends.'

'Is he going to get married soon?'

'I don't think he's in any hurry. . . .'

'Is his fiancée a secretary too?'

'She's Doctor Parendon's, the boss's brother's assistant.'

Maigret smoked his pipe in short puffs, trying to soak up everything germane to this world which he had not known anything about the previous day, and which had just welled up in his life.

'Since we're talking about such things, I'm going to ask you another indiscreet question. Do you go to bed with Monsieur Parendon?'

It was her way of doing things. She listened attentively to the question, her face serious. She took her time and then, at the moment of answering, she began to smile, a smile both mischievous and spontaneous, while her eyes twinkled behind her glasses.

'In a sense, yes. We make love, but it's always on t

37

so to speak, so the word bed isn't appropriate, since we've never been to bed together.'

'Does Tortu know?'

'We've never spoken about it, but he must guess.'

'Why?'

'When you know the flat better, you'll understand. Let's see, how many people are around here during the day? . . . Monsieur and Madame Parendon and the two children, that's four. Three in the office, seven. Ferdinand, the cook, the maid and the cleaning-woman, brings us to eleven. Not to mention Madame's masseur, who comes four mornings a week, or her sisters, or her friends. . . . Even though there are a lot of rooms, one meets everyone else. Especially in here.'

'Why in here especially?'

'Because it's in here everyone comes to get paper, stamps, paperclips. . . . If Gus needs a piece of string, it's these drawers he comes to look in. . . . Bambi always needs stamps or scotch tape. As for Madame . . .'

He watched her, curious to see how she would continue.

'She's everywhere. Oh, yes, she goes out a lot, but one never knows if she's out or in. You will have noticed that all the corridors and most of the rooms are carpeted. You can't hear anyone coming. The door opens and in pops someone you weren't expecting. For example, she sometimes pushes open my door and mutters, "Oh, excuse me!" as if she'd made a mistake . . .'

'Is she inquisitive?'

'Or scatterbrained. Unless she has a thing about it.'

'Has she never surprised you with her husband?'

'I'm not sure. Once, not long before Christmas, when we thought she was at the hairdresser's, she came in at a rather delicate moment. We had time to look normal, at least I think we did, but I'm not sure. She seemed very natural and began to talk to her husband about the present she had just bought for Gus.'

'Hasn't she changed in her attitude to you?'

'No. She is nice to everyone, a kind of niceness that is peculiarly her own, a little as if she were floating around

38

above us to protect us. . . . I've secretly nicknamed her the angel. . . .'

'Don't you like her?'

'I wouldn't have her for a friend, if that's what you mean.'

A bell rang and the girl got up suddenly.

'Will you excuse me? The boss is calling me.'

She was at the door already, having picked up a pencil and a shorthand notebook on the way.

Maigret remained alone, watching the chauffeur in the courtyard not yet reached by the sun. He was polishing the Rolls with a chamois and whistling a repetitive jingle.

Mademoiselle Vague did not come back, and Maigret remained seated by the window—he who had such a horror of waiting. He could have gone along to the end of the corridor to the office occupied by Tortu and Julien Baud, but it was as if he was in a pleasant stupor, his eyes half-closed, looking first at one thing, then at another.

The table which served as a desk had heavy oak legs, tastefully carved, and it must have stood previously in another room. Its surface was polished by long use. There was a beige blotter with four leather corners. The pen-tray was very ordinary, made of a kind of plastic. It held fountain pens, pencils, a rubber and an erasing-knife. There was a dictionary near the typing table.

Suddenly he frowned. He stood up rather regretfully and went over to look more closely at the table. He had not been mistaken. There was a thin slit, still fresh, such as the erasing-knife would have made cutting a sheet of paper.

Near the pen-tray there was a flat metal ruler.

'You've noticed that too?'

He jumped. It was Mademoiselle Vague who had come in, still holding her notebook.

'What do you mean?'

'The scratch. Isn't it awful to spoil such a lovely table?'

'Have you any idea who did it?'

'Anyone who had access to this room, that is to say, anyone at all. I told you everybody treated this place as their own.'

So he wouldn't have to search. He had promised himself the previous day that he would examine all the tables in the house, for he had noticed that the paper had been cut cleanly, as if with a guillotine.

'Did you tell him what we were talking about?'

She answered, not in the least embarrassed:

'Yes.'

'Even about your relationship with him?'

'Of course.'

'Is that why he called you?'

'No. He really had something to ask me about the case he's working on just now.'

'I'll come back in a moment. I suppose you don't need to show me in any more?'

She smiled.

'He told you to make yourself at home, didn't he?'

So he knocked at the tall oak door, opened it and found the little man sitting at his desk, which was covered this morning with official-looking documents.

'Come in, Monsieur Maigret. I'm sorry I interrupted you. I didn't know you were with my secretary. You're getting to know a bit more about our household.

'Would it be indiscreet to ask you if I could look at the second letter?'

Maigret gave it to him willingly, and he had the impression that Parendon's face, which was already colourless, grew waxy. The blue eyes no longer sparkled behind the thick glasses, but stared at Maigret with an anguished, questioning look.

' "From now on, the crime may be committed at any time." Do you believe that?'

Maigret, who was staring at him equally hard, said only:

'Do you?'

'I don't know. I don't know any longer. Yesterday I took the affair lightly more than anything. Although I did not believe it was a spiteful joke, I was tempted to think it was a minor revenge, treacherous and naïve at the same time. . . .'

'Against whom?'

'Against me, against my wife, against anyone in the house.
. . . A clever way of getting the police here and having us
harassed by questions.'

'Have you mentioned it to your wife?'

'I had to, since she met you in my office.'

'You could have told her that I had come to ask your
opinion on a professional matter.'

Parendon's face expressed mild surprise.

'Would Madame Maigret be satisfied with an explanation
like that?'

'My wife never asks questions.'

'Mine does. And she goes on asking, just like your interro-
gations, if one can believe what one reads, until she thinks
she has got to the bottom of things. Then she checks on them
with little questions, seemingly harmless, which she shoots
at Ferdinand, at the cook, at my secretary, at the children. . . .'

He was not complaining. There was no bitterness in his
voice. More a kind of admiration, in fact. He seemed to be
talking about a phenomenon whose merits are widely known.

'What was her reaction?'

'That it must be revenge on the part of one of the domestics.'

'Have they any grounds for complaint?'

'They always have grounds for complaint. For example,
Madame Vauquin, the cook, works late when we give a
dinner, and the cleaning-woman goes at six o'clock whatever
happens. On the other hand, the cleaning-woman earns two
hundred francs less. You understand?'

'What about Ferdinand?'

'Did you know that Ferdinand, who is so correct, so formal,
was a legionnaire and has taken part in commando raids?
No one checks what he does in the evenings in his room above
the garages, whom he sees or where he goes. . . .'

'Is that the kind of thing you suspect too?'

The lawyer hesitated a second and decided to be honest.

'No.'

'Why?'

'None of them would have written the sentences in the
letter, or used certain of the words.'

41

'Are there any guns in the house?'

'My wife has two shotguns, because she is often invited on a shoot. I don't shoot.'

'Have you a revolver?'

'I have an old Browning in a drawer of my bedside table. Lots of people do, I think. One tells oneself that if burglars. . . .'

He laughed softly.

'I could give them a fright, anyway. Here . . .'

He opened a drawer of the desk and took out a box of cartridges.

'The gun is in my room at the other end of the flat, and the cartridges are here, a habit I got into when the children were younger and I was afraid of accidents. This makes me realize that they're now over the age of reason and I could load my Browning. . . .'

He kept on rummaging in the drawer and this time he pulled out a cosh, an American model.

'Do you know where I got this toy? Three years ago, I was surprised to be called to the police station to see the superintendent. When I got there I was asked if I had a son called Jacques. He was twelve at the time.

'A fight had broken out as the boys were coming out of school, and the policeman found Gus in possession of this cosh. . . .

'I questioned him when I got home and learned that he had got it from a friend in exchange for six packets of chewing gum.' He smiled, amused at the memory.

'Is he a violent boy?'

'He went through a difficult period between the ages of twelve and thirteen. He used to get into violent but short-lived tempers, especially when his sister taunted him. After that it wore off. I would say he's too calm, too solitary a boy for my liking. . . .'

'Hasn't he any friends?'

'I only know of one, a boy called Génuvier who comes quite often to listen to music with him. His father is a *pâtissier* in the Rue du Fauborg-Saint-Honoré—you must have heard the name—ladies go there from all over town. . . .'

'If you will excuse me now, I'll go back to your secretary.'

'What do you think of her?'

'She is intelligent, both spontaneous and thoughtful. . . .'

That seemed to please Parendon, who purred:

'I find her invaluable. . . .'

While Parendon immersed himself in his files once again, Maigret rejoined Mademoiselle Vague in her office. She was not even pretending to work and was obviously waiting for him.

'One question which you will find ridiculous, mademoiselle —has the Parendon boy . . .'

'Everyone calls him Gus.'

'Right! Has Gus ever tried to make love to you?'

'He's fifteen years old.'

'I know. That's just the age to be curious about certain things, or for sentimental attachments.'

She thought for a moment. Like Parendon, she took time to think before answering. It was as if he had taught her exactitude.

'No,' she said finally. 'When I first knew him, he was a little boy who came in to ask me for stamps for his collection, a boy who scrounged an incredible amount of pencils and scotch tape. And sometimes he asked me to help him with his homework. He would sit where you are and watch me with a serious expression. . . .'

'And now?'

'He is half a head taller than I am and he has been shaving for a year. If he scrounges anything from me now, it's cigarettes, when he has forgotten to buy any.'

She lit one suddenly, while Maigret filled his pipe slowly.

'Aren't his visits any more frequent?'

'Quite the opposite. I think I told you he leads his own life, apart from the family except for meals. And he even refuses to appear at table when there are guests. He prefers to eat in the kitchen.'

'Does he get on well with the staff?'

'He doesn't make any distinctions between people. Even if he is late, he won't let the chauffeur drive him to school, in case the other boys see him in a limousine.'

43

'In fact, he is ashamed of living in a house like this?'

'It's a bit like that, yes.'

'Has his relationship with his sister improved?'

'You must remember that I never have meals with them and that I rarely see them together. As far as I can see, he thinks of her as a curious creature and tries to understand how she works, rather the way he would think of an insect.'

'What about his mother?'

'She's a bit flamboyant for him. I mean she is always on the move, always talking to a crowd of people. . . .'

'I understand. And the girl? Paulette, I think her name is.'

'Everyone here says Bambi. Don't forget that both children have nicknames. Gus and Bambi. I don't know what they call me among themselves—it should be quite funny.'

'How does Bambi get on with her mother?'

'Badly.'

'Do they quarrel?'

'Not even that. They hardly speak to each other.'

'On whose side is the animosity?'

'On Bambi's. You'll be seeing her. Although she's young, she passes judgment on everyone around her, and you can tell by her look that she is judging them cruelly.'

'Unjustly?'

'Not always.'

'Does she get on with you?'

'She accepts me.'

'Does she ever come to see you in your office?'

'When she needs me to type a lecture or photocopy a document.'

'Does she ever talk to you about her friends?'

'Never.'

'Do you think that she knows about your relationship with her father?'

'I've sometimes wondered about that. I don't know. Anyone could have looked in on us without our knowing.'

'Does she love her father?'

'She has taken him under her protection. She seems to

44

think of him as her mother's victim and that is why she hates her for taking so much of the limelight.'

'In fact Monsieur Parendon doesn't play an important rôle in the family, does he?'

'Not an obvious rôle.'

'Has he never tried?'

'Perhaps he did a long time ago, before I came. He must have seen that the battle was already lost and . . . and he retreated into his shell.'

She laughed.

'Not as much as you'd think. He knows everything that goes on, too. He doesn't ask questions like Madame Parendon —he contents himself with listening, observing, deducing. . . . He is an extremely intelligent man.'

'I had that impression.'

He saw that she was delighted. Suddenly she looked on him as a friend, as if he had won her over. He realized that if she and Parendon made love it was not because he was her boss, but because she felt a real passion for him.

'I imagine you don't have a lover. . . .'

'That's right. I don't want one.'

'Don't you mind living alone?'

'On the contrary. I would find it unbearable to have someone around all the time. Even more so to have someone in my bed.'

'No passing affairs?'

Still that slight hesitation between the truth and a lie.

'Sometimes. Very rarely.'

And, with a pride which was quite comic, she added as if she were making a profession of faith:

'But never in my flat.'

'What kind of relationship is there between Gus and his father? I did ask before, but we got side-tracked.'

'Gus admires him. But he admires him from a distance, without letting him see it, with a kind of humility. You see, to understand them you must know the whole family, and your investigations will go on for ever. . . .

'You know that the flat belonged to Monsieur Gassin de

Beaulieu, and it is full of reminders of him. The former president has been ill for three years and never leaves the manor-house in the Vendée. But before that he sometimes came to spend a week or two here—he still has a room—and, from the moment he came in, he was master of the house again.'

'So you knew him?'

'Very well. He used to dictate all his letters to me.'

'What kind of a man is he? From his portrait . . .'

'The one in Monsieur Parendon's office? If you have seen the portrait, you have seen the man. What is called an upright and honest judge and a cultivated man. You know what I mean? A man who walked around larger than life and who acted as if he had just stepped down from his pedestal.

'While he was here, no one in the flat was allowed to make any noise. Everyone walked on tiptoe. They whispered. The children, who were younger then than they are now, lived in terror . . .

'Monsieur Parendon's father, the surgeon, on the other hand. . . .'

'Does he still come?'

'Not very often. That's just what I was going to tell you. You will have heard the stories about him, everyone has. He was the son of peasants in Berry, and he always behaved like a peasant. His speech is rough and colourful on purpose, even in his lectures.

'A few years ago he was still a force of nature. Since he lives very near here, in the Rue de Miromesnil, he often used to drop in for a visit, just in passing, and the children adored him.

'That didn't please everyone. . . .'

'Particularly Madame Parendon. . . .'

'It's true there was no love lost between them. I don't know anything for sure. The servants have talked about a violent scene which took place. At any rate, he doesn't come any more, but his son goes to visit him every two or three days.'

'So the Gassins, in fact, have beaten the Parendons.'

'More than you think.'

The air was blue with smoke from Maigret's pipe and

Mademoiselle Vague's cigarettes. The girl walked over to the window which she opened wider to let in the fresh air.

'Because,' she went on in an amused tone, 'the children have aunts, uncles and cousins. Monsieur Gassin de Beaulieu had four daughters, and the other three live in Paris too. They have children ranging in age from ten to twenty-two. In fact, last spring one of the girls married an officer who works at the Ministry for the Navy.

'So much for the Gassin de Beaulieu clan. If you want, I will make up a list for you, with their husbands' names.'

'I don't think that will be necessary just now. Do they often come here?'

'Sometimes one of them, sometimes another, Although they've been married for a long time, they still consider this house as the family home.'

'While on the other hand . . .'

'You have understood what I was going to say before I said it. Monsieur Parendon's brother, Germain, is a doctor, a specialist in infantile neurology. He is married to a former actress who still looks young and vivacious. . . .'

'Does he look like . . . ?'

Maigret was a little embarrassed by his question, and she understood.

'No. He's just as broad and powerful as his father, and much taller. He is an extremely handsome man, and it is surprising to find he's so gentle. He and his wife have no children. They don't go out much and only entertain close friends. . . .'

'But they don't come here,' sighed Maigret, who was beginning to form a fairly accurate picture of the family.

'Monsieur Parendon goes to see them on the evenings when his wife plays bridge, since he loathes cards. Sometimes Monsieur Germain comes to visit him in his office. I can tell if he has been when I come in in the morning because the rooms smells of cigars.'

Maigret seemed suddenly to change his tone of voice. He did not grow menacing or severe, but the trace of badinage and amusement in his voice and eyes was no longer there.

'Listen to me, Mademoiselle Vague. I am sure you have

answered me with complete honesty, and sometimes you have even anticipated my questions. I still have one more to ask you and I beg you to be just as sincere. Do you think these letters are a joke?'

She answered without hesitation:

'No.'

'Before they were written, had you ever felt that something terrible was about to take place in this house?'

This time she took her time, lit another cigarette, then said:

'Perhaps . . .'

'When?'

'I don't know. I'm thinking. . . . Perhaps after the summer holidays. Round about then, anyway.'

'What did you notice?'

'Nothing in particular. Just something in the air. . . . I'm tempted to say a sort of oppression.'

'Who, in your opinion, is the person who is being threatened?'

She blushed suddenly and was silent.

'Why won't you answer?'

'Because you know perfectly well what I would say: Monsieur Parendon.'

He stood up, sighing.

'Thank you. I think I have tormented you enough this morning. I'll probably come back to see you again soon.'

'Do you want to question the others?'

'Not before lunch. It's almost noon. I expect I'll see them afterwards.'

She watched him leave, tall, bulky, awkward, then suddenly, when the front door had closed again, she began to cry.

CHAPTER THREE

IN THE RUE DE MIROMESNIL there was a dark little restaurant, a relic of former days, where the menu was still written on a slate and where one could see the proprietor's wife through a glass door, a big woman with legs like columns, standing over her stove.

The regulars each had their napkin in a pigeon-hole and frowned when someone took their seat. That was a rare occurrence since the waitress, Emma, didn't like new faces. Some of the older inspectors from the Rue de Saussaies frequented the place and so did clerks of the type one hardly ever sees any more, the type one imagines seated in front of ancient black desks, wearing cotton lustre over-sleeves.

The proprietor, seated at his desk, recognized the superintendent and came over to welcome him.

'It's a long time since we've seen you round here. Anyway, you can congratulate yourself on your sense of smell—there are *andouillettes* today.'

Maigret liked to eat alone like that from time to time, letting his eye wander over an old-fashioned décor, over characters who mainly worked in back yards or in unexpected offices— disputed claims offices, security loans offices, orthopaedists, timber merchants. . . .

As he himself said, he ruminated. He didn't think. His mind wandered from one idea to another, sometimes tying in old cases with the one on hand.

Parendon fascinated him. In his mind, as he ate the crisp, juicy *andouillette* served with chips that didn't taste of grease, the gnome assumed aspects which were both moving and frightening.

'Article 64, Monsieur Maigret! Don't forget Article 64!'

Was it really an obsession with him? Why did this important

lawyer, a man people came from all over the world to consult at great expense on maritime matters, why did he hypnotise himself to such an extent about the only article of the Penal Code which in fact dealt with human responsibility?

Oh, yes, it did it prudently. Without giving the slightest definition of dementia. And limiting it to the moment of the action, that is to say, to the moment of the actual crime.

He knew some psychiatrists of the old school, the men the judges like to choose as experts because they do not look for subtleties. Those men, in delimiting the responsibility of a criminal, only take brain lesions or malformations into account, or, since the Penal Code mentions it in the next article, epilepsy.

But how can one establish that a man, at the moment when he killed another, at the precise moment of the death blow, was in full possession of his faculties? How, even more important, can one swear that he was capable of resisting the impulse?

Article 64, yes . . . Maigret had often argued about it, particularly with his old friend Pardon. It was argued over, too, at almost every congress of the International Society of Criminology, and there were fat volumes on the subject, the very volumes which filled a large part of Parendon's library.

'Well? Is it good?'

The jovial proprietor refilled his glass with a Beaujolais which was perhaps on the young side but had exactly the right fruity taste.

'You wife hasn't lost her touch.'

'She'd be pleased if you would go and tell her that before you leave.'

The house was made in the image of a man like Gassin de Beaulieu, a man of noble birth, a Commander of the Legion of Honour, a man who had never entertained any doubts about the Code, about the law, or about himself.

Seated at the tables round about Maigret were thin men, fat men, men in their thirties, men in their fifties. Almost all of them were eating alone, staring into space or at a newspaper. They had in common that particular patina given by a humble, monotonous way of life.

There is a tendency to imagine people the way one wishes them to be. Here, one man had a crooked nose or a receding chin, another had one shoulder too low, while his neighbour was obese. Half of the heads were bald, and more than half of those eating wore glasses.

Why did Maigret think of that? For no reason in particular. Because Parendon, in his huge study, looked like a gnome; others, more cruel, might have said like a monkey.

As for Madame Parendon. . . . He had hardly seen her. She had only put in a rapid appearance, as if to give him a sample of her brilliant personality. How had that pair got together? By what happy meeting or through what clever stroke of family business?

As well as those two there was Gus, who worked at his hi-fi and electronics in his bedroom with the *pâtisser*'s son. He was taller, stronger than his father, luckily, and, if one could believe Mademoiselle Vague, he was a well-balanced boy.

There was also his sister Bambi, studying archaeology. Did she really intend to dig in the deserts of the Near East some day, or were those studies only a blind?

Mademoiselle Vague fiercely defended her employer with whom she could only make love in the corner of the office, on the sly. Why in heaven's name didn't they meet somewhere else? Were they both so afraid of Madame Parendon? Or was it through a sense of guilt that they had to keep the furtive, impromptu element in their relationship?

There was also the former legionnaire turned butler; the cook and the housekeeper who detested each other because of their hours of work and their wages; and a maid called Lise whom Maigret hadn't yet met and who had scarcely been mentioned to him.

There was René Tortu, who had slept just once with the secretary and was at present dragging out a long engagement to another girl. Finally there was Julien Baud, who was learning about Paris as a lawyer's copying clerk before breaking into the world of the theatre.

Whose side were they on, each one of them? The Gassins'? The Parendons'?

Someone in that list wanted to kill someone else.

And, by an ironic touch, a former inspector of the Sûreté Nationale held the post of concierge downstairs.

The gardens of the President of the Republic were across the street and, through the trees which were beginning to turn green although it was early yet, the well-known steps where he was photographed shaking hands with his important guests.

Wasn't there a certain incoherence? The bistros, the things around Maigret, seemed more real, more solid. It was everyday life. Unimportant people, yes, but there are more unimportant people than there are others, even if they are less often noticed, dress soberly, speak more quietly, hug the walls as they walk along or huddle together in the métro.

He was automatically served a *baba au rhum* liberally covered with *crème Chantilly*, another of the proprietor's wife's specialities. Maigret remembered to go into the kitchen to shake hands with her. He even had to kiss her on both cheeks. It was the tradition.

'I hope it won't be so long before you come again.'

If the murderer took his time, Maigret might well be back often. . . .

For his thoughts kept returning to the murderer. To the murderer who wasn't yet a murderer. To the potential murderer.

Are there not thousands and thousands of potential murderers in Paris?

Why had this one felt it necessary to warn Maigret in advance? Through a kind of romanticism? To make himself interesting? Or did he want to be stopped before he did anything?

How could he be stopped?

Maigret walked up as far as Saint-Philippe-du-Roule in the sunshine and turned to the left, stopping from time to time in front of a shop window: very expensive things, often quite useless, which people bought anyway.

He passed the Papeterie Roman, where he amused himself

by reading names straight out of the Almanach de Gotha on visiting cards or engraved invitations. This was where the paper which had started it all had come from. Without the anonymous letters, Maigret would still not have known the Parendons, the Gassin de Beaulieus, the aunts, the uncles, the cousins.

Like him, other people were walking along the pavements just for the pleasure of screwing up their eyes in the sunlight and breathing the air with its little gusts of warmth. He felt like shrugging his shoulders, jumping on the first open bus that came along and going back to the Quai.

'To hell with the Parendons!'

Back there he might find some poor man who had really killed, because he could no longer do anything else, or perhaps a young tough from Pigalle, newly arrived from Marseilles or Bastia, who had done in a rival to prove he was a man.

He took a seat on a café terrace, near a brazier, to drink his coffee. Then he went inside and shut himself in the telephone booth.

'Maigret here. . . . Get me someone from my office, please. . . . It doesn't matter. Janvier, Lucas or Lapointe if you can. . . .'

It was Lapointe who answered.

'Anything new, son?'

'A phone call from Madame Parendon. She wanted to speak to you in person, and I had a terrible time getting her to understand that you have lunch just like anyone else. . . .'

'What did she want?'

'She wants you to go and see her as soon as possible.'

'At home?'

'Yes. She'll wait for you until four o'clock. She has an important appointment after that.'

'With her hairdresser, no doubt. Is that all?'

'No, but the other might be a joke. . . . Half an hour ago the telephonist had someone on the line, a man or a woman, she couldn't tell which, an odd voice, or it might have been a child's. . . . Anyway the person was breathing hard, in a hurry or upset, and he said very quickly:

' "Tell Superintendent Maigret to hurry. . . ." '

53

'The telephonist had no time to ask anything—the person had already hung up.

'It isn't a letter this time, and that's why I'm asking myself. . . .'

Maigret almost told him:

'Don't ask yourself anything.'

He wasn't asking himself any questions. He wasn't trying to play guessing games, but that didn't stop him from being worried.

'Thank you, my boy. I'm just going back to the Avenue Marigny. If anything comes up, you can call me there.'

The fingerprints on the two letters hadn't been any use. For years incriminating fingerprints have been getting rarer and rarer because they have been talked about so much in the papers, in novels and on television that even the most obtuse criminals take precautions.

He walked past the lodge where the former inspector from the Rue de Saussaies greeted him with respectful familiarity. The Rolls stood in front of the porch, with no one in it except the chauffeur. Maigret climbed up to the first floor and rang the bell.

'Good afternoon, Ferdinand.'

He was becoming a part of the household, wasn't he?

'I'll take you to Madame. . . .'

Ferdinand had had his instructions. She had left nothing to chance. His hat was taken away as if he were in a restaurant, and for the first time he walked through an immense drawing-room such as a minister of state might have. There were no personal objects lying around—no scarf, no cigarette-holder, no open book. Not a speck in the ash-trays. Three tall open windows looked out on the quiet courtyard which was now bathed in sunshine and where no cars were now being washed.

A corridor. A sharp turn. The flat seemed to be formed of a central body and two wings, like an old château. A strip of red carpeting on the white marble floor. Always the too-tall ceilings which dwarfed everyone.

Ferdinand knocked gently at a double door, which he opened without waiting for a reply, and announced:

'Superintendent Maigret.'

He found himself in an empty boudoir, but Madame Parendon appeared immediately from a neighbouring room, her arm outstretched, walking in front of Maigret, whose hand she shook vigorously.

'I am a little ashamed, Superintendent, of having telephoned you, or rather of having telephoned one of your subordinates. . . .'

Here everything was blue, the silk brocade covering the walls, the Louis XV armchairs, the upholstery, even the yellow-patterned Chinese carpet had a blue background.

Was it by chance that, at two in the afternoon, she was still wearing a négligé, a turquoise blue négligé?

'Forgive me for receiving you in my den, as I call it, but it is the only place where one isn't incessantly interrupted. . . .'

The door through which she had come was still ajar, and he caught a glimpse of a dressing-table, also Louis XV, which indicated that it was her bedroom.

'Do sit down.'

She pointed to a fragile chair into which the superintendent eased himself carefully, telling himself not to move too much.

'Do smoke your pipe. . . .'

Even if he didn't want to! She wanted him to be like the newspaper photographs. The photographers, too, never failed to remind him:

'Your pipe, Superintendent. . . .'

As if he puffed at his pipe from morning till night! What if he wanted to smoke a cigarette? Or a cigar? Or not to smoke at all?

He did not like the chair he was sitting in, which he expected to break at any moment. He did not like this blue boudoir or this woman in blue who was giving him a veiled smile.

She was sitting in a bergère chair. She lit a cigarette with a gold lighter such as he had seen in Cartier's window. The cigarette case was gold. Quite a few things in these rooms must be gold.

'I am a little jealous of the fact that you went to see the little Vague girl before you came to see me. This morning. . . .'

'I shouldn't have dared to disturb you so early. . . .'

Was he going to turn into a diplomatic Maigret? He was annoyed at his own suavity.

'No doubt you have been told that I get up late and that I keep to my rooms until midday. . . . It is true and it isn't. I lead a very busy life, Monsieur Maigret, and in fact I start my days early.

'First of all there is this big house to run. If I did not telephone to the shops myself, I don't know what we should eat, nor what kind of bills we should get at the end of the month. Madame Vauquin is an excellent cook, but the telephone still frightens her and makes her stammer. The children take up my time. Even though they are grown up now, I have to take an interest in their clothes, their activities. . . .

'If it weren't for me, Gus would live in jeans, a sweater and tennis shoes all the year round. . . .

'It doesn't matter. I won't mention the charity work I am involved in. Other people are content to send a cheque or to attend a cocktail party, but when it's a question of real work, you won't find anyone. . . .'

He waited patiently, politely, so patiently and so politely that he did not bring her back to the matter in hand.

'I imagine you lead a very busy life too.'

'You understand, Madame, I am only a civil servant.'

She laughed, showing all her teeth, the tip of a pink tongue. Her tongue was very pointed, he noticed. She was blonde, almost a strawberry blonde, and her eyes were the colour usually called green, but which is more often a dark grey.

Was she forty? A bit more? A bit less? Forty-five? It was impossible to say, so strong was the effect of the beautician's work.

'I must tell that to Jacqueline. . . . She is the wife of the Minister of the Interior, one of my best friends. . . .'

Good! He had been warned. She had wasted no time in playing her first trump.

'I may appear to be joking . . . I am joking. . . . But you must realize that that is only a front. In fact, Monsieur Maigret, I am tormented by what is happening, more than tormented. . . .'

Then, straight to the point:

'What did you think of my husband?'

'He is very pleasant. . . .'

'Of course. That's what everyone says. I mean. . . .'

'He is very intelligent, remarkably intelligent.'

She was growing impatient. She knew what she was getting at and he was interrupting her. Maigret, looking at her hands, noted that they were older than her face.

'I think that he is very sensitive, too.'

'If you were being quite honest, wouldn't you say he is over-sensitive?'

He opened his mouth to reply, but this time it was she who won, adding:

'Sometimes he frightens me, he is so introspective. He is a man who suffers. I have always known that. When I married him there was at first a certain amount of pity in my love for him.'

Maigret played the idiot.

'Why?'

For a moment she was put out of her stride.

'But . . . but you have seen him. Right from childhood, he must have been ashamed of his looks.'

'He isn't tall. Many other men. . . .'

'Look here, Superintendent.' She braced herself. 'Let us lay our cards on the table. I don't know what his heredity is, or rather I know only too well—his mother was a young nurse at Laënnec, a ward maid really, and she was only sixteen when Professor Parendon gave her a child. Why on earth, since he was a surgeon, didn't he perform an abortion? Did she threaten to expose him? I don't know. . . . What I do know is that Emile was a seven months' baby. . . . That is, a premature baby.'

'Most premature babies grow into normal children. . . .'

'Do you think he is normal?'

57

'In what sense?'

She stubbed her cigarette out nervously, only to light another.

'Excuse me. You seem to be avoiding the issue, to be trying not to understand.'

'To understand what?'

She couldn't stand it any longer, got up suddenly and began to pace the Chinese carpet.

'To understand why I am worried, why, as they say, I am all churned up. For almost twenty years I have forced myself to protect him, to make him happy, to give him a normal life. . . .'

He kept on smoking his pipe in silence, his eyes following her. She was wearing extremely elegant slippers which must have been made to measure.

'Those letters he told me about. . . . I don't know who wrote them, but they reflect my own fears quite closely.'

'Has this been going on for a long time?'

'Weeks . . . Months . . . I hardly dare say years. When we were first married he went places with me, we went out, we went to the theatre, we dined in town. . . .'

'Did that make him happy?'

'It relaxed him, at any rate. I suspect now that he never feels at ease, that he is ashamed that he is not like other men, that he has always felt like that. . . .

'Wait! Even his choice of Maritime Law as a career. . . . Can you tell me for what reason a man like him could have chosen Maritime Law? It was a sort of act of defiance. Since he couldn't plead at assizes. . . .'

'Why not?'

She looked at him helplessly.

'Well really, Monsieur Maigret, you know that as well as I do. Can you see that pale, insignificant little man in the great hall of the assizes, defending a criminal's life?'

He decided not to tell her in turn that one noted barrister of the previous century was only four foot three.

'He is bored. As time goes on, as he grows older, he shuts himself away more and more, and, when we give a dinner, I have a dreadful time to get him to be present. . . .'

He also refrained from asking her who made up the invitation list.

He listened, and he watched.

He watched and tried not to worry, because the picture this taut-nerved woman with her burning energy was painting of her husband was both true and false.

True in what respect?

False in what respect?

That was what he would have liked to unravel. His vision of Emile Parendon was becoming like a blurred photograph. The contours were not clear. The features changed expression according to the angle from which they were viewed.

It was true that he was enclosed in a world of his own, the world, one might say, of Article 64. Was he a responsible person? An irresponsible one? Other men besides him were passionately interested in that most important question and councils had argued over it since the Middle Ages.

In his case, had the thought not become an obsession? Maigret remembered his own entry into the study the previous day, and the look which Parendon had shot at him, as if the superintendent was for him at that moment a sort of incarnation of the celebrated article or was capable of giving him an answer to it.

The lawyer had not asked him what he had come about, what he wanted. He had spoken of Article 64, his mouth almost trembling with passion.

It was true that . . .

Yes, he did lead an almost solitary life in this house which was as much too big for him as a giant's coat would have been.

How, with his stunted body, with all the thoughts which whirled around in his head, did he face this woman daily—this woman who was so nervous that her nervousness was communicated to everything around her?

It was true that . . .

A half-pint, maybe! A gnome—that too, perhaps.

But sometimes, when the neighbouring rooms appeared to

be empty, when the time seemed right, he made love to Mademoiselle Vague.

What was true? What was false? Didn't even Bambi protect herself from her mother by taking refuge in archaeology?

'Listen to me, Monsieur Maigret. I am not the empty-headed woman you may have been told about. I am a woman with specific responsibilities—a woman, moreover, who makes a great effort to lead a useful life. Our father brought us up like that, my sisters and me. He was a man of duty. . . .'

Oh, oh! The superintendent did not like the sound of those words: the righteous judge, the pride of the Bench, teaching his daughters the sense of duty. . . .

With her, however, it rang a little false. She did not give her mind time to fasten itself on to a sentence, for her face, her whole body quivered and word succeeded word, idea followed idea, images changed in quick succession.

'There is fear in this house, that is true. . . . And I am the one who feels that fear most. . . . No! You mustn't believe that I wrote those letters. . . . I am too direct to use such devious methods. . . .

'If I had wanted to see you, I would have telephoned you, as I did this morning. . . .

'I am afraid. . . . Not so much for me, but for him. . . . I don't know what he might do, but I feel he may do something, that he has reached the brink, that a sort of demon inside him is impelling him to take some dramatic action. . . .'

'What makes you think that?'

'You have seen him, haven't you?'

'He seemed to me to be very calm and well-balanced, and I found he had a well-developed sense of humour.'

'An irritating sense of humour, not to say macabre. . . . That man is eating himself away. . . . His work only takes up two or three days a week, and the greater part of his research is done by René Tortu. . . .

'He reads journals, writes letters to all parts of the world, to people he has never met but whose articles he has read.

'He often spends days at a time without setting foot outside, happy just to watch the world go by through the windows. . . .

Always the same chestnut trees, the same wall around the gardens of the Elysée Palace. . . . I nearly said even the same people going by. . . .

'You have come here twice and you have not asked to see me. . . . But unfortunately I am the most interested party. . . . I am his wife, do not forget that, even if he seems to forget it sometimes. . . . We have two children who still need to be taken care of. . . .'

She gave him a moment's breathing space when she lit a cigarette. It was the fourth. She smoked greedily, without slowing her rate of speech, and the boudoir was already filled with clouds of smoke.

'I don't think that you can foresee any better than I can what he will do. . . . Would he take his own life? . . . It is possible, and I would be very upset after having tried for so many years to make him happy. . . .

'Is it my fault if I haven't succeeded?

'Perhaps I shall be the victim, which is more likely, because he has come to hate me, little by little. . . . Can you understand that? . . . His brother, who is a neurologist, could explain. . . . He needs to project his disillusionment, his bitterness, his humiliations on to someone. . . .'

'Excuse me if . . .'

'Let me finish, please. Tomorrow, the next day, some day, you will perhaps be called here and you will find yourself in front of a dead woman who will be me. . . .

'I forgive him in advance, because I know he is not responsible and that medicine, in spite of all its progress . . .'

'Do you consider your husband to be a medical case?'

She looked at him with a kind of defiance.

'Yes.'

'A mental case?'

'Perhaps.'

'Have you consulted any doctors?'

'Yes.'

'Doctors who know him?'

'We have several doctors among our friends.'

'What exactly have they told you?'

61

'To take care. . . .'

'To take care of what?'

'We haven't gone into details. They were not consultations, but social conversations.'

'Are they all of the same opinion?'

'Several of them are.'

'Can you give me their names?'

Maigret said that so that he could take his black notebook out of his pocket. The gesture was enough to make her beat a retreat.

'It wouldn't be right to give you their names, but if you want to have him examined by an expert . . .'

Maigret had put aside his patient, bland manner. His face too was strained, for things were beginning to happen quickly.

'When you telephoned my office to ask me to come to see you, did you already have that in mind?'

'Have what in mind?'

'To ask me more or less directly to have your husband examined by a psychiatrist.'

'Did I say that? That is a word I never even mentioned.'

'But the thought showed clearly behind everything you said. . . .'

'In that case either you have misunderstood me or I have expressed myself badly. Perhaps I am too frank, too spontaneous. . . . I don't take the trouble to choose my words. . . . What I said to you, what I am repeating now, is that I am afraid, that there is fear running loose in this house. . . .'

'And I am repeating to you, fear of what?'

She sat down again as if she were exhausted, and looked at him hopelessly.

'I don't know what I can say to you now, Superintendent. I thought you would understand without my having to go into details. I am afraid for myself, for him. . . .'

'In other words, you are afraid that he may kill you or that he may commit suicide?'

'Put that way, it seems ridiculous, I know, when everything around us is so peaceful.'

'Forgive me if I seem indiscreet. Does your husband still have sexual relations with you?'

'Up until a year ago. . . .'

'What happened a year ago to change the situation?'

'I came upon him with that girl. . . .'

'Mademoiselle Vague?'

'Yes.'

'In the office?'

'It was so sordid. . . .'

'And after that you shut your door to him? Did he ever try to come in?'

'Only once. I told him what my reasons were and he understood.'

'Didn't he insist?'

'He didn't even apologize. He went away just like someone who has got out at the wrong floor.'

'Have you had any lovers?'

'What?'

Her eyes had grown hard, her look sharp and spiteful.

'I am asking you,' he repeated calmly, 'if you have had any lovers. These things happen, don't they?'

'Not in our family, Superintendent, and if my father were here . . .'

'In his capacity as judge, your father would understand that it is my duty to ask you the question. You have just spoken to me of an atmosphere of fear, of a threat hanging over you and your husband. You suggest, in veiled terms, that I should have him examined by a psychiatrist. So it is natural . . .'

'Forgive me. I let myself get carried away. No, I have not had any lovers, and I never shall have.'

'Do you have a gun?'

She got up, walked quickly to the neighbouring room, returned and handed Maigret a small mother-of-pearl-handled revolver.

'Take care. It is loaded.'

'Have you had it long?'

'One of my friends, a woman with a really black sense of humour, gave it to me when I got married.'

'Aren't you afraid that the children, playing around . . . ?'

'They rarely come into my bedroom, and when they were younger this gun was kept in a locked drawer.'

'Your shotguns?'

'They are in a case and the case is in the coach-house, with our trunks, suitcases and golf-bags.'

'Does your husband play golf?'

'I've tried to get him interested, but he gets out of breath by the third hole.'

'Is he often ill?'

'He has few serious illnesses. The worst, if I remember rightly, was an attack of pleurisy. On the other hand, he is constantly afflicted by little things, laryngitis, influenza, head colds. . . .'

'Does he call in his doctor?'

'Of course.'

'One of your friends?'

'No. A local practitioner, Dr Martin, who lives in the Rue du Cirque, the street behind this one.'

'Has Dr Martin ever spoken to you privately?'

'No, he hasn't, but I have often waited to catch him as he left, to make sure that my husband had nothing serious.'

'What did he say?'

'He said no. . . . That men like him often live the longest. He told me about Voltaire, who . . .'

'I know about Voltaire. Has he ever suggested that your husband consult a specialist?'

'No. . . . Only . . .'

'Only what?'

'What's the use? You will only misinterpret my words again.'

'Try, anyway.'

'I can tell from your attitude that my husband has made an excellent impression on you, and I was sure that that would be the case. I won't say that he plays a part consciously. With strangers, he is a lively man, making a great show of stability. With Dr Martin, he speaks and acts as he does with you. . . .'

'And with the servants?'

'He is not responsible for the work of the domestics.'

'What does that mean?'

'That he does not have to reprimand them. He leaves that task to me, so that I have to do the dirty work. . . .'

Maigret was stifling in the over-soft chair, in the boudoir whose blue was becoming unbearable to him. He got up and nearly stretched himself as he would in his own office.

'Have you anything else to tell me?'

She too stood up and looked him up and down as one equal to another.

'There would be no point.'

'Do you want me to send an inspector to keep permanent watch in the flat?'

'The idea is quite ridiculous.'

'Not if I am to believe your presentiments.'

'It is not a question of presentiments.'

'It is not a question of facts, either.'

'Not yet. . . .'

'Let us recap. . . . For some time, your husband has been showing signs of mental derangement. . . .'

'That's it exactly!'

'He retreats into himself and his behaviour worries you. . . .'

'That is nearer the truth.'

'You are afraid for his life or for yours. . . .'

'I admit that.'

'Which one do you think it will be?'

'If I knew that, I would be slightly less worried.'

'Someone living in this house, or someone who has easy access to it, sent us at the Quai two letters announcing that a murder would take place shortly. I may add, now, that as well as the letters there has been a telephone call in my absence. . . .'

'Why did you not tell me about that?'

'Because I was listening to you. This message, a very brief one, only confirms the ones which preceded it. The unknown man, or woman, said, more or less, "Tell Superintendent Maigret it will be soon. . . ." '

He watched her grow pale. She was not acting. Her face suddenly became lifeless, except for patches of rouge. The corners of her lips collapsed.

'Oh! . . .'

She lowered her head, and her thin body seemed to have lost its prodigious energy.

At that moment he forgot his annoyance and pitied her.

'Do you still not want me to send you someone?'

'What good would that do?'

'What do you mean?'

'If something is going to happen, the presence of a policeman who will be stationed heaven knows where won't stop it. . . .'

'Do you know that your husband has an automatic?'

'Yes.'

'Does he know that you have this revolver?'

'Of course.'

'And your children?'

Her nerves so stretched she was almost weeping, she cried:

'My children have nothing to do with this, can't you understand that? They mind their own business and not ours. They have their own lives to live. They laugh at ours, what there is left of it. . . .'

She had spoken vehemently again, as if certain subjects unleashed her anger automatically.

'You may go now! Forgive me for not showing you out. I don't know what I expected. . . . Whatever is going to happen, let it happen! . . . Go and find my husband, or that girl. . . . Goodbye, Monsieur Maigret. . . .'

She had opened the door for him, waited until he was gone and shut it again. Already, in the corridor, it seemed to the superintendent that he had come out of another world, and the blue of the boudoir he had just left haunted him still.

He looked out through a window into the yard where a different chauffeur from the one in the morning was polishing a different car. It was still sunny, with a light breeze.

He was tempted to take his hat from the cloakroom, as

he knew where it was, and to leave without saying anything. Then, as if in spite of himself, he went to Mademoiselle Vague's office.

She was wearing a white smock over her dress and was photocopying documents. The venetian blinds were closed, letting in only a few rays of light.

'Do you want to see Monsieur Parendon?'

'No.'

'That's just as well, because he's in conference with two important clients. One of them has come from Amsterdam and the other from Athens. They are both shipowners who . . .'

He wasn't listening, and she went to open the venetian blinds, flooding the narrow room with sunshine.

'You look tired.'

'I've spent an hour with Madame Parendon.'

'I know.'

He looked at the telephone switchboard.

'Did you put through her call to the Quai des Orfèvres?'

'No. I didn't even know she had phoned. It was Lise who told me when she came in and asked me for a stamp. . . .'

'Who is Lise?'

'Her maid.'

'I know. I mean what kind of person is she?'

'An ordinary girl like me. We are both from the provinces. I'm from a small town and she's from the country. Since I had some education, I became a secretary, and since she hadn't, she became a maid. . . .'

'How old is she?'

'Twenty-three. I know how old everyone is, because I fill out the forms for the Social Security.'

'Is she a devoted servant?'

'She does what she is told to do very conscientiously and I don't think she has any desire to change her job.'

'Has she any lovers?'

'When she has her day off, Saturday. . . .'

'Is she intelligent enough to have written the letters you have read?'

'Certainly not.'

67

'Did you know that Madame Parendon came upon you with her husband about a year ago?'

'I told you that it had happened once, but there have been other times when she could have opened and shut the door again without being heard. . . .'

'Has Parendon told you that his wife has refused to have sexual relations with him since then?'

'They were so infrequent anyway!'

'Why?'

'Because he doesn't love her.'

'Doesn't love her, or doesn't love her any longer?'

'That depends on what you mean by the word love. He was no doubt flattered that she married him and for years he forced himself to show his gratitude. . . .'

Maigret smiled, thinking that on the other side of the wall two important shipowners who had come from the opposite ends of Europe were putting their prosperity into the hands of the little man whom Mademoiselle Vague and he were discussing in such a way.

To them, he was not an odd, half-impotent gnome, closed in on himself, mulling over unhealthy thoughts, but one of the luminaries of Maritime Law. Were the three of them not playing with hundreds of millions while Madame Parendon, furious or depressed, disappointed in any case, dressed for her four o'clock appointment?

'Won't you sit down?'

'I think I'll have a look next door.'

'You'll only find Julien Baud there. Tortu is at the Palais de Justice.'

He gestured vaguely.

'Well, Julien Baud, then.'

CHAPTER FOUR

IT SEEMED TO MAIGRET as if he had gone into another flat. Just as the rest of the house was orderly, mummified in a solemnity previously set out by President Gassin de Beaulieu, so in the office René Tortu shared with young Julien Baud disorder and carelessness struck one's eye immediately.

By the window, a desk of the kind common to all businesses was covered with dossiers, and there were green files on the pine shelving which had been added progressively as it was needed. There were files on the ground, on the waxed floor.

As for Julien Baud's desk, it was an old kitchen table covered with wrapping paper held on with drawing pins. Photographs of nudes cut out of magazines were stuck up on the walls with scotch tape. When the superintendent pushed open the door, Baud was sticking stamps on envelopes, weighing them one by one. He raised his head and looked at him without surprise, without any emotion, appearing to be wondering what Maigret wanted.

'Are you looking for Tortu?'

'No. I know he's at the Palais.'

'He'll be back before long.'

'I'm not looking for him.'

'For whom, then?'

'No one.'

A well-built young man with red hair and freckled cheeks. His porcelain-blue eyes reflected absolute calm.

'Would you care to sit down?'

'No.'

'As you like. . . .'

He went on weighing the letters, some of which were in large manila envelopes, then he consulted a little booklet giving the postal rates for the different countries.

'Do you find that interesting?' Maigret asked.

'You know, since I first came to Paris. . . .'

He had a trace of a delightful accent, drawing out certain syllables.

'Where do you come from?'

'From Morges. . . . On the shore of Lake Geneva. . . . Do you know it?'

'I've been through it. . . .'

'It's lovely, *n'est-ce pas?*'

The 'lovely' became 'loovely' and the *n'est-ce pas* was a sing-song.

'Yes, it is lovely. . . . What do you think of this household?'

He mistook the word 'household' for 'house.'

'It's big. . . .'

'How do you get on with Monsieur Parendon?'

'I don't see him much. In my position I stick on stamps, I go to the post, I run the errands, I tie up parcels. . . . I'm not very important. From time to time the boss comes into the office and claps me on the shoulder and asks, "Everything all right, young man?"

'As for the servants, they all call me the little Swiss, even though I'm five foot eleven in my socks.'

'Do you get on well with Mademoiselle Vague?'

'She's nice. . . .'

'What do you think of her?'

'Well, you see, she's on the other side of the fence too, the boss's side.'

'What do you mean?'

'What I say, of course. They have their work there, and we have ours. When the boss needs someone, it's not me, it's her. . . .'

His face had an expression of naïveté, but the superintendent was not sure that it was not a calculated naïveté.

'I understand you want to be a playwright?'

'I try to write plays. I have already written two, but they're bad. When one comes from the canton of Vaud, like me, one has to get used to Paris first. . . .'

'Does Tortu help you?'

'Help me what?'

'To get to know Paris. By taking you around, for example. . . .'

'He has never taken me anywhere. He has other things to do.'

'What?'

'His fiancée, his friends. . . . As soon as I got off the train at the Gare de Lyon, I understood. . . . Here, it's everyone for himself.'

'Do you often see Madame Parendon?'

'Quite often, especially in the mornings. When she has forgotten to telephone one of the tradesmen, she comes to find me.

' "My dear little Baud, would you be so good as to order a leg of lamb and ask them to send it round at once. If they haven't anyone to send, run round to the butcher's, will you?"

'So I go to the butcher's, to the fishmonger's, to the grocer's. . . . I go to her shoemaker if there's a scratch on a shoe. It's always "My dear little Baud" . . . Do this or stick on the stamps. . . .'

'What is your opinion of her?'

'Maybe I'll put her in one of my plays. . . .'

'Because she is somewhat out of the ordinary?'

'There's no one quite ordinary here. They're all nuts.'

'Your boss too?'

'He's intelligent, that's for sure, because if he wasn't he wouldn't do the job he does, but he's a nut-case, isn't he? With all the money he makes he could do something other than stay sitting all the time at his desk or in an armchair. He's not very strong, I know, but still. . . .'

'Do you know about his relationship with Mademoiselle Vague?'

'Everyone knows about that. But he could afford to pay for ten women, for a hundred, if you see what I mean. . . .'

'And his relationship with his wife?'

'What relationship? They live in the same house and meet each other in the corridors like people passing in the street. Once I had to go into the dining-room during lunch, because I was alone in the office and there had just been an urgent

71

telegram . . . Well! They were all sitting there like strangers in a restaurant. . . .'

'You don't seem very fond of them.'

'I'm not so badly off. They provide characters for me.'

'Comic ones?'

'Comic and tragic at the same time. . . . Like life. . . .'

'Have you heard about the letters?'

'Of course.'

'Have you any idea who could have written them?'

'It could have been anyone. . . . It could have been me. . . .'

'Did you do it?'

'No . . . I didn't think of it. . . .'

'Does the girl get on well with you?'

'Mademoiselle Bambi?'

He shrugged his shoulders.

'I wonder if she would recognize me in the street. When she needs something, paper, scissors, anything, she comes in and helps herself without saying anything, then she goes away again, still not saying anything.'

'Is she a snob?'

'Maybe she isn't. Maybe it's just the way she is.'

'Do you believe, too, that something terrible is going to happen?'

He looked at Maigret with his big blue eyes.

'Tragedy can strike anywhere. . . . Listen, last year, one sunny day just like this, a little old lady who was walking along was run over by a bus just outside the house. . . . Well, a few seconds before, she didn't know anything was going to happen. . . .'

There were hurried steps in the corridor. A young man of about thirty, brown-haired, tall, stopped short in the doorway. He was carrying a briefcase and had an air of importance about him.

'Superintendent Maigret, I suppose.'

'You suppose correctly.'

'Did you wish to see me? Have you been waiting for me long?'

'I wasn't waiting for anyone, in fact. . . .'

He was quite handsome, with his dark hair, his well-defined features, his aggressive way of looking at people. One could tell that he was determined to be successful.

'Won't you sit down?' he asked, going over to the desk where he set down his briefcase.

'I've been sitting down a good part of the day. We were just chatting, your young colleague and I. . . .'

The word colleague visibly shocked René Tortu, who shot a dirty look at the young Swiss.

'I had an important case at the Palais. . . .'

'I know . . . Do you often plead?'

'Whenever a conciliation becomes impossible. Maître Parendon rarely appears in person before the judges. We prepare the dossiers and then it is my duty. . . .'

'I understand.'

The young man had no doubts as to his own importance.

'What do you think of Maître Parendon?'

'As a man or as a jurist?'

'As both.'

'As a jurist, he is head and shoulders above his colleagues and there is no one more able than he at picking out the weak point in an adversary's argument.'

'And as a man?'

'Working for him, being so to speak his sole assistant, it is not my place to judge him on that basis.'

'Do you think he is vulnerable?'

'I would not have thought of that word. Let's say that in his place I would lead a more active life.'

'Being present at the receptions given by his wife, for example, going to the theatre with her, or dining in town?'

'Perhaps. . . . There are other things to life than books and dossiers.'

'Have you read the letters?'

'Maître Parendon has shown me the photostats.'

'Do you believe it is a joke?'

'Perhaps. I must confess I haven't thought about it much.'

'And yet they announce that something terrible is going to happen imminently, in this house.'

Tortu said nothing. He took some papers out of his brief-case and put them in the files.

'Would you marry a girl who was a younger edition of Madame Parendon?'

Tortu looked at him in amazement.

'I'm already engaged, didn't you know? So there's no question. . . .'

'It's a way of asking you what you think of her.'

'She is active, intelligent, and she knows how to treat. . . .'

He looked towards the door suddenly and there, standing in the doorway, was the woman they were talking about. She was wearing a leopard-skin coat over a black silk dress. She was either going out or she had just come in.

'Are you still here?' she asked in astonishment, giving the superintendent a calm, cold look.

'You can see that I am. . . .'

It was difficult to know how long she had been in the corridor and how much of the conversation she had heard. Maigret understood what Madcmoiselle Vague had meant when she spoke of a house where one never knew if one was being spied on.

'My dear little Baud, would you ring the Comtesse de Prange immediately and tell her that I shall be at least a quarter of an hour late because I was held up at the last moment? . . . Mademoiselle Vague is occupied with my husband and those gentlemen. . . .'

She left, after a last hard look at Maigret, Julien Baud picked up the telephone receiver. As for Tortu, he must have been pleased, because if Madame Parendon had heard his last words she could only be grateful to him.

'Hello. . . . Is that the residence of the Comtesse de Prange?"

Maigret shrugged his shoulders and left. Julien Baud amused him and he wasn't at all sure that the boy wouldn't make a success of a career as a dramatist. As for Tortu, he did not like him at all, for no reason in particular.

Just as he reached the cloakroom, to get his hat, Ferdinand appeared as if by chance.

'Do you stay near the door all day?'

'No, Superintendent . . . I only thought it would not be long before you left. . . . Madame went out a few moments ago.'

'I know. . . . Have you ever been in jail, Ferdinand?'

'Only military prison, in Africa.'

'Are you French?'

'I'm from Aubagne.'

'Then why did you enlist in the Foreign Legion?'

'I was young . . . I had done some stupid things. . . .'

'In Aubagne?'

'In Toulon. Bad company, that sort of thing. . . . When I thought things were about to go badly for me, I enlisted in the Legion saying I was Belgian.'

'Have you ever been in trouble since?'

'I've been in service with Monsieur Parendon for eight years and he has never made any complaint.'

'Do you like this job?'

'There are worse. . . .'

'Does Monsieur Parendon treat you well?'

'They don't come any better than him. . . .'

'And Madame?'

'Between you and me, she's a bitch.'

'Does she give you a hard life?'

'She gives everyone a hard life. . . . She is everywhere, sticks her nose into everything, complains about everything. . . . Thank God my room is over the garage.'

'So that you can have your girl-friends in?'

'If I were as foolish as to do that and she found out, she'd sack me on the spot. As far as she's concerned, servants should be castrated. . . . No, but being over there lets me breathe easy. It also lets me go out when I want, even though there's a bell in my flat and I'm supposed to be on call, she says, twenty-four hours a day. . . .'

'Has she ever called you at night?'

'Three or four times. Probably just to make sure that I was there.'

'What was her excuse?'

'Once, she had heard a suspicious noise and she made a tour of the rooms with me looking for a burglar. . . .'

'Was it a cat?'

'There isn't a cat or dog in the house—she wouldn't stand for it. When Monsieur Gus was younger, he asked for a puppy for Christmas, but he got an electric train instead. I've never seen a boy throw such a fit of temper.'

'And the other times?'

'One time, it was a smell of burning. The third . . . wait a minute . . . oh, yes! . . . She had been listening at Monsieur's door and she hadn't heard his breathing. She sent me to see that nothing had happened to him.'

'Couldn't she have gone in herself?'

'I suppose she had her reasons. Mind you, I'm not complaining. Since she goes out in the afternoons and almost every evening, there are long periods of peace.'

'Do you get on well with Lise?'

'Not too badly. She's a pretty girl. For a time . . . well, you know what I mean. . . . She needs to change. . . . Almost every Saturday it's a different man. . . . Well, since I don't like to share. . . .'

'What about Madame Vauquin?'

'That old cow!'

'Doesn't she like you?'

'She measures out our food as if we were boarders and she's even more miserly with the wine, no doubt because her husband's a drunk who beats her at least twice a week— naturally she has it in for all men.'

'Madame Marchand?'

'I hardly see her except when she's pushing her vacuum cleaner. That woman never talks, but she moves her lips whenever she's alone. Maybe she's praying.'

'Mademoiselle?'

'She isn't proud, or affected. It's a pity she's always so sad.'

'Do you think she's unhappy in love?'

'I don't know. Maybe it's just the atmosphere in the house. . . .'

'Have you heard about the letters?'

He seemed embarrassed.

'I may as well tell you the truth . . . Yes . . . But I haven't read them.'

'Who told you about them?'

Even more embarrassed, he pretended to search his memory.

'I don't know. . . . I come, I go, I say a few words to someone, a few to someone else. . . .'

'Was it Mademoiselle Vague?'

'No. She never talks about Monsieur's business.'

'Monsieur Tortu?'

'That chap thinks he's my boss all over again.'

'Julien Baud?'

'Perhaps. . . . Really, I don't remember. . . . It was maybe in the office. . . .'

'Do you know if there are any guns in the house?'

'Monsieur has a Browning in the drawer of his bedside table, but I haven't seen any cartridges in the room.'

'Do you do his room?'

'That's part of my duties. I serve at table too, of course.'

'Don't you know of any other gun?'

'There's Madame's little toy, a 6.33 made at Herstal. . . . You'd need to fire it point-blank to hurt anyone. . . .'

'Have you felt any change in the atmosphere in the house lately?'

He seemed to think.

'Possibly. They never talk much at table. Now I might say they never talk at all. Only a few words between Monsieur Gus and Mademoiselle, from time to time. . . .'

'Do you believe the letters?'

'About as much as I believe in astrology. According to the horoscopes in the paper I ought to get a fat sum of money at least once a week. . . .'

'So you don't think that something might happen?'

'Not because of the letters.'

'Because of what, then?'

'I don't know.'

'Does Monsieur Parendon seem odd to you?'

'That depends on what you mean by odd. Everyone has his

77

own idea about the life he leads. If he's happy like that . . . Anyway, he's not mad. I would even say, quite the opposite. . . .'

'That she is the one who is mad?'

'Not that either! Good Lord! That woman is as wily as a fox.'

'Thank you, Ferdinand.'

'I do my best, Superintendent. I've learned that it pays to be honest with the police.'

The door shut behind Maigret. He went down the broad staircase with its wrought-iron balustrade. He waved a hand to the concierge who was braided like a hotel porter, and breathed the fresh air again with a sigh of relaxation.

He remembered a pleasant bar on the corner of the Avenue Marigny and the Rue de la Cirque, and it wasn't long before he was leaning at the counter. He wondered what he would drink, and ended up by ordering a pint of beer. The atmosphere of the Parendons still stuck to him. But would it not have been the same if he had spent as long with any family?

With less intensity, perhaps. He would doubtless have found the same spites, the same pettinesses, the same fears, in any case the same incoherence.

'Don't philosophize, Maigret!'

Didn't he forbid himself to think, on principle? Good! He had not seen the two children, nor the cook, nor the cleaning-woman. He had only seen the maid in the distance, in a black uniform with a lace cap and apron.

Because he was on the corner of the Rue du Cirque he remembered Dr Martin, Parendon's personal physician.

'I suppose I should see you?' he said to himself.

He caught sight of the plate on the front of the building, climbed to the third floor, was shown into a waiting room where there were already three people and, discouraged, came out again.

'Aren't you waiting to see the doctor?'

'I didn't come for a consultation. I'll ring him.'

'What name?'

'Superintendent Maigret.'

'Wouldn't you like me to tell him that you are here?'

'I would rather not make his patients wait any longer than they have to. . . .'

There was the other Parendon, the brother, but he was a doctor too, and Maigret knew enough about the routine of Parisian doctors, through his friend Pardon.

He didn't want to take the bus, or the métro. He felt weary, heavy with tiredness, and he let himself collapse into a taxi.

'Quai des Orfèvres. . . .'

'Yes, Monsieur Maigret. . . .'

That did not please him. He used to be rather proud of being recognized, but for some years he had grown rather more irritated by it.

What kind of a fool would he look if nothing happened in the house in the Avenue Marigny? He had not even dared to mention the letters at the briefing. For two days he had neglected his office and had spent most of his time in a flat where the people led a kind of life which had nothing to do with him.

There were cases in progress, not, happily, very important ones, to which he should still be giving his attention.

Was it the letters, plus the midday telephone call, which were twisting his view of people? He could not think of Madame Parendon as an ordinary woman he might meet anywhere. He saw her again in his mind's eye, pathetic in all the blue of her boudoir and her négligé, putting on some kind of act for his benefit.

Parendon too had stopped being an ordinary man. The gnome looked at him with his pale eyes made bigger by the thick lenses, and Maigret tried in vain to read his thoughts in them.

The others . . . Mademoiselle Vague . . . that big red-headed boy Julien Baud . . . Tortu looking suddenly at the door where Madame Parendon had appeared as if by magic.

He shrugged his shoulders and, since the car was coming to a stop in front of the main door of the Police Judiciaire, he went through his pockets looking for change.

Some ten inspectors filed into his office, each one with a

79

problem to hand over to him. He opened the mail which had come in in his absence and signed a pile of documents, but all the time that he was working in the sunny calm of his office, the house in the Avenue Marigny remained at the back of his mind.

He felt an uneasiness which he could not throw off. And yet he had done everything he could. No crime, no misdemeanour had been committed. No one had called the police officially for a special reason. No one had lodged a complaint.

Nevertheless he had devoted hours of studying the little world which revolved around Emile Parendon.

He searched his memory in vain for a precedent. Yet he had dealt with all kinds of situations.

At a quarter past five someone brought him an express letter which had just arrived, and he recognized the block letters at once.

The stamp showed that the sheet had been lodged at half-past four at the post office in the Rue de Miromesnil. That is to say, a quarter of an hour after he had left the Parendons' house.

He tore off the strip on the dotted line. Because of the size of the sheet, the writing was smaller than in the previous letters, and Maigret noted, comparing them, that this one had been written more quickly, less carefully, possibly in a kind of feverish haste.

'Dear Superintendent,
    'When I wrote my first letter to you and asked you to give me your answer in the guise of an advertisement, I could not have imagined that you would charge head first into this case about which I had hoped later to give you indispensable details.
    'Your haste has spoiled everything, and now you yourself must realize that you are all at sea. Today you have provoked the murderer in some way, and I am sure that he will feel obliged to strike because of you.
    'I may be wrong, but I believe it will be sometime in the

next few hours. I cannot help you. I am sorry. I do not hold it against you.'

Maigret re-read the letter with a grave expression on his face and went to the door to call Janvier and Lapointe. Lucas was not there.

'Read this, boys.'

He watched them with some anxiety, as if to see if their reactions were the same as his. They had not been intoxicated by the time spent in the flat. They could only judge by the bits of evidence they had seen.

Leaning together over the sheet of paper, they showed an increasing interest and grew rather worried.

'It looks as if things are hotting up,' murmured Janvier, laying the express letter on the desk.

'What are these people like?' asked Lapointe.

'Like everybody else and like no one at all. . . . What I'm wondering is what we can do. I can't leave a man in the flat permanently, and anyway that wouldn't do any good— the place is so vast that anything could happen in one part without someone in another part noticing. Have someone posted in the building? I'm going to do that tonight to ease my conscience, but, if the letters are not a joke, the blow won't come from outside the flat. . . .

'Are you free, Lapointe?'

'I haven't anything special on, chief.'

'Right, you'll go there. You'll find the concierge in the lodge, a man called Lamure who used to work in the Rue de Saussaies. Spend the night in his room and go up to the first floor from time to time. Get Lamure to make you a list of all the people living in the building, including the staff, and check all points of entry.'

'I see.'

'What do you see?'

'That this way, if anything happens, we'll at least have something to work on. . . .'

It was true, but the superintendent hated to look at the situation in that light. If anything happened. . . . All right!

Since it wasn't a question of theft, it could only be a death. . . .
Whose death? . . . Killed by whom? . . .

People had talked to him, had answered his questions, had
seemed to be telling the truth. Was it up to him, dammit, to
tell who was lying and who was telling the truth, or even if
one of the people in the case was crazy?

He strode up and down his office with furious steps and
talked as if to himself, while Lapointe and Janvier exchanged
glances.

'It's quite simple, Superintendent. . . . Someone writes to
you and says that someone is going to kill. . . . The only thing
is, he can't tell you in advance who will kill whom, or when,
or how. . . . Why does he write to you? . . . Why warn you? . . .
For no reason at all . . . to amuse himself. . . .'

He seized a pipe and filled it, tapping it nervously with his
index finger.

'Who does he take me for, anyway? . . . If something
happens, they'll say it's my fault. . . . That woman in the blue
chiffon thinks it is already. . . . It seems I've gone to work too
quickly. . . . What should I have done? . . .

'Waited for an invitation? . . . All right! And if nothing
happens, *I* look like a mug, *I'm* the man who has wasted the
tax-payers' money for two days. . . .'

Janvier remained serious, but Lapointe could not help
smiling and Maigret saw him. For a moment he stopped, still
angry, then he laughed, clapping his assistant on the shoulder.

'I'm sorry, boys. This case will drive me mad. Over there
everybody goes around on tiptoe and I began to go on tiptoe too, to tread as if I were walking on eggshells. . . .'

This time Janvier had to laugh too, imagining Maigret
walking on eggshells.

'At least I can burst out here. . . . That's it. . . . Let's talk
seriously. Lapointe, you can go now. Get something to eat and
go and take up your post in the Avenue Marigny. If anything
at all odd happens, don't hesitate to telephone me at home,
even if it should be the middle of the night.

'Good night. See you tomorrow. Someone will relieve you
at about eight in the morning. . . .'

He went over to the window and stood there. His eyes following the course of the Seine, he went on for Janvier's benefit:

'Are you on any particular case at the moment?'

'I arrested the two boys this morning, two kids of sixteen. . . . You were right. . . .'

'Will you take over from Lapointe tomorrow morning? It seems stupid, I know, and that's why I'm annoyed, but I feel obliged to take these precautions which in any case don't serve any useful purpose.

'You'll see, if anything happens everyone will blame me. . . .'

While he spoke the last sentence he was staring at one of the lamp-posts on the Pont Saint-Michel.

'Give me the express letter.'

He had remembered a word, one he had not paid any attention to before, and he wondered if his memory was at fault.

'. . . I am sure that he will feel obliged to strike because of you. . . .'

The word 'strike' was indeed there. Obviously that could mean strike a hard blow. But, in the three letters, the anonymous correspondent had shown a certain meticulousness in his choice of words.

'Strike, you see? Both the man and the woman have a gun. I was in fact going to demand that they be handed over to us, the way I would take matches away from children. But I can't take away all their kitchen knives and all the paper-knives. . . . One can strike with pokers too, and there is no lack of fireplaces there . . . nor of candlesticks . . . nor of statues. . . .'

Suddenly changing his tone, he said:

'Try and get me Germain Parendon on the phone. He's a neurologist, lives in the Rue d'Aguesseau, my Parendon's brother.'

He lit his pipe while he waited. Janvier, sitting on a corner of the desk, fiddled with the telephone.

'Hello? Is that Dr Parendon's house? . . . This is the Police Judiciaire, Mademoiselle. . . . Superintendent Maigret's office. . . . The superintendent would like to speak to the

doctor for a moment. . . . What? . . . In Nice? . . . Yes. . . .
Just a moment. . . .'

For Maigret was signalling to him.

'Ask her where he's staying.'

'Are you still there? Could you tell me where the doctor is staying? At the Negresco? . . . Thank you. . . . Yes, I expect so . . . I'll try anyway. . . .'

'Is he seeing a patient?'

'No. It's a conference on infantile neurology. It seems it's a very heavy programme and the doctor has to give a paper tomorrow. . . .'

'Ring the Negresco. It's only six o'clock. . . . Today's programme ought to be over. They're bound to have a big dinner somewhere at eight, at the Préfecture or somewhere else. If he isn't at a cocktail party. . . .'

They had to wait ten minutes or so, because the Negresco's lines were always engaged.

'Hello, this is the Police Judiciaire in Paris, Mademoiselle. . . . Could you get me Dr Parendon, please. . . . Yes, Parendon. . . . He is one of the conference delegates. . . .'

'She is going to see if he is in his room or at the cocktail party which is going on just now in the main reception hall.

'Hello! . . . Yes, doctor. . . . Excuse me, I'll hand you over to Superintendent Maigret.'

Maigret took the receiver awkwardly, for at the last moment he didn't know what to say.

'I am sorry to disturb you, Doctor. . . .'

'I was just going to give my paper a last look over. . . .'

'That's what I imagined you would be doing. I have spent a long time with your brother, yesterday and today. . . .'

'How did you two get together?'

The voice was gay, pleasant, much younger than Maigret had imagined.

'It's quite complicated, and that's why I took the liberty of ringing you. . . .'

'Is my brother in trouble?'

'Not as far as I know. . . .'

'Is he ill?'

84

'What is your opinion of his health?'

'He seems much weaker and frailer than he really is. I couldn't stand up under the amount of work he manages to get through in a few days. . . .'

Maigret decided to come to the point.

'I'll explain as briefly as I can what the situation is. Yesterday morning I received an anonymous letter telling me that a murder was going to be committed. . . .'

'At Emile's?'

The voice was full of laughter.

'No. It would take too long to tell you how we got to your brother's house. In any case, it turned out that that letter and the next did come from his house, both written on his writing paper, with the heading carefully cut off.'

'I suppose my brother reassured you? It's a joke of Gus's, isn't it?'

'As far as I know, your nephew is not in the habit of playing practical jokes. . . .'

'That is true. Bambi isn't either. . . . I don't know. . . . Maybe the young Swiss clerk? . . . Or a housemaid? . . .'

'I have just received a third message, an express letter this time. It says that the event is about to take place.'

The doctor's tone changed.

'Do you believe it?'

'I've only known the household since yesterday. . . .'

'What does Emile have to say about it? I suppose he just shrugs it off?'

'He doesn't take it quite as lightly as that, in fact. On the contrary, I have the impression that he believes there's a real threat.'

'Against whom?'

'Perhaps against himself. . . .'

'Who on earth would want to harm him? And why? Apart from his passion for the revision of Article 64, he's the most inoffensive, friendly soul in the world. . . .'

'I liked him very much. . . . You spoke of passion just now, Doctor. . . . Would you, as a neurologist, go so far as to say mania?'

'In the medical sense, certainly not.'

His tone had become drier, for he had taken the superintendent's meaning.

'In fact, you are asking me if my brother is sane. . . .'

'I wouldn't have gone that far.'

'Are you having the house guarded?'

'I have already sent one of my inspectors over.'

'Has my brother had to deal with any shady characters lately? He hasn't set himself against business interests which are too powerful for him?'

'He didn't talk about his business affairs, but I know that this very afternoon he had a Greek shipowner and a Dutch one in his office.'

'They come from as far away as Japan. . . . We can only hope it is just a joke. . . . Have you any other questions to ask me?'

Maigret had to think quickly, as the neurologist at the other end of the line was probably looking at the Promenade des Anglais and the blue waters of the Baie des Anges.

'What is your opinion of your sister-in-law's stability?'

'Between ourselves, and I would certainly not repeat it in the witness box, if all women were like her, I would have remained a bachelor. . . .'

'I said her stability. . . .'

'I understood that. Let's say that she goes to extremes in everything . . . and, to be fair, I must admit that she is the first to suffer for it. . . .'

'Is she the kind of woman to have fixed opinions?'

'Certainly, if those opinions are plausible and spring from precise facts. I can assure you that if she told you a lie, it was so perfect a lie that you haven't noticed it. . . .'

'Would you say she is a hysteric?'

There was a fairly long silence.

'I wouldn't quite dare to go that far, although I've seen her in states which could be called hysteria. Mind you, although she is neurotic, she manages by some kind of miracle to find the strength to control herself.'

'Did you know she has a gun in her room?'

'She told me about it one evening. She even showed it to me. It's more of a toy than anything else.'

'A deadly toy. Would you let her keep it in her drawer?'

'You know, if she took it into her head to kill, she would manage it in any case, with or without a firearm.'

'Your brother has a gun, too.'

'I know.'

'Would you say the same thing about him?'

'No. I am sure, not just as a man, but as a doctor, that my brother would never kill. . . . The only thing which might happen to him would be to kill himself one evening in a fit of despair. . . .'

His voice had cracked.

'You're very fond of him, aren't you?'

'There are only the two of us. . . .'

The sentence struck Maigret. Their father was still alive and Germain Parendon too was married. Now he said:

'There are only the two of us. . . .'

As if each one had only the other in the world. Was the brother's marriage also a broken one?

Parendon, in Nice, pulling himself together. Perhaps he had looked at his watch.

'Well! Let's hope nothing happens. Goodbye, Monsieur Maigret.'

'Goodbye, Doctor Parendon.'

The superintendent had telephoned to reassure himself. But what had happened was just the opposite. After his talk with the lawyer's brother, he felt more worried than ever.

'The only thing which might happen to him . . . one evening in a fit of despair. . . .'

And was it precisely that which was going to happen?

What if it were Parendon himself who had written the anonymous letters? To stop himself from acting? To put a kind of barrier between the impulse and the act?

Maigret had forgotten Janvier, who had taken up his stand near the window.

'Did you hear that?'

'I heard what you said. . . .'

87

'He doesn't like his sister-in-law. He believes that his brother would never kill anyone, but he is less sure that he wouldn't be tempted to commit suicide some day. . . .'

The sun had gone in and it was suddenly as if something was missing. It was not yet dark. There was no need to put on the lights. The superintendent did so anyway, as if to chase the evil spirits away.

'Tomorrow you will see the house and you'll understand better. There's nothing to stop you ringing and telling Ferdinand who you are and walking round the flat and into the offices. . . . They are prepared for it. . . . They expect it. . . .

'The only thing that might happen to you would be to have Madame Parendon appear in front of you when you least expect it—I almost believe she gets around without even displacing air. . . . Well, she'll look at you and you will feel vaguely guilty. That's the impression she makes on everybody.'

Maigret called the office boy to give him the signed documents and the letters to post.

'Nothing new? No one to see me?'

'No one, Superintendent.'

Maigret was not expecting any visitors. But he was surprised that neither Gus nor his sister had appeared at any time. They, like the rest of the household, must be fully aware of what had happened since the previous day. They would certainly have heard people talking about Maigret's questionings. Perhaps they had even seen him rounding a corner in the corridor?

If Maigret, at fifteen, had heard someone say. . . .

He would of course have hastened to question the superintendent thoroughly, ready to take over from him.

He realized that time had passed, that that was another world.

'Shall we have a drink at the Brasserie Dauphine and go home for dinner?'

That is what they did. Maigret walked a good bit of the way before taking a taxi, and when his wife, hearing his footsteps, opened the door, his expression was not too careworn.

'What is there to eat?'

88

'Lunch warmed up.'

'And what was there for lunch?'

'Cassoulet.'

They both smiled, but she had guessed his state of mind nevertheless.

'Don't worry, Maigret. . . .'

He hadn't told her anything more about the case he was working on. Aren't all cases the same, when you get right down to it?

'You're not the one who's responsible. . . .'

After a moment, she added:

'It gets cold suddenly at this time of year. . . . I'd better close the window. . . .'

CHAPTER FIVE

AS ON EVERY OTHER MORNING, his first contact with life was the smell of coffee, then his wife's hand touching his shoulder and finally the sight of Madame Maigret, already fresh and alert, wearing a flowered housecoat, holding his cup out to him.

He blinked and asked, rather stupidly:

'The telephone hasn't rung, has it?'

If it had, he would have been awake as soon as she. The curtains were open. Spring, though it had come early, was still there. The sun was up and the noises of the street stood out clearly.

He gave a sigh of relief. Lapointe had not telephoned. Therefore nothing had happened in the Avenue Marigny. He drank half the cup, got up gaily and went into the bathroom. He had been wrong to worry. When the first letter arrived, he should have realized that it was not serious. This morning he was a little ashamed of having let himself panic like a child who still believes in ghost stories.

'Did you sleep well?'

'Very well.'

'Do you think you'll be in to lunch?'

'I think so.'

'Would you like fish?'

'Skate in black butter, if you can get any.'

Half an hour later he was surprised and annoyed, when he pushed open the door of his office, to find Lapointe in the armchair. The poor boy was a bit pale and almost asleep. He had felt it better to wait rather than leave a report and go home to bed, no doubt because the superintendent had seemed so worried the night before.

'Well, Lapointe, my boy?'

The inspector had stood up when Maigret sat down in front of the pile of letters on his desk.

'Just a minute, please. . . .'

He wanted to reassure himself first of all that there was no new anonymous letter.

'Good! Now tell me. . . .'

'I got there a little before six in the evening and made contact with Lamure, the concierge, who insisted that I have dinner with him and his wife. The first person to come into the building after me, at ten past six, was young Parendon, the one they call Gus.'

Lapointe pulled a notebook out of his pocket so that he could refer to his notes.

'Was he alone?'

'Yes. He had several schoolbooks under his arm. Then, a few minutes later, an effeminate-looking man holding a leather bag. . . . Lamure told me that it was the Peruvian woman's hairdresser.

' "There must be a ball or a big party somewhere," he said calmly, and drained his glass of red wine.

'By the way, he emptied a bottle by himself and he was surprised, and a bit annoyed, that I didn't do the same.

'Let's see. . . . At 7.45, a woman arrived in a chauffeur-driven car—Madame Hortense, the concierge called her.

'She's one of Madame Parendon's sisters, the one that goes out most often with her. She's married to a Monsieur Benoît-Biguet, an important man, very rich, and they have a Spanish chauffeur. . . .'

Lapointe smiled.

'I'm sorry to be giving you the uninteresting details, but since I had nothing else to do I wrote everything down. . . . At 8.30 the Peruvians' limousine drew up and the couple came down in the lift. He was wearing tails and she had on a formal evening gown with a chinchilla stole. One doesn't see that sort of thing very often now. . . .

'At five to nine Madame Parendon and Madame Hortense went out. I found out afterwards where they went—the chauffeurs are in the habit of coming in to have a drink in

91

the lodge with Lamure when they get back. He always has a litre of red wine at hand. . . .

'There was a charity bridge evening at the Crillon and that's where they went. They came back a little after midnight. The sister went upstairs and stayed there for half an hour. That's when the chauffeur came in for his drink.

'Nobody paid any attention to me. I just looked like one of them, no one of importance. . . . The hardest thing was not to empty the glasses I was given.

'Mademoiselle Parendon, they call her Bambi, came in at about one o'clock. . . .'

'When did she go out?'

'I don't know. I didn't see her leave. That means she didn't have dinner at home. She was accompanied by a young man whom she kissed at the foot of the stairs. . . . She wasn't at all worried that we were there. . . .

'I asked Lamure if she always did that. He said she did and it was always the same boy, but he didn't know who he was. . . . He was wearing an anorak and shapeless moccasins, and his hair was on the long side. . . .'

Lapointe sounded as if he was repeating by rote, fighting sleep, his eyes on his notebook.

'You haven't mentioned the departure of Mademoiselle Vague, Tortu and Julien Baud. . . .'

'I didn't write it down, in fact, because I thought it was part of the routine. They came down at six o'clock, by the stairs, and once on the pavement they each went their own way.'

'What else?'

'I went up as far as the fourth floor two or three times, but I saw and heard nothing. I could have been wandering about in a church at night.

'The Peruvians came in at about three o'clock. They'd had supper at Maxim's. Before that they had been to a big film première in the Champs-Elysées. It seems they're real Parisian personalities.

'That's all that happened at night. Not even a cat, one really can say that, because there isn't an animal in the place except for the Peruvians' parakeet.

'Did I tell you that Ferdinand, the Parendons' butler, went off to bed at about ten? That the cook left at nine o'clock?

'It was Ferdinand who appeared first in the morning, at seven o'clock. He went out, because he usually goes to the bar at the corner of the Rue du Cirque to have his first coffee of the day, and fresh croissants. . . . He stayed out for about half an hour. During that time the cook arrived, and the cleaning-woman, Madame Marchand.

'The chauffeur came over from his room, which is over the garages, near Ferdinand's, and went upstairs for breakfast. . . .

'I didn't write everything down straightaway. That's why my notes are a bit confused. During the night I went to listen at the Parendons' door at least ten times and I didn't hear a thing.

'The Peruvians' chauffeur brought out his employers' car to wash it, just as he does every morning. . . .'

Lapointe put his notebook back in his pocket.

'That's all, chief. Janvier came. I introduced him to Lamure, who seemed to know him already, and I left. . . .'

'Well, get to bed quickly now, boy. . . .'

In a few moments the bell for the briefing would ring in the corridors. Maigret filled a pipe, grabbed his paper-knife and went swiftly through the mail.

He was relieved. He had every reason to be. But there was still a weight in the pit of his stomach, a vague apprehension.

The main subject under discussion in the director's office was the son of a Minister of State who had had a car crash at four in the morning, at the corner of the Rue François Ier, in unpleasant circumstances. Not only was he drunk, but one could hardly reveal, without causing a scandal, the name of the girl with him, who had had to be taken to hospital. As for the driver of the car that had been run into, he had died instantly.

'What's your opinion, Maigret?'

'Me? Nothing, sir.'

When it was a matter of politics or of anything concerning politics, Maigret just wasn't there. He had the knack of looking vague, almost stupid, at such times.

'Still, we must find an answer. . . . The newspapers don't know anything about it yet, but in an hour or two they will. . . .'

It was ten o'clock. The telephone on the director's desk rang. He picked it up nervously.

'Yes, he's here. . . .'

He held the receiver out to Maigret.

'It's for you. . . .'

He had a premonition. He knew before putting the receiver to his ear that something had happened in the Avenue Marigny, and it was indeed Janvier's voice at the other end of the line. It was low, almost as if he were embarrassed.

'Is that you, chief?'

'Yes, it's me. . . . Well, who is it?'

Janvier understood the meaning of his question at once.

'The young secretary. . . .'

'Dead?'

'Unfortunately.'

'Shot?'

'No. . . . There was no noise. . . . No one noticed anything. . . . The doctor hasn't got here yet. . . . I'm calling you before I have any details because I was downstairs when it happened. . . . Monsieur Parendon is here beside me; he's quite shattered. . . . We're waiting for Dr. Martin to arrive at any moment.'

'Was she stabbed?'

'Butchered, more like. . . .'

'I'll be right over.'

The director and Maigret's colleagues looked at him, surprised to see him so pale, so affected by the call. At the Quai des Orfèvres, particularly in the Criminal Division, didn't they deal in murder daily?

'Who is it?' asked the director.

'Parendon's secretary.'

'The neurologist?'

'No. his brother, the lawyer. . . . I'd had some anonymous letters.'

He pushed through the door without giving any more explanations and went straight to the inspectors' office.

'Lucas?'

'Yes, chief. . . .'

He looked around.

'You, Torrence. . . . Right. . . . You two come into my office. . . .'

Lucas, who knew about the letters, asked:

'Has there been a murder?'

'Yes.'

'Parendon?'

'His secretary. . . . Ring Moers and tell him to get over there with his technicians. . . . I'm calling the Public Prosecutor's Office. . . .'

It was always the same. For at least an hour, instead of working in peace, he was going to have to give explanations to the Deputy Public Prosecutor and to whichever examining magistrate was appointed.

'Go on, boys. . . .'

He was overcome, as if it had been someone in his own family. Of all the members of the household, Mademoiselle Vague was the last he would have thought of as a victim.

He had taken a liking to her. He liked the way she had spoken of her relationship with her employer, a mixture of jauntiness and matter-of-factness. He had felt that at bottom, in spite of the difference in ages, she felt for him a passionate fidelity which is perhaps one of the truest kinds of love.

Then why was she the one to be killed?

He climbed into the little black car while Lucas took the wheel and big Torrence got in behind.

'What's it all about?' he asked as they moved off.

'You'll find out,' replied Lucas, who knew how Maigret was feeling.

Maigret didn't notice the streets, the passers-by, the trees which were growing greener every day, the huge buses which passed dangerously close to their car.

He was there already. He visualized Mademoiselle Vague's little office, where he had sat by the window at the same time on the previous day. She had sat right opposite him, as if to show him the sincerity in her eyes. And when she had hesitated after a question it was because she was looking for the right words.

There was a car at the door already. It belonged to the local superintendent, whom Janvier must have notified. Whatever happens, the correct procedure must be followed.

Lamure was standing gloomily in the doorway of his luxurious lodge.

'Who would have thought . . . ?' he began.

Maigret walked past him without answering and started up the stairs, since the lift was at one of the other floors. Janvier was waiting for him on the landing. He said nothing. He too could guess how his chief was feeling. Maigret didn't notice Ferdinand taking his hat, at his post as if nothing had happened.

He strode into the corridor, passed the door of Parendon's office and came to Mademoiselle Vague's, which was standing open. At first he only saw two men, the local superintendent, Lambilliote, whom he had met frequently, and one of his colleagues.

He had to look at the floor, almost under the Louis XIII table which was used as a desk.

She was wearing an almond-green spring frock, probably for the first time that season, since on the previous day and the day before that he had seen her in a navy-blue skirt and a white blouse. He had thought that she must consider it a kind of uniform.

After the blow she must have slid out of her chair, and her body was doubled over, oddly twisted. Her throat was gaping open and she had lost a considerable quantity of blood which would still be warm.

It took him some time to realize that Lambilliote was shaking his hand.

'Did you know her?'

He looked at Maigret, astounded to see him so moved by the sight of a body.

'Yes, I knew her,' he said in a hoarse voice.

And he rushed into the office at the end of the corridor where Julien Baud, eyes reddened, stood before him. His breath smelled of spirits. There was a bottle of brandy on the desk. In the corner René Tortu held his head in his hands.

'Was it you who found her?'

The word '*tu*' came naturally to his lips, since the big Swiss seemed suddenly like a child.

'Yes, sir.'

'Did you hear anything? Did she cry out? Did she groan?'

'Nothing. . . .'

He could hardly speak. There was a lump in his throat and tears poured from his blue eyes.

'Excuse me. . . . It's the first time. . . .'

It seemed as though he had been waiting to cry until that moment, and he pulled his handkerchief from his pocket.

'I . . . Just a minute. . . . I'm sorry. . . .'

He wept copiously, standing in the middle of the room, looking taller than his five foot eleven. There was a sharp little sound. It was the stem of Maigret's pipe breaking under the pressure of his bite. The bowl fell to the floor. He bent down to pick it up and put it in his pocket.

'Please forgive me. . . . It's stronger than I am. . . .'

Baud got his breath back, dried his eyes and glanced at the bottle of brandy but didn't dare touch it.

'She came in here at about ten past nine to bring me some documents to check. . . . I can't remember where I put them, in fact. . . . It's the proceedings of yesterday's session, with notes and references. . . . I must have left them in her office. . . . No. . . . Oh! They're on my table. . . .'

Creased by a clenched hand.

'She asked me to take them back to her as soon as I had finished. I went along . . .'

'At what time?'

'I don't know. . . . I must have worked for about half an hour. . . . I was very happy, very pleased with life. . . . I like working for her. . . . I looked around. . . . I didn't see her. . . . Then, when I looked down. . . .'

Maigret poured a little brandy into the glass which Ferdinand must have brought, and gave it to him.

'Was she still breathing?'

He shook his head.

'The men from the Public Prosecutor's Office are here, Chief.'

'Didn't you hear anything either, Monsieur Tortu?'

'No, nothing. . . .'

'Were you in here all the time?'

'No. . . . I went to see Monsieur Parendon for about ten minutes about the case I dealt with at the Palais yesterday. . . .'

'What time was that?'

'I didn't look at my watch. . . . About nine-thirty. . . .'

'How was he?'

'The same as usual. . . .'

'Was he alone?'

'Mademoiselle Vague was with him. . . .'

'Did she go out as soon as you came in?'

'A few seconds later. . . .'

Maigret would have liked a brandy too, but he didn't dare have one.

He had to go through the formalities. He grumbled about it, but in fact it wasn't a bad thing because it made him come out of the nightmare he was living in.

The Public Prosecutor's Office had appointed Daumas as examining magistrate. Maigret had worked with him several times, a pleasant man, a little on the timid side, whose only fault was excessive attention to detail. He must have been about forty. With him was the Deputy Public Prosecutor, De Claes, a tall fair man, very thin, perfectly turned out. He always held a pair of light-coloured gloves in his hand, summer and winter.

'What do you think, Maigret? I'm told you had an inspector in the building, is that right? Were you expecting anything to happen?'

Maigret shrugged his shoulders and gestured vaguely.

'It would take too long to tell you everything. . . . I spent almost all day in this flat yesterday and the day before, following up some anonymous letters.'

'Did the letters say who the victim would be?'

'No, that's just it. That is why it was impossible to avoid

98

the murder. I would have had to have a policeman standing behind each person, following them step by step through the house. Lapointe spent the night downstairs. This morning Janvier took his place. . . .'

Janvier was standing in a corner, his head bowed. From the courtyard came the sound of the Peruvians' chauffeur washing the Rolls.

'Who did tell you, Janvier?'

'Ferdinand. He knew I was down there. . . . I had spoken to him. . . .'

There were heavy footsteps in the corridor. The experts had arrived with their apparatus. One little man, completely round, didn't seem to fit in with the group, and he looked at all the people in the room, wondering which one to speak to.

'Dr. Martin. . . .' he murmured finally. 'I'm sorry to have got here so late, but I had a patient at the surgery and she took so long to get dressed. . . .'

He saw the body. He opened his bag and knelt on the floor. He was the least moved of anyone.

'She's dead, of course.'

'Did she die instantly?'

'She must have lived for a few seconds, let's say thirty or forty seconds, and since her throat was cut she couldn't possibly have cried out.'

He pointed to an object half hidden by the table. It was the erasing-knife Maigret had noticed the previous day. Now it was stuck in the pool of thick blood.

In spite of himself the superintendent looked at the girl's face, her glasses askew, her eyes blue and staring.

'Would you close her eyes, Dr. Martin?'

Except at the beginning of his career, he had rarely been so shaken by the sight of a corpse.

As the doctor was about to obey, Moers grabbed Maigret by the sleeve.

'The photographs . . .' he reminded him.

'Of course. . . . No, don't do anything. . . .'

It was up to him not to look. They still had to wait for the medical expert. Dr. Martin, a lively man in spite of his stoutness, asked:

'May I go now, gentlemen?'

Then, looking at each in turn, he finally addressed Maigret.

'Are you Superintendent Maigret? I wonder if I shouldn't go and see Monsieur Parendon. Do you know where he is?'

'In his office, I imagine.'

'Does he know? . . . Has he seen? . . .'

'Probably.'

In fact, no one knew anything for certain. The whole atmosphere was one of incoherence. A photographer set up an enormous camera on a tripod, while a grey-haired man took measurements on the floor and the magistrate's clerk scribbled in a notebook.

Lucas and Torrence, who had not as yet received any instructions, stood in the corridor.

'What do you think I should do?'

'Go and see him if you think he might need you.'

Dr. Martin had just reached the door when Maigret called him back.

'I will undoubtedly have questions to ask you sometime today. Will you be at home?'

'Except between eleven and three—I have a clinic at the hospital.'

He pulled out a fat pocket-watch, looked startled and went off rapidly.

Judge Daumas coughed.

'I suppose, Maigret, you'd rather I left you to work in peace? I only wanted to know if you suspect anyone in particular. . . .'

'No. . . . Yes. . . . Frankly, sir, I don't know. This case isn't like any other I have had, and I'm a little confused. . . .'

'Do you need me any more?' asked Superintendent Lambilliote.

'Not any more,' Maigret replied vaguely.

He was in a hurry to see them all go. The office emptied little by little. Suddenly a flashbulb went off in the already bright room. Two men, going about their work as matter-offactly as joiners or locksmiths, took fingerprints from the dead girl.

Maigret slipped quietly out of the room, signalled to Lucas and Torrence to wait for him and went into the office at the end of the corridor, where Tortu was answering the telephone while Baud, his elbows on the table, stared blankly ahead.

He was drunk. The level of the brandy in the bottle had gone down by three good fingers. Maigret picked it up and, quite unashamedly, because it was really necessary, poured himself a drink in the Swiss boy's glass.

He went about his work like a sleepwalker, stopping at times, his eyes staring blankly, afraid that he had forgotten something essential. He shook hands absent-mindedly with the medical expert whose real work would only begin at the Medico-Legal Institute.

The ambulance men were already there with a stretcher, and Maigret took a last glance at the almond-green dress which had been meant to celebrate a lovely spring day.

'Janvier, you'd better see to her parents. Their address must be there, in the office at the end of the hall. Look in her handbag, too. . . . Anyway, do what has to be done. . . .'

He led the other two men towards the cloakroom.

'You two draw me up a plan of the flat, then question everyone in it and note down where each person was between nine-fifteen and ten. And note down everything everybody saw, everyone who went out and in. . . .'

Ferdinand was standing there waiting, his arms folded.

'He will help you with the plan. Tell me, Ferdinand, I suppose Madame Parendon is in her room?'

'Yes, Monsieur Maigret.'

'How did she react?'

'She didn't react at all, sir, because she doesn't know anything about it yet. As far as I know she is sleeping, and Lise hasn't dared take it on herself to waken her.'

'Hasn't Monsieur Parendon gone to see her either?'

'Monsieur hasn't left his office.'

'Hasn't he seen the body?'

'Excuse me. He did leave it for a minute, when Monsieur Tortu went to tell him. He took a quick look into Mademoiselle Vague's office and then went back to his own.'

Maigret had been wrong the previous evening in believing that because his anonymous correspondent had a precise style he should take the word 'strike' literally.

She hadn't been struck. Nor had she been shot. She had literally been slaughtered.

He had to move aside to let the stretcher-bearers pass, and a few moments later he knocked at the enormous door of Parendon's office. He heard no reply. Still, it was a thick oak door.

He turned the knob, pushed one of the panels and saw the lawyer sitting in one of the leather armchairs.

For a second he was afraid that something terrible had happened to him too, he was so bent over, his chin resting on his chest, one soft hand touching the carpet.

Maigret walked over and sat in a chair opposite him so that they were face to face, close together, just as they had been at their first meeting. On the shelves, the gilt-lettered names of Lagache, Henri Ey, Ruyssen and other psychiatrists shone brightly on the leather bindings.

He was surprised to hear a voice murmur:

'What do you think about it, Monsieur Maigret?'

The voice was remote, dull. It was the voice of a man prostrated with grief. The lawyer could scarcely make the effort to sit up or to raise his head. Suddenly his glasses fell to the ground, and without the thick lenses his eyes looked like those of a frightened child. He bent forward to pick them up with an effort and put them on again.

He spoke again:

'What are they doing?'

And he pointed with his white hand to the girl's office.

'The formalities are over. . . .'

'The . . . the body?'

'They have just taken the body away.'

'Don't worry. . . . I'm going to pull myself together.'

He placed his right hand automatically over his heart while

the superintendent looked at him as fixedly as he had on the first day.

Parendon managed to pull himself together, took a handkerchief out of his pocket and mopped his face with it.

'Would you like something to drink?'

He looked towards the part of the panelling which hid a little bar.

'Will you have one too?'

Maigret took advantage of the offer to get up and take out two glasses and the bottle of armagnac.

'It wasn't a joke,' the lawyer said slowly.

And although his voice had grown strong again, it was still strange, mechanical, without intonation.

'It puts you in an awkward situation, doesn't it?'

And, since Maigret still stared at him without answering, he added:

'What are you going to do now?'

'Two of my men are busy establishing how everyone in the flat spent their time between nine-fifteen and ten o'clock. . . .'

'It happened before ten o'clock. . . .'

'I know.'

'Ten to ten. . . . It was exactly ten to ten when Tortu came in and told me. . . .'

He glanced at the bronze clock which showed twenty-five minutes to twelve.

'Did you stay in that chair after that?'

'I followed Tortu across the corridor, but I couldn't stand the sight for more than a few seconds. . . . I came back here and . . . you are right . . . I haven't moved from this chair. . . .

'I vaguely remember that Dr. Martin came in, that he spoke to me, that I shook my head, that he took my pulse and left in a hurry. . . .'

'He had to go to the hospital for his clinic, in fact.'

'He must have thought that I was drugged.'

'Have you ever taken anything like that?'

'Never. I can imagine what it's like.'

The trees outside rustled softly and one could hear the rumble of the buses in the Place Beauveau.

'I could never have suspected. . . .'

He spoke incoherently, leaving his sentences unfinished, and Maigret kept on staring at him. Maigret always carried two pipes in his pocket and he took out the unbroken one, filled it and puffed deeply, as if to recover his equilibrium.

'Suspected what?'

'How far. . . . In what way. . . . The importance. . . . Yes, the importance, that's the word, of relationships. . . .'

His hand pointed once more to the secretary's office.

'It was so unexpected!'

Would Maigret have been any surer of himself if he had read all the books on psychiatry and psychology on the library shelves?

He could not remember ever having watched a man as intensely as he did at that moment. He did not miss a movement, not a twitch of a facial muscle.

'Did you think it would be her?'

'No,' admitted the superintendent.

'Did you think it would be me?'

'You or your wife.'

'Where is *she*?'

'Apparently she is asleep and doesn't yet know anything about it.'

The lawyer frowned. He was making a great effort to concentrate.

'Hasn't she left her rooms?'

'Not according to Ferdinand.'

'It isn't part of Ferdinand's duties. . . .'

'I know. One of my inspectors is probably questioning Lise right now.'

Parendon began to grow agitated, as if something he had not previously thought of had suddenly worried him.

'Well then, are you going to arrest me? . . . If my wife didn't leave her room . . .'

Had it then seemed evident to him that Madame Parendon was the murderer?

'Tell me, are you going to arrest me?'

'It is too soon to arrest anyone.'

He got up and swallowed a mouthful of armagnac, wiping the back of his hand across his forehead.

'I don't understand anything any more, Maigret. . . .'

He took a grip on himself.

'Excuse me . . . Monsieur Maigret. . . . Did anyone who doesn't belong to the household get into the flat?'

He was returning to his normal self again. His eyes were growing lively.

'No. One of my men spent the night in the lodge and another relieved him at about eight this morning.'

'We must read the letters again,' Parendon murmured.

'I read them several times late yesterday afternoon.'

'There is something that doesn't hang together in all this, as if events suddenly took an unexpected turn. . . .'

He sat down again and Maigret considered what he had said. He too, when he learned that Mademoiselle Vague was dead, had thought that it was a mistake.

'You know, she was very, very . . . devoted to me.'

'More than that,' affirmed the superintendent.

'Do you think so?'

'When she spoke to me of you yesterday, she spoke with real passion.'

The little man blinked, incredulous, as if he could not believe that he had inspired such feelings.

'I had a long talk with her while you were seeing the two shipowners.'

'I know. She told me. . . . What had happened to the documents?'

'Julien Baud had them in his hand when he discovered the body and rushed back to his office in a panic. The papers are a bit crumpled.'

'They are very important. Those people must not suffer because of what has happened in my house.'

'May I ask you a question, Monsieur Parendon?'

'I have been waiting for it ever since I saw you come in. It is your duty to ask it, of course, and also not to take my word for it. . . . No, I did not kill Mademoiselle Vague.

'There are words which I have hardly ever spoken in my

life, which I have almost erased from my vocabulary. Today I am going to use one, because there is no other to express the truth which I have just discovered: I loved her, Monsieur Maigret.'

He said that calmly, and it was all the more impressive. The rest was more easily said.

'I thought I felt no more than a slight attachment for her, apart from physical desire. I was a little ashamed of it, because I have a daughter who is almost as old as she was. Antoinette had . . .'

That was the first time Maigret had heard anyone say Mademoiselle Vague's Christian name.

'She had a kind of . . . wait a minute . . . of spontaneity which I found refreshing. . . . You see, there is hardly any spontaneity in this house. She brought it in from outside, like a present, as one might bring in fresh flowers.'

'Do you know with what weapon the crime was committed?'

'A kitchen knife, I suppose?'

'No. . . . A type of erasing-knife which I noticed on your secretary's desk yesterday. . . . It caught my eye because it isn't the usual model. The blade is longer, sharper. . . .'

'It comes from the Papeterie Roman, like all the office furniture.'

'Did you buy it?'

'Certainly not. She must have chosen it herself.'

'Mademoiselle Vague was sitting at her desk, probably going over some documents. She had given some to Julien Baud to check.'

Parendon did not seem like a man on his guard, a man waiting for a trap. He listened carefully, possibly rather surprised at the importance Maigret attached to these details.

'The person who killed her knew that the erasing-knife was there in the pen-tray, or he would have brought a gun. . . .'

'What makes you think that he wasn't armed and then changed his mind?'

'Mademoiselle Vague saw him pick up the knife and that did not make her suspicious. She did not get up. She went on working while he walked behind her. . . .'

Parendon was thinking, reconstructing in his mind the scene that Maigret had just described, with the precision of the great business lawyer that he was.

There was nothing woolly in his attitude. A gnome he might be, if one can poke fun at people of small stature, but a gnome of astonishing intelligence.

'I think you'll be obliged to arrest me before the day is over,' he said suddenly.

There was nothing sarcastic in his manner. He had come to a certain conclusion after weighing up the pros and cons.

'It will be a chance for my counsel,' he added, with some irony this time, 'to get some practice on Article 64.'

Maigret was confused once more. He was even more so when the door leading to the big drawing-room opened and Madame Parendon stood in the doorway. She had not done her hair or put on any make-up. She wore the same blue négligé as the day before. She was holding herself very erect, but she still looked much older than she was.

'I am sorry to disturb you. . . .'

She spoke as if nothing had happened.

'I suppose, Superintendent, that I have no right to speak to my husband alone? We do not often do so, but under the circumstances. . . .'

'For the moment I can only allow you to speak to him in my presence.'

She did not come forward into the room but remained standing, the sun-filled drawing-room behind her. The two men had stood up when she appeared.

'Very well. You are doing your job.'

She took a puff at the cigarette she was holding and looked hesitatingly at each in turn.

'May I first ask you, Monsieur Maigret, if you have come to a decision?'

'On what?'

'On what happened this morning. . . . I have just heard about it and I suppose you are about to make an arrest. . . .'

'I have not made any decision.'

'Good. The children will be home soon and it would be

better to have everything clear. Tell me, Emile, was it you who killed her?'

Maigret couldn't believe his eyes or his ears. They were facing each other, ten feet apart, their expressions hard, their features strained.

'Are you daring to ask me if . . . ?'

Parendon choked, his little fists clenched with rage.

'Stop play-acting. Answer me yes or no.'

Then, suddenly, he lost his temper, a thing which had probably happened to him very few times in his life, and, raising his arms in a sort of entreaty to heaven, he shouted:

'You know very well I did not, for God's sake!'

He was dancing with rage. He was almost on the point of attacking her.

'That is all I wanted to hear. Thank you.'

And she went back into the drawing-room in a most natural manner, closing the door behind her.

CHAPTER SIX

'I AM SORRY I lost my temper, Monsieur Maigret. It is most unusual for me. . . .'

'I know.'

It was precisely because he knew it that Maigret was thoughtful.

The little man, still standing, got back his breath and his self-control and wiped his face once more. It was not flushed, but yellowish.

'Do you hate her?'

'I don't hate anybody. . . . Because I don't believe that a human being is ever fully responsible. . . .'

'Article 64!'

'Yes, Article 64. . . . I don't care if it makes me appear to be mad, but I will not change my opinion. . . .'

'Even if it should concern your wife?'

'Even if it should concern her.'

'Even if she killed Mademoiselle Vague?'

For a moment his face seemed to dissolve, his eyes to dilate.

'Even then.'

'Do you think she is capable of such an action?'

'I am not going to accuse anyone.'

'A few moments ago I asked you a question. I am going to ask you another and you will be able to answer yes or no. My anonymous correspondent is not necessarily the murderer. Someone, sensing disaster in the air, might have thought that by introducing the police into the house he could avert it.'

'I can anticipate the question. I did not write the letters.'

'Could the murdered girl have done so?'

He reflected for a few moments.

'It's not impossible. But it doesn't fit in with her character.

She was more direct than that—I was just telling you about her spontaneity. . . .

'In fact, wouldn't she have been more likely to come to me, since she knew quite well . . . ?'

He bit his lip.

'Knew what quite well?'

'That if I had felt I was being threatened I would have done nothing about it.'

'Why?'

He looked hesitantly at Maigret.

'It's hard to explain. . . . One day I made my choice. . . .'

'By getting married?'

'By embarking on my chosen career. . . . By getting married. . . . By living in a certain way. . . . So I must take the consequences. . . .'

'Isn't that contrary to your views on human responsibility?'

'Perhaps. It would seem so, anyway. . . .'

He seemed tired, helpless. One could guess at the turmoil of thoughts he was forcing himself to organize behind his domed forehead.

'Do you believe, Monsieur Parendon, that the person who wrote to me thought that the victim would be your secretary?'

'No.'

In spite of the closed doors they heard a voice in the drawing-room, crying:

'Where is my father?'

Then almost immediately the door opened abruptly and a very tall young man with unkempt hair took two or three steps into the room and stopped in front of the two men.

He first looked from one to the other, then his eyes rested on the superintendent with an almost menacing gleam.

'Are you going to arrest my father?'

'Calm down, Gus. . . . Superintendent Maigret and I . . .'

'Are you Maigret?'

He looked at him with more than mere curiosity.

'Whom are you going to arrest?'

'No one, at the moment.'

'Anyway, I can swear it wasn't my father. . . .'

'Who told you what has happened?'

'The concierge first of all, but he didn't give me any details, then Ferdinand. . . .'

'Weren't you half expecting it?'

Parendon took advantage of the situation to sit down at his desk, as if he wanted to be in his most accustomed place once more.

'Is this an interrogation?'

And the boy turned to his father to ask his advice.

'My rôle, Gus . . .'

'Who told you I'm called Gus?'

'Everybody I've met here. . . . I'm going to ask you questions, just as I shall ask everyone, but it isn't an official interrogation. . . . I asked you if you weren't half expecting it?'

'Expecting what?'

'What happened this morning.'

'If you mean was I expecting someone to cut Antoinette's throat, no. . . .'

'Did you call her Antoinette?'

'I've called her that for a long time. We were good friends.'

'What did you expect?'

His ears suddenly flamed.

'Nothing in particular. . . .'

'But something drastic?'

'I don't know. . . .'

Maigret noted that Parendon was watching his son carefully, as if he too had asked a question, or as if he was making a discovery.

'Are you fifteen, Gus?'

'I'll be sixteen in June.'

'Would you rather I talked to you in front of your father, or alone in your room or any other room?'

The boy hesitated. Although his anger had subsided, he was still very nervous. He turned towards the lawyer again.

'Which would you prefer, Father?'

'I think you would both be more at ease in your room. . . . Just a minute, Gus. . . . Your sister will be coming in at any minute, if she isn't here already. . . . I want you to have lunch together as usual, without worrying about me. . . . I won't come into the dining room.'

'Aren't you going to have anything to eat?'

'I don't know. I may have a sandwich. . . . I need a little peace.'

The boy was on the point of rushing to give his father a hug. It was not Maigret's presence which stopped him, but a fear, which must always have existed between father and son, of showing too much emotion.

Neither of them was inclined to sentimental effusions or embraces, and Maigret could easily visualize a younger Gus coming to sit silent and motionless in his father's office, just to watch him reading or working.

'If you want to come to my room, come on. . . .'

As they went through the drawing-room, Maigret found Lucas and Torrence waiting for him, ill at ease in the enormous, sumptuously-furnished room.

'Finished, boys?'

'Yes, chief. . . . Do you want to see the plan and who went where when?'

'Not just now. What time did it happen?'

'Between half past nine and a quarter to ten. . . . Almost certainly at 9.37.'

Maigret turned towards the wide-open windows.

'Were they open this morning?' he asked.

'From a quarter past eight onwards.'

Behind the garages rose the many windows of a six-storey block of flats in the Rue du Cirque. It was the back of the building. A woman was walking across a kitchen, pot in hand. Another, on the third floor, was changing her baby's nappy.

'You two go and have something to eat before you do anything else. Where is Janvier?'

'He has found the mother, in a village in Berry. She's not on the telephone and he has asked someone to get her to the post office. . . . He's waiting in the end office for the call.'

'He can join you after that. You'll find a restaurant that's not bad in the Rue de Miromesnil—it's called "Au Petit

Chaudron." After you've eaten, divide the floors to those flats you can see from here in the Rue du Cirque between you. Question the tenants whose windows look out on this side. They might, for instance, have seen someone going through the drawing-room between 9.30 and 9.45. . . . They must see into other rooms. . . .'

'Where will we find you?'

'At the Quai, when you've finished. Unless you find something important. . . . I might still be here.'

Gus waited, interested in what was going on. The tragedy which had taken place did not stop him from having a slightly childish curiosity about police procedure.

'Now I'm all yours, Gus.'

They went down a corridor, narrower than the one in the other wing, past a kitchen. They could see a fat woman dressed in black through the glass-panelled door.

'It's the second door.'

The room was big, its whole feeling different from the rest of the flat. The furniture was in the same style, undoubtedly because it had had to be used somewhere. Gus had changed its character by piling it up with all kind of things, adding pin-boards and shelves.

There were four loudspeakers, two or three gramophone turntables, a microscope on a whitewood table, copper wires forming a complicated circuit fixed on to another table. There only was one armchair, by the window, with a piece of red cotton laid haphazardly over it. There was a length of red cotton covering the bed too, turning it into a sort of divan.

'You've kept it?' Maigret remarked, pointing to a large teddy bear on a shelf.

'Why should I be ashamed of it? My father gave it to me for my first birthday.'

He spoke the word 'father' proudly, almost defiantly. He was ready to spring fiercely to his defence.

'Did you like Mademoiselle Vague, Gus?'

'I've told you already. She was my friend.'

He must have been flattered that a girl of twenty-five should treat him as a friend.

'Did you often go into her office?'

'At least once a day.'

'Did you ever go out with her?'

The boy looked at him, surprised. Maigret filled his pipe.

'Go out where?'

'To the pictures, maybe. . . . Or dancing. . . .'

'I don't dance. I've never been out with her.'

'Did you ever go to her flat?'

The boy's ears flamed again.

'What are you trying to make me say? What are you thinking?'

'Did you know of Antoinette's relationship with your father?'

'Why not?' he replied, his head held proudly. 'Do you see anything wrong with that?'

'It doesn't matter what I think, but what you think.'

'My father's a free agent, isn't he?'

'What about your mother?'

'It wasn't any of her business.'

'What do you mean by that?'

'It's a man's right . . .'

He didn't finish the sentence, but what he had said showed his meaning clearly.

'Do you think that's the reason for what happened this morning?'

'I don't know.'

'Were you expecting something to happen?'

Maigret had sat down in the red chair and he lit his pipe slowly, watching the boy, who was still in the adolescent period of growth, his arms too long, his hands too big.

'I was expecting it and not expecting it. . . .'

'Express yourself more clearly. Your teachers at the Lycée Racine would not accept that for an answer.'

'I didn't imagine you were like this. . . .'

'Do you think I'm hard?'

'I think you don't like me, that you suspect me of something, I don't know what. . . .'

'That's right.'

114

'Not of having killed Antoinette, though? Besides, I was at school.'

'I know. And I also know that you really worship your father.'

'Is that wrong?'

'Not at all. At the same time, you feel he's defenceless.'

'What are you insinuating?'

'Nothing bad, Gus. Your father is inclined not to fight, except possibly in his work. He believes that everything which happens to him only happens because of his own short-comings.'

'He's an intelligent and honest man. . . .'

'Antoinette was defenceless too, in her own way. In fact there were two of you keeping guard over your father, she and you. That's why there was a sort of complicity between you.'

'We never said anything about that. . . .'

'I'm sure you didn't. But you still felt you were on the same side. That's why, even if you had nothing to say to her, you never missed a chance of going to see her.'

'What are you getting at?'

For the first time the boy, who had been fiddling with a piece of copper wire, turned his head away.

'I'm there already. It was you who sent me those letters, Gus, and you who telephoned the Police Judiciaire yesterday.'

Maigret could only see his back. There was a long pause. Finally the boy turned to him, his face scarlet.

'Yes, it was me. . . . You would have found out anyway, wouldn't you?'

He no longer looked defiantly at Maigret. On the contrary, the superintendent had risen in his esteem again.

'How did you come to suspect me?'

'The letters could only have been written by the murderer or by someone who was trying to protect your father indirectly.'

'It could have been Antoinette.'

Maigret thought it better not to tell him that the girl wasn't a child any more and would not have gone about things in such a complicated, or such a childish, way.

'Have I been a disappointment to you, Gus?'

'I thought you would go about things differently.'

'How, for instance?'

'I don't know. I've read all about your cases. I thought you were the man who would understand everything. . . .'

'And now?'

'Now I don't think anything at all.'

'Whom did you want me to arrest?'

'I didn't want you to arrest anyone.'

'Well, then? What should I have done?'

'You're the one who's in charge of the Crime Squad, not me.'

'Had any crime been committed yesterday, or even at nine o'clock this morning?'

'Of course not.'

'What did you want me to protect your father from?'

There was another silence.

'I felt he was in danger.'

'What kind of danger?'

Maigret was sure that Gus understood the real meaning of the question. The boy had wanted to protect his father. From whom? Couldn't it also have been to protect him from himself?

'I don't want to answer any more questions.'

'Why not?'

'Because!'

He added, in a firm voice:

'Take me to the Quai des Orfèvres if you want. Ask me the same questions for hours on end. . . . Maybe you think I'm only a boy, but I swear I won't say any more. . . .'

'I'm not asking you any more. It's time you were going to lunch, Gus.'

'It won't matter if I'm late back to school today.'

'Where is your sister's room?'

'Two doors along this corridor.'

'No hard feelings?'

'You're doing your job. . . .'

And the boy slammed the door. A moment later Maigret knocked at Bambi's door, through which he could hear the droning of a vacuum cleaner. It was a young girl in uniform who opened the door. She had soft blonde hair.

'Were you looking for me?'

'Are you Lise?'

'Yes. I'm the maid. You've already walked past me in the corridors.'

'Where is Mademoiselle Bambi?'

'She might be in the dining-room. Or perhaps in her father's room, or her mother's—that's in the other wing.'

'I know. I was in Madame Parendon's rooms yesterday.'

An open door showed him a dining-room panelled from floor to ceiling. The table, which could have seated twenty, was set for two. In a little while Bambi and her brother would be here, separated by a vast stretch of tablecloth, with Ferdinand, formal in white gloves, to serve them.

As he passed, he opened the door of the lawyer's office slightly. Parendon was sitting in the same chair as in the morning. There was a bottle of wine, a glass and some sandwiches on a folding table. He did not move. Perhaps he had not heard anything. There was a spot of sunlight on his head. It looked bald like that.

The superintendent shut the door again and found the corridor he had gone along the day before, and the door of the boudoir. Through it he could hear a voice he did not recognize, insistent, tragic.

He could not make out the words, but he could feel the unbridled passion.

He knocked very loudly. The voice stopped suddenly and a second later the door opened and a girl stood in front of him, still breathless, her eyes shining.

'What do you want?'

'I am Superintendent Maigret.'

'I thought so. So what? Haven't we the right to be in our own house any more?'

She was not beautiful, but she had a pleasant face and a well-proportioned figure. She wore a simply-cut suit and her hair was held back by a ribbon, although it was not the fashion.

'I would like to have a short talk with you before you have lunch, Mademoiselle.'

'Here?'

He hesitated. He had seen her mother's shoulders trembling.

'Not necessarily. Wherever you like. . . .'

Bambi came out of the room without a backward glance, shut the door and said:

'Where do you want to go?'

'To your room?' he suggested.

'Lise is doing my room.'

'To one of the offices?'

'I don't mind.'

Her hostility was not directed towards Maigret in particular. It was more a state of mind. Now that her violent harangue had been interrupted, her nerves had relaxed and she followed him dully.

'Not in . . .' she began.

Not in Mademoiselle Vague's room, of course. They went into Tortu's and Julien Baud's office. They were out having lunch.

'Have you seen your father? . . . Sit down.'

'I'd rather not sit.'

She was too overwrought to sit still in a chair.

'As you like.'

He did not sit, either, but leaned on Tortu's desk.

'I asked you if you had seen your father?'

'No, not since I came home.'

'When did you get back?'

'At twelve-fifteen.'

'Who told you what had happened?'

'The concierge.'

It appeared that Lamure had lain in wait for both Gus and his sister, so as to be the first to tell them the news.

'And then?'

'And then what?'

'What did you do?'

'Ferdinand wanted to say something to me. I didn't listen and I went straight to my room.'

118

'Was Lise there?'

'Yes. She was cleaning the bathroom. Everything's late because of what has happened.'

'Did you cry?'

'No.'

'Didn't it occur to you to go and see your father?'

'Maybe. . . . I don't remember. . . . I didn't go.'

'Did you stay in your room long?'

'I didn't look at the time. Five minutes, maybe a little longer. . . .'

'What were you doing?'

She looked at him, hesitating. That seemed to be a habit in the household. Everyone had a tendency to weigh their words before they spoke.

'Looking in the mirror.'

It was a challenge. That habit too could be found in other members of the family.

'Why?'

'You want me to be honest, don't you? Well, I will be! . . . I was trying to see who I look like.'

'You mean your father or your mother?'

'Yes.'

'What conclusion did you come to?'

Her expression hardened and she shouted at him angrily: 'My mother!'

'Do you hate your mother, Mademoiselle Parendon?'

'I don't hate her. I want to help her. I've often tried.'

'To help her do what?'

'Do you think this is getting us anywhere?'

'What are you talking about?'

'Your questions. . . . My answers. . . .'

'They may help me to understand.'

'You spend a few hours here and there in the midst of a family and you think you can understand them? Don't think I'm hostile to you. I know you have been wandering around the house since Monday.'

'Do you know who sent me the letters?'

119

'Yes.'

'How did you find out?'

'I walked in while he was cutting the sheets of paper.'

'Did Gus tell you what they were for?'

'No. I only understood afterwards, when I heard people talking about the letters.'

'Who told you about them?'

'I don't remember, Julien Baud, maybe. I like him. He looks scatterbrained, but he's a nice boy.'

'There's one thing that intrigues me. . . . It was you who chose the nickname Bambi and who called your brother Gus, wasn't it?'

She looked at him, smiling slightly.

'Does that surprise you?'

'Was it a protest?'

'That's right. A protest against this huge, solemn barracks of a place, against the way we live, against the kind of people who come here. . . . I wish I'd been born in an ordinary family and had to struggle to make my way in life.'

'You are struggling, in your own way.'

'Archaeology, you know. I didn't want to take up a career where I would be taking a place from someone else.'

'It's your mother who irritates you above all, isn't it?'

'I would much rather not talk about her.'

'Unfortunately she is what matters just now, isn't she?'

'Perhaps. . . . I don't know. . . .'

She stole a glance at him.

'You think she is guilty,' Maigret insisted.

'What makes you think that?'

'When I went to her room I heard you speaking angrily. . . .'

'That doesn't mean that I think she's guilty. . . . I don't like the way she behaves. . . . I don't like the life she leads, the life she makes us lead. . . . I don't like . . .'

She was less in control of herself than her brother, although she looked calmer.

'Do you blame her for not making your father happy?'

'You can't make people happy in spite of themselves. As for making them unhappy . . .'

'Did you like Mademoiselle Vague, as you like Julien Baud?'

She didn't hesitate before replying.

'No!'

'Why?'

'Because she was a little schemer who made my father believe she loved him.'

'Did you ever hear them speak of love?'

'Certainly not. She wouldn't coo over him in front of me. You only had to see her when she was with him. I don't know what went on when the door was closed.'

'Were you upset on moral grounds?'

'To hell with morals. . . . And anyway, what morals? . . . Those of what environment? Do you think that the moral standards of this district are the same as those of a small town in the provinces or those of the 20th *Arrondissement*?'

'Do you think she hurt your father?'

'Perhaps she isolated him too much.'

'Do you mean that she estranged him from you?'

'Those are questions I've never thought about. Nobody thinks about them. Let's say that if she hadn't been there, there might have been some chance. . . .'

'Of what? Of a reconciliation?'

'There wasn't anything to reconcile. My parents have never loved each other and I don't believe in love either. Nevertheless there is a possibility of living in peace, in a kind of harmony. . . .'

'Is that what you have tried to bring about?'

'I've tried to calm my mother's frenzies, to lessen her rantings and ravings. . . .'

'Hasn't your father helped you?'

Her ideas were not at all like those of her brother and yet they coincided on a few points.

'My father has given up.'

'Because of his secretary?'

'I'd rather not answer that, not say any more. Put yourself in my place—I come home from the Sorbonne and I find . . .'

'You're right. Believe me, I am doing this so that the least possible harm will come of it. Can you imagine an investigation dragging on for several weeks, the uncertainty, the interviews at the Police Judiciaire, then in the magistrate's office. . . .'

'I hadn't thought of that. What are you going to do?'

'I haven't made any decisions yet.'

'Have you had lunch?'

'No. Neither have you, and your brother must be waiting for you in the dining-room.'

'Isn't my father having lunch with us?'

'He'd rather have it alone in his office.'

'Aren't you having lunch?'

'I'm not hungry just now, but I must confess I'm dying of thirst.'

'What would you like to drink? Beer? Wine?'

'Anything, as long as it's in a big glass. . . .'

She couldn't help smiling.

'Wait here a minute. . . .'

He had understood the reason for her smile. She didn't see him going to the kitchen or the butler's pantry to have a drink, like one of the servants. Nor did she see him sitting with Gus and herself in the dining-room while they lunched in silence.

When she came back, he saw she hadn't bothered with a tray. She held a bottle of Saint-Emilion, six years old, in one hand, and a cut glass tumbler in the other.

'Don't hold it against me if I was rude to you, or if I haven't been very helpful. . . .'

'You are all very helpful. . . . Run along and eat now, Mademoiselle Bambi.'

It was an odd sensation to be there at one end of the flat, in the office belonging to Tortu and the young Swiss, alone with a bottle and a glass. Because he had said a big glass, she had brought a water tumbler and he was not ashamed of filling it full.

He was really thirsty. He needed some kind of stimulation too, for he had just spent one of the most exhausting mornings of his career. Now he was sure that Madame Parendon was waiting for him. She knew that he had questioned the entire household except for her and she would be kicking her heels wondering when he would finally come.

Had she, like her husband, had lunch brought to her room?

He sipped his wine standing in front of the window, looking vaguely at the courtyard which he saw for the first time empty of cars, with only a ginger cat stretched out in a patch of sunlight. Since Lamure had told him that except for the parakeet there wasn't an animal in the house, it must be a neighbouring cat, looking for a peaceful spot.

He hesitated before taking a second glass, filled it half full, and took time to fill a pipe before drinking it.

After that he heaved a sigh and went to the boudoir, along the corridors he was beginning to recognize.

He had no need to knock. His steps had been heard in spite of the carpet, and the door opened as soon as he approached. Madame Parendon, still wearing her blue silk négligé, had had time to put on her make-up and do her hair, and her face looked almost as it had the previous day.

Was it more tense or more relaxed? He would have found it difficult to say. He felt there was a difference, some sort of flaw, but he was unable to pick it out.

'I was expecting you.'

'I know. Well, now I am here. . . .'

'Why did you have to see everyone else before me?'

'What if it was to give you time to think things over?'

'I don't need to think things over. . . . To think what things over?'

'The things that have happened. . . . The things that are inevitably going to happen. . . .'

'What are you talking about?'

'When a murder has been committed it is followed, sooner or later, by an arrest, a preliminary investigation, a trial. . . .'

'What has that got to do with me?'

'You hated Antoinette, didn't you?'

'So you call her by her Christian name too?'

'Who else does?'

'Gus, for one. I don't know about my husband. . . . He's

123

probably capable of saying "Mademoiselle" very politely while making love.'

'She's dead.'

'So what? Just because someone is dead do we have to impute only good characteristics to her?'

'What did you do last night when your sister left after bringing you back from the Crillon?'

She frowned, remembered, sneered:

'I had forgotten that you had filled the house with policemen. . . . Well . . . I had a headache, I took an aspirin and tried to read while I waited for it to take effect. See, the book is still there and you'll find a bookmark at page 10 or 12. . . . I didn't get very far. . . .

'I went to bed and tried to sleep, without success. . . . That happens not infrequently and my doctor knows all about it.'

'Dr Martin?'

'Dr Martin is my husband's doctor, and the children's. My doctor is Dr Pommeroy, who lives in the Boulevard Haussmann. I'm not ill, thank God!'

She spoke these words forcefully, threw them out like a challenge.

'I'm not undergoing any treatment or following any diet. . . .'

He thought she was going to say, under her breath:

'Not like my husband.'

She did not say it, and went on:

'The only thing I have to complain about is lack of sleep. Sometimes I am still awake at three in the morning. . . . It's both tiring and a strain. . . .'

'Was that the case last night?'

'Yes. . . .'

'Were you worried?'

'By your visit?' she retorted in a flash.

'It might have been by the anonymous letters, by the atmosphere they had created. . . .'

'I have slept badly for years and there have never been any anonymous letters. . . . I always end up by getting up again and taking a sleeping pill which Dr Pommeroy has prescribed for me. If you want to see the box. . . .'

'Why should I want to see it?'

'I don't know. Judging by the questions you asked me yesterday, I can expect anything. . . . In spite of the sleeping pill, it took me a good half hour to get to sleep and when I woke up I was surprised to see that it was half past eleven.'

'I thought you often got up late.'

'Not that late. I rang for Lise. . . . She brought me a tray with tea and toast. It wasn't until she opened the curtains that I saw her eyes were all red.

'I asked her why she had been crying. She burst into tears again and told me that something dreadful had happened, and I at once thought of my husband. . . .'

'What did you think might have happened to him?'

'Do you think that man is strong? Don't you think that his heart might give out at any moment, like the rest?'

He did not comment on 'like the rest', but reserved it for later.

'She finally told me that Mademoiselle Vague had been murdered and that the house was full of policemen.'

'What was your first reaction?'

'I was so shattered that I began by drinking my tea. Then I rushed to my husband's office—what's going to happen to him?'

He pretended not to understand.

'To whom?'

'To my husband. You aren't going to throw him in prison? With his health . . .'

'Why should I put your husband in prison? In the first place, that's not my job, but the judge's. Furthermore, I don't see any reason at this moment for arresting your husband.'

'Well, whom do you suspect then?'

He did not answer. He walked slowly over the blue carpet with its yellow pattern while she sat down, as she had the day before, in the easy chair.

'Why, Madame Parendon,' he asked, putting emphasis on each syllable, 'would your husband have killed his secretary?'

'Must there have been a reason?'

'One doesn't usually commit murder without a motive.'

'Some people could imagine a motive, couldn't they?'

'Such as . . . ?'

'For example, if she were pregnant?'

'Do you have any reason to believe that she was pregnant?'

'None. . . .'

'Is your husband a Catholic?'

'No. . . .'

'Even suppose she had been pregnant, it's quite possible that he might have been very pleased. . . .'

'It would have been an embarrassment to him.'

'You forget that we no longer live in the times when unmarried mothers were looked down on. Times change, Madame Parendon. . . . Then, too, many people have no hesitation in finding a broad-minded gynaecologist. . . .'

'I only used that as an example.'

'Think of another reason.'

'She might have been blackmailing him. . . .'

'For what reason? Are your husband's business affairs shady? Do you believe he is capable of serious irregularities which might cast a slur on his honour as a member of the Bar?'

She resigned herself, tight-lipped, to saying:

'Certainly not.'

She lit a cigarette.

'That kind of girl always ends up trying to make the man marry her.'

'Has your husband spoken to you about a divorce?'

'Not so far.'

'What would you do if he did?'

'I would feel obliged to resign myself to it and to stop taking care of him. . . .'

'I understand you have considerable means of your own. . . .'

'More than he does. This is my house. I own the whole building.'

'In that case I can see no reason for blackmail.'

'Perhaps he was growing tired of a make-believe love?'

'Why make-believe?'

'Because of his age, his background, his kind of life, everything. . . .'

'Is your love more real?'

'I gave him two children.'

'Do you mean you gave them to him as a wedding present?'

'Are you daring to insult me?'

She looked furiously at him again while he, on the other hand, took care to appear calmer than he was.

'I have no such intention, Madame, but it usually takes two people to make children. Let us say more simply that you and your husband have had two children.'

'What are you trying to get at?'

'I am trying to get you to tell me simply and sincerely what you did this morning.'

'I have told you.'

'Neither simply nor sincerely. You told me a long story about insomnia, so that you could skip over the whole morning.'

'I was asleep.'

'I would like to be sure about that. . . . I will probably know for certain in a very short time. My inspectors have taken note of what everyone did, and where, between 9.15 and 10. I am well aware that one can get to the offices by different routes.'

'Are you accusing me of lying?'

'Of not telling me the whole truth, at least.'

'Do you think my husband is innocent?'

'I don't think anyone is innocent, *a priori*, just as I don't think anyone is guilty. . . .'

'Yet the way you are interrogating me. . . .'

'What was your daughter accusing you of when I came to look for her?'

'Didn't she tell you?'

'I didn't ask her.'

She sneered once more. It was a bitter twist of the lips, an irony she wanted to be cruel, scornful.

'She is luckier than I am.'

'I asked you what she was accusing you of. . . .'

'Of not being beside her father at a time like this, if you must know.'

'Does she think that her father is guilty?'

'What if she does?'

'Gus too, of course?'

'Gus is still at the age where the father is a kind of god and the mother is a shrew.'

'When you appeared in your husband's study just now, you knew I would be there with him. . . .'

'You aren't necessarily everywhere, Monsieur Maigret, and I might have wanted to see my husband alone. . . .'

'You asked him a question. . . .'

'A simple question, a natural question, the question any wife in my position would have asked in the same circumstances. You saw his reaction, didn't you? Did you think it was normal? Would you say that a man who dances with rage, shouting insults, is a normal man?'

She felt that she had scored a point and she lit another cigarette after stubbing out the first in a blue marble ash-tray.

'I am waiting for your other questions, if you have any more to ask. . . .'

'Have you had lunch?'

'Don't worry about that. If you are hungry . . .'

Her expression, as well as her attitude, was capable of changing from one moment to the next. She became very much the society woman again. Leaning back slightly, her eyes half-closed, she was mentally cocking a snook at him.

CHAPTER SEVEN

MAIGRET had managed to keep himself under control from the beginning of his interview with Madame Parendon. And it was sadness which overcame his irritation little by little. He felt heavy, awkward. He realized how much he lacked knowledge which might have helped him carry out this interrogation well.

Finally he sat down in one of the chairs which were too delicate for him, his unlit pipe in his hand, and in a calm but lifeless voice he said:

'Listen to me, Madame. Contrary to what you may think, I am not hostile to you. I am only a civil servant whose job is to look for the truth with the means at his disposal.

'I am going to ask you again the question I asked you a moment ago. I must ask you to think before you answer, to weigh the pros and cons. I must warn you that if it is later proved that you have lied to me, I shall draw my own conclusions and I shall ask the judge for a warrant for your arrest.'

He watched her, particularly her hands, which betrayed her inner tension.

'Did you leave your rooms after nine o'clock this morning, and did you go in the direction of the offices, for any reason whatsoever?'

She did not blink, did not turn her eyes away. She took her time, as he had asked, but it was obvious that she was not thinking, that she had already taken her stand once and for all. Finally she said:

'No.'

'You did not set foot in the corridors?'

'No.'

'You did not go through the drawing-room?'

'No.'

'You did not, even with no evil intent, go into Mademoiselle Vague's office?'

'No. I may add that I consider these questions an insult.'

'It is my duty to ask them.'

'You forget that my father is still alive. . . .'

'Is that a threat?'

'I am simply reminding you that you are not in your office at the Quai des Orfèvres. . . .'

'Would you rather I took you there?'

'I dare you to. . . .'

He thought it better not to take her at her word. He often went fishing when he was at Meung-sur-Loire, and once he had landed an eel which he had tremendous difficulty in taking off the hook. It kept slipping between his fingers and finally it fell on the grass on the bank and slid back into the water.

He was not here for his own pleasure. He was not fishing.

'Do you then deny having killed Mademoiselle Vague?'

The same words, over and over, the same look of a man who is desperately trying to understand another human being.

'You know perfectly well.'

'What do I know?'

'That it was my poor husband who killed her.'

'For what reason?'

'I have already told you. . . . In his condition, there is no need for a precise reason. . . .

'I am going to tell you something which I alone know, apart from him, because he told me before we were married. He was afraid of the marriage. He put it off time and time again. At that time I didn't know that he was consulting several doctors.

'Did you know that when he was seventeen he tried to commit suicide because he was afraid he wasn't a normal man? He cut his wrist. When the blood spurted out he panicked and called for help, pretending there had been an accident. . . .

'Do you know what this tendency to suicide means?'

Maigret was sorry that he had not brought the bottle of wine with him. Tortu and young Julien Baud must have been surprised to find it in their room when they came back, and they would probably have emptied it by now.

'He had scruples . . . He was afraid that our children wouldn't be normal. When Bambi began to grow, and to talk, he watched her anxiously. . . .'

It might have been true. There was certainly some truth in what she was saying, but he still had the impression of a sort of displacement, of a split between the words, the sentences, and the truth.

'He is haunted by the fear of illness and death. Dr Martin knows about that. . . .'

'I saw Dr Martin this morning.'

She appeared to mark a point up to him, then quickly regained her assurance.

'Didn't he mention it to you?'

'No. And he did not for one moment think that your husband could be the murderer.'

'You are forgetting a doctor's professional secrets, Superintendent.'

He began to see a glimmer of light, but she remained vague, distant.

'I also spoke to his brother on the telephone. He is in Nice, at a conference.'

'Was that after what has happened?'

'Before.'

'Wasn't he concerned?'

'He did not advise me to have your husband watched.'

'And yet he must know. . . .'

She lit yet another cigarette. She was chain-smoking, inhaling deeply.

'Have you never met people who have lost contact with life, with reality, who turn in on themselves rather as one turns a glove inside out?

'Question our friends, both men and women. Ask them if my husband takes any interest now in human beings. He

131

does dine with some people, because I insist, but he hardly notices that they are there, and as for speaking to them. . . .

'He doesn't listen, he sits as if he were shut in. . . .'

'Are the friends you are speaking of the friends of his choice?'

'They are people whom we, in our position, ought to meet, normal people who lead a normal life. . . .'

He did not ask her what she considered a normal life. He felt it better to let her go on talking. Her monologue was growing more and more interesting.

'Do you think that he went to the beach even once last summer, or to the swimming pool? He spent his time sitting under a tree in the garden. What I took for distraction, when I was a girl, when he suddenly stopped listening to me, is a real inability to live with other people.

'That is why he shuts himself in his office, why he hardly comes out of it, and when he does he looks at us like an owl surprised by the light.

'You have been quick to judge, Monsieur Maigret. . . .'

'I have another question to ask you. . . .'

He was sure before he asked it what the answer would be.

'Have you handled your revolver since yesterday evening?'

'Why should I have handled it?'

'I am waiting for an answer from you, not a question.'

'The answer is no.'

'How long is it since you held it in your hand?'

'Months. . . . It's a long time since I tidied up that drawer.'

'You handled it yesterday, when you showed it to me.'

'I had forgotten that.'

'But, since I handled it, my fingerprints will be on top of the others.'

'Is that all you have found out?'

She looked at him as if she were disappointed at discovering that Maigret was so stupid, so bad at his job.

'You have just told me, with a certain self-satisfaction, of your husband's isolation and of his lack of contact with reality. Now, as recently as yesterday he was in his office dealing with an extremely important case with men who most certainly have their feet on the ground. . . .'

'Why do you think he chose Maritime Law? . . . He has never set foot on a boat in his life. . . . He has no contact with seamen. . . . Everything takes place on paper. Everything is abstract, don't you see? It's another proof of what I keep telling you, of what you refuse to see. . . .'

She got up and began to pace about the room as if she were thinking.

'Even his hobby, the celebrated Article 64—isn't that proof that he is afraid, afraid of himself, and that he is trying to reassure himself? He knows that you are here, that you are questioning me. . . . In this house everyone is aware of what everyone else is doing. . . . Do you know what he is thinking? . . . He is hoping that I will become impatient, that I will appear nervous, that I will get angry, so that I will be suspected instead of him. . . .

'If I were in prison, he would be free. . . .'

'Just a minute. I don't understand. What freedom would he have that he doesn't have now?'

'His complete freedom.'

'To do what, now that Mademoiselle Vague is dead?'

'There are other Mademoiselle Vagues.'

'So now you think that your husband would take advantage of your being away from home to have mistresses?'

'Why not? It's another way of reassuring oneself. . . .'

'By killing them one after the other?'

'He wouldn't necessarily kill the others.'

'I thought you said he was incapable of making contact with people.'

'With normal people, people of our social standing. . . .'

'So people who are not of your social standing are not normal?'

'You know very well what I mean. I mean that it is not normal for him to seek their company.'

'Why not?'

Someone knocked at the door. It opened to reveal Ferdinand in a white jacket.

133

'One of the gentlemen wishes to speak to you, Monsieur Maigret.'

'Where is he?'

'Here, in the corridor. He told me it was extremely urgent and so I took the liberty of bringing him. . . .'

The superintendent could make out Lucas's figure in the darkened corridor.

'If you will excuse me, Madame Parendon?'

He shut the door behind him while Ferdinand disappeared and the lawyer's wife remained alone in her room.

'What is it, Lucas?'

'She went through the drawing-room twice this morning.'

'Are you sure?'

'You can't see it from here, but from the drawing-room you can, quite clearly . . . There is an invalid who sits almost all day at one of the windows in the Rue du Cirque. . . .'

'A very old man?'

'No. It's a man who had an accident to his legs. He's about fifty. He is interested in everything that goes on in this house, and the car-washing, especially when it's the Rolls, fascinates him. Judging by his replies to the other questions I asked him, we can believe what he says. . . . His name is Montagné. . . . His daughter is a midwife. . . .'

'At what time did he see her first?'

'Shortly after nine-thirty.'

'Was she going towards the offices?'

'Yes. He is more familiar than we are with the layout of the place. That's how he knows about Parendon and his secretary. . . .'

'What was she wearing?'

'A blue housecoat.'

'And the second time?'

'She went through the room in the opposite direction less than five minutes later. One detail struck him—the maid was dusting at the far end of the room and she didn't see her. . . .'

'Madame Parendon didn't see the maid?'

'No.'

'Have you questioned Lise?'

134

'Yes, this morning.'

'Didn't she mention the incident?'

'She says she didn't see anything.'

'Thank you. . . .'

'What shall I do now?'

'You can both wait here for me. Was there any confirmation of what the man Montagné said?'

'Only a young maid on the fifth floor who thinks she saw something blue at the same time.'

Maigret knocked on the boudoir door and went in just as Madame Parendon was coming out of her bedroom. He took time to empty his pipe and fill it again.

'Would you be so good as to ring for your maid?'

'Do you need something?'

'Yes.'

'As you wish.'

She pressed a button. Several minutes passed in silence and Maigret, watching the woman he was tormenting, could not help having a constricted feeling in his chest.

He went over in his mind the terms of Article 64, which had taken on such importance in the past three days:

'There is no crime or misdemeanour if the accused was in a state of dementia at the time of the act, or if he was driven to it by an irresistible impulse.'

Could the man Madame Parendon had just described to him, her husband, have acted in a state of dementia at any given moment?

Had she too read the books on psychiatry, or . . . ?

Lise came in. She was afraid.

'Did you send for me, Madame?'

'The Superintendent wishes to speak to you.'

'Shut the door, Lise. There's nothing to be afraid of. . . . When you answered my inspectors' questions this morning you were upset, and you obviously did not realize how important their questions were.'

The poor girl looked from the superintendent to her mistress, who was sitting in the armchair, her legs crossed, leaning back, as if it had nothing to do with her.

'I don't know what you are talking about. . . .'

'The actions of all the staff between nine-fifteen and ten o'clock have been established. Shortly after nine-thirty, let's say at nine thirty-five, you were dusting in the drawing-room. Is that right?'

Another look at Madame Parendon, who did not look at her, then a faint voice:

'Yes, it's true.'

'At what time did you go into the drawing-room?'

'About nine-thirty. . . . A little later. . . .'

'So you didn't see Madame Parendon going in the direction of the offices?'

'No.'

'But shortly after you got there, when you were at the far end of the room, you saw her going in the opposite direction, that is to say, going towards these rooms. . . .'

'What should I do, Madame?'

'That is your affair, my child. Answer the questions put to you. . . .'

Tears were flowing down Lise's cheeks. She had rolled the handkerchief she had taken from her apron pocket into a ball.

'Did someone tell you something?' she asked naïvely.

'Answer the question, as Madame has just advised you. . . .'

'Will it mean that Madame is charged?'

'It will confirm another witness's statement, someone who lives in the Rue du Cirque and who saw both of you from his window.'

'Oh, well, there's no point in lying. It's true. I'm sorry, Madame. . . .'

She wanted to rush to her mistress, possibly to throw herself on her knees, but Madame Parendon spoke coldly to her.

'If the superintendent has finished with you, you may go.'

She went out and burst into tears in the doorway.

'What does that prove?' asked the woman, on her feet again, a cigarette trembling at her lips, her hands in the pockets of her blue négligé.

'That you have lied at least once.'

'I am in my own house and I do not have to give an account of my actions.'

'In a case of murder, you do. I warned you when I asked you the question.'

'Does that mean you are going to arrest me?'

'I am going to ask you to come with me to the Quai des Orfèvres.'

'Have you a warrant?'

'A blank one. An order to appear, where I have only to write in your name.'

'And then?'

'That won't depend on me any more.'

'On whom?'

'On the magistrate. Then, probably, on the doctors.'

'Do you think I am mad?'

He read the panic in her eyes.

'It isn't up to me to answer that.'

'I am not mad, do you hear? . . . And even if I did kill her, which I still deny, it was not in a moment of madness. . . .'

'May I ask you to give me your revolver?'

'Get it yourself. It's in the top drawer of my dressing-table.'

He went into the bedroom. Everything there was pale pink. The two rooms, one blue, the other pink, reminded him of a picture by Marie Laurencin.

The bed, a big low bed, Louis XVI in style, was still un-made. The furniture was painted a pale grey. On the dressing-table he saw pots of cream, little bottles, the whole range of products women use to fight the ravages of time.

He shrugged his shoulders. This intimate display made him melancholy. He thought of Gus, who had written the first letter.

Would things have happened in the same way if he had not intervened?

He took the revolver out of the drawer, in which there were also jewel-boxes.

He did not know how to answer the question. Would Madame Parendon perhaps have attacked her husband instead of attacking the girl? Would she have waited a few days more? Would she have used another weapon?

He frowned as he went back into the boudoir where the woman was standing in front of the window, her back to him. He saw that her back was beginning to grow bent. Her shoulders seemed narrower, bonier.

He held the gun in his hand.

'I am going to be open with you,' he said. 'I can't prove anything yet, but I am sure that this revolver was in the pocket of your housecoat when you went through the drawing-room just after nine-thirty. . . .

'I even wonder if at that particular moment you did not intend to kill your husband. . . . The testimony of the invalid in the Rue du Cirque may help us to prove that. . . . You must have gone up to his door, didn't you? You heard voices, because your husband was talking to René Tortu at that time. . . .

'It then occurred to you to do a sort of substitution. . . . Would you not wound your husband just as deeply, if not more so, by killing Antoinette Vague instead of killing him? . . . Not counting the fact that, at the same time, you were casting suspicion on him.

'You have been preparing the ground since our talk yesterday. . . . You went on doing so today. . . .

'Under the pretext of looking for a stamp, or for writing paper, or something, you went into the secretary's office. She greeted you absently and went back to her work. . . .

'You saw the erasing-knife, which made the revolver unnecessary and was even better, since someone might hear the gun. . . .'

He stopped speaking, lit his pipe rather reluctantly and stood there waiting. He had slipped the mother-of-pearl gun into his pocket.

A long time went by. Madame Parendon's shoulders did not move. So she was not crying. She kept her back to him and, when she finally turned to look at him, her face was pale and immobile.

No one looking at her could have imagined what had

taken place that morning in the Avenue Marigny, and even less what had taken place in the overwhelming blue of the boudoir.

'I am not mad,' she said emphatically.

He did not answer. What good would it have done? And besides, what did he know about it?

CHAPTER EIGHT

'GET YOURSELF DRESSED, MADAME,' Maigret said gently. 'You can pack a suitcase with a change of underwear and some personal belongings. . . . Perhaps you should ring for Lise?'

'To be sure that I won't commit suicide? Don't worry, there's no danger of that, but you may push the button on your right.'

He waited for the maid to appear.

'Give Madame Parendon a hand. . . .'

Then he walked along the corridor, his head bowed, looking at the carpet. He lost his way, mistook one corridor for another, and saw Ferdinand and fat Madame Vauquin through the glass door of the kitchen. There was an almost half-full bottle of red wine in front of Ferdinand. The butler had just poured himself a glass and was sitting with his elbows on the table, reading a newspaper.

He went in.

The other two were startled and Ferdinand jumped to his feet at once.

'Would you give me a glass of wine, please?'

'I brought the other bottle from the office. . . .'

What did it matter? In the state he was in, vintage Saint-Emilion or some rough red. . . .

He didn't dare say that he would have preferred the rough red.

He drank slowly, staring into space. He did not protest when the butler refilled his glass.

'Where are my men?'

'Waiting near the cloakroom. They didn't want to sit in the drawing-room.'

They were guarding the exit instinctively.

'Lucas, go back into the corridor where you were a few minutes ago. Stand outside the boudoir door and wait there for me.'

He went back to see Ferdinand.

'Is the chauffeur in?'

'Do you want him? I'll call him straightaway.'

'What I want is for him to be at the door with the car in a few minutes. . . . Are there any journalists waiting in the street?'

'Yes, sir.'

'Photographers?'

'Yes.'

He knocked at the door of Parendon's office. He was alone, sitting in front of scattered papers which he was annotating in red pencil. He saw Maigret and remained motionless, looking at him, not daring to ask any questions. His blue eyes behind their thick lenses had an expression which combined softness and a sadness such as Maigret had rarely seen before.

Did he need to speak? The lawyer had understood. While waiting for the superintendent he had clung on to his papers as if he were clinging to a wreck.

'I think you will have the occasion to study Article 64 some more, Monsieur Parendon. . . .'

'Has she confessed?'

'Not yet.'

'Do you think she will confess?'

'There will come a time, tonight, in ten days' time or in a month, when she will crack; and I would rather not be there. . . .'

The little man took his handkerchief from his pocket and began to clean his glasses as if it were a matter of prime importance. Suddenly the irises of his eyes seemed to melt, to dissolve into the whites. Only his mouth remained, showing an almost childish emotion.

'Are you taking her away?'

His voice was scarcely audible.

'In order to avoid the reporters' comments and to give

141

her departure some dignity, she will take her own car. I shall give the instructions to the chauffeur, and we shall arrive at the Police Judiciaire at the same time.'

Parendon gave him a look of gratitude.

'Don't you want to see her?' asked Maigret, knowing what the answer would be.

'What could I say to her?'

'I know. You're right. Are the children here?'

'Gus is at school. I don't know if Bambi is in her room or if she has a class this afternoon. . . .'

Maigret was thinking both of the woman who was about to leave and of those who would be left behind. Life would be difficult for them too, for a time at least.

'Didn't she say anything about me?'

The lawyer asked the question timidly, almost fearfully.

'She spoke about you a lot. . . .'

The superintendent understood now that Madame Parendon had not found the words which seemed to accuse her husband in books. They had been in herself. She had worked a kind of transference, projecting her own worries on to him.

He looked at his watch, and gave the reason for looking.

'I am giving her time to dress, to pack her suitcase. . . . The maid is with her. . . .'

". . . if the accused was in a state of dementia at the time of the act or if he was driven to it by an irresistible. . . ."

Some men he had arrested because it was his job to do so had been acquitted by the court, others found guilty and sentenced. Some, particularly at the beginning of his career, had been condemned to death, and two of them had asked him to be there at the final moment.

He had begun by studying medicine. He had regretted having to give it up because the circumstances so required. If he had been able to go on with his medical studies, would he not have chosen psychiatry?

In that case it would have been he who had to answer the question:

". . . if the accused was in a state of dementia at the time of the act or if he was driven to it by. . . ."

Perhaps he didn't regret the interruption of his studies so much. He would not be required to decide.

Parendon got up and walked hesitantly, awkwardly, towards him and held out his little hand.

'I. . . .'

But he was unable to speak. It was sufficient for them to shake hands silently, looking each other in the eye. Then Maigret went to the door which he closed behind him without looking back.

He was surprised to see Lucas standing by the door with Torrence. A glance from his assistant in the direction of the drawing-room explained why Lucas had left his post in the corridor.

Madame Parendon stood there in the middle of the enormous room, dressed in a light-coloured suit, with a hat and white gloves. Lise was standing behind her, holding a suitcase.

'You two go to the car and wait for me.'

He felt that he was acting like a master of ceremonies, and he knew that he would always hate the moments he was living through.

He went towards Madame Parendon and bowed slightly. It was she who spoke, her voice calm and natural.

'I shall follow you.'

Lise went down with them in the lift. The chauffeur rushed to open the car door and was surprised that Maigret did not follow his employer into the car.

He put the suitcase in the boot.

'Drive Madame Parendon directly to 36, Quai des Orfèvres, go in through the archway and turn left in the courtyard. . . .'

'Very good, Superintendent.'

Maigret gave the car time to break through the hedge of journalists who had not understood what was happening. Then, while they bombarded him with questions, he rejoined Lucas and Torrence in the little black police car.

'Are you going to make an arrest, Superintendent?'

'I don't know. . . .'

'Do you know who's guilty?'

'I don't know, boys. . . .'

He was being honest. The words of Article 64 came flooding into his memory one by one, terrifying in their imprecision.

The sun still shone, the chestnut trees were still growing greener, and he could see the same people prowling around the palace of the President of the Republic.

MAIGRET TAKES
THE WATERS

*

*Translated from
the French by*
EILEEN ELLENBOGEN

CHAPTER ONE

'DO YOU KNOW THEM?' Madame Maigret asked in an undertone, observing that her husband was looking back over his shoulder at the couple who had just gone past.

The man, too, had turned his head and was smiling. He seemed hesitant, as though considering retracing his steps to shake the Chief Superintendent by the hand.

'No, I don't think so . . . I don't know. . . .'

He was a squat little man. His wife, too, was small and plump, though perhaps an inch or so taller. Why was it Maigret had the impression that she was a Belgian? Because of her fair skin, her hair that was almost buttercup yellow, her protuberant blue eyes?

This was their fifth or sixth encounter. The first time, the man had stopped dead, beaming in delighted surprise. He had stood there uncertainly, as if about to speak, while the Chief Superintendent, frowning, searched his memory in vain.

There was certainly something familiar about that face and figure, but what the devil was it? Where had he last seen this cheerful little man, with the wife who looked as though she were made of brightly coloured marzipan?

'I really can't think. . . .'

It didn't much matter. Besides, everybody here was different from the people one met in everyday life. Any minute now, there would be a burst of music. On the bandstand, with its slender columns and ornate canopy, the uniformed bandsmen, their eyes fixed on the conductor, sat waiting to raise the brass instruments to their lips. This presumably was the Municipal Band, made up of firemen and other Council workers. Their uniform was splendid, with scarlet tabs, white sashes, and enough gold braid and embroidery to satisfy a South American General.

147

Hundreds—thousands it seemed to him—of iron chairs done up with yellow paint were set out in concentric circles round the bandstand, and nearly all were occupied by silent, waiting men and women with solemn faces.

In a minute or two, at nine o'clock, amid the great trees of the park, the concert would begin. After an oppressively hot day, the evening air seemed almost cool, and a light breeze rustled the leaves. Here and there, lamp standards surmounted by milky globes lightened the dark foliage with patches of paler green.

'Do you want to sit down?'

There were still a few empty chairs, but they did not avail themselves of them. This evening, as always, they preferred to walk about in a leisurely way. Other couples, like themselves, came and went, half-listening to the music, but there was also a number of solitary men and women, almost all elderly.

Nothing seemed quite real somehow. The white casino, plastered with the ornate mouldings so much in vogue at the turn of the century, was floodlit. Except for the occasional blare of a motor horn in the Rue Georges-Clemenceau, one could almost believe that here time had stood still.

'There she is . . .' whispered Madame Maigret, pointing with her chin.

It had become a sort of game. She had got into the habit of following her husband's glance, watching for any glimmer of surprise or interest.

What else was there for them to do with their time? They walked, or rather strolled, about the streets. From time to time they paused, not because they were out of breath, but to look more closely at the play of light on a tree, a house or a face.

They felt as though they had been in Vichy since the dawn of time, although, in fact, this was only their fifth day. Already they had established a routine, to which they adhered rigorously, as though it really mattered, and their days were given up to a succession of rituals, which they performed with the utmost solemnity.

How seriously, in fact, did Maigret take it all? His wife sometimes wondered, stealing a covert glance at him, trying to read his mind. He was not the man he was in Paris. His walk was less brisk, his features less drawn. He went about most of the time smiling but abstracted. His expression suggested a degree of satisfaction, certainly, but also, perhaps, a touch of sardonic self-mockery.

'She's wearing her white shawl.'

Each new day found them in the same place at the same hour, in one of the shaded park walks, beside the Allier, on a boulevard lined with plane-trees, or in a crowded or a deserted side-street, and, because of this, they had come to recognize, here and there, a face or a figure, and these were already getting to be part of their world.

Was it not the case that everyone here was going through the same motions at the same time every hour of the day, and not just at the mineral springs, where they all forgathered for the hallowed glass of water?

Maigret's eyes rested on a figure in the crowd, and sharpened. His wife followed his glance.

'Is she a widow, do you think?'

They could well have christened her 'the lady in mauve,' or rather 'the lady in lilac,' because that was the colour she always wore. Tonight, she must have arrived late, because she was sitting in one of the back rows.

The previous evening, at about eight o'clock, the Maigrets had come upon her unexpectedly as they were walking past the bandstand. There was still an hour to go before the concert. The little yellow chairs were so neatly arranged in concentric rings that they might have been circles drawn with a compass. All the chairs were vacant except one, in the front row, where the lady in lilac was sitting. There was something pathetic about her. She did not attempt to read by the light of the nearby lamp. She was not knitting. She was not doing anything. She did not seem in the least restless. She sat motionless, very upright, with her hands lying flat in her lap, looking straight in front of her, like a public figure avoiding the stares of the crowd.

She could have come straight out of a picture book. Unlike most of the women here, who went about bareheaded, she wore a white hat. The filmy shawl draped over her shoulders was white too. Her dress was of that distinctive lilac colour that she seemed so much attached to.

She had an unusually long, narrow face and thin lips.

'She must be an old maid, don't you think?'

Maigret was unwilling to commit himself. He was not conducting an enquiry or following a trail. Here, he was under no obligation to study people's faces, hoping that they would reveal the truth about themselves.

All the same, every now and then he caught himself doing it. He couldn't help it. It had become second nature. For no reason at all, he would find himself taking an interest in someone in the crowd, trying to guess their occupation, their domestic circumstances, the kind of life they led when they were not taking the waters.

It was by no means easy. After the first few days, sometimes after the first few hours, everyone seemed to become assimilated. Almost all wore the same expression of slightly vacant serenity, except those who were seriously ill, and who stood out from the rest by virtue of their deformities, their painful movements, and, still more, the unmistakable look in their eyes of pain tempered with hope.

The lady in lilac was one of what might be described as Maigret's circle of intimates, one of those who had attracted his attention and intrigued him from the first.

It was hard to guess her age. She might be forty-five or fifty-five. Time had not imprinted any tell-tale lines on her face.

She gave the impression of a woman accustomed to silence, like a nun, used to solitude, even perhaps enjoying it. Whether walking or, as at present, sitting, she totally ignored the people around her. No doubt it would have surprised her to know that Chief Superintendent Maigret, not as a matter of professional duty but simply for his own satisfaction, was studying her, in the hope of finding out what she was really like.

'She's never lived with a man, I'd say,' he replied, as the opening burst of music came from the bandstand.

'Nor with children, either. Perhaps with someone very old, though. She might, perhaps, have had an aged mother to look after.'

If so, she was unlikely to have been a good nurse, since she appeared unbending and unsociable. If she failed to see the people around her, it was because she did not look at them. She looked inwards. She looked within herself, seeing no one but herself, deriving, no doubt, some secret satisfaction from this self-absorption.

'Shall we go?'

They had not come to listen to the music. They had simply got into the habit of walking past the bandstand at this time of the evening. Besides, it was not every night that there was a concert. Some evenings, it was virtually deserted on this side of the park. They strolled across the park, turning right into the colonnade which ran beside a road brilliant with neon signs. They could see hotels, restaurants, shops, a cinema. They had not yet been to the cinema. It did not fit in with their time-table.

There were other people taking a walk like themselves, at more or less the same leisurely pace, some coming, some going. A few had cut short their walk to go to the casino theatre. They were late, and could be seen hurrying in, one or two here and there in evening dress.

Every one of these people lived a quite different life some-where else, in a district of Paris, in some little provincial town, in Brussels, Amsterdam, Rome or Philadelphia.

Each was a part of some pre-determined social order, with its own rules, taboos and passwords. Some were rich, others poor. Some were so ill that the treatment could do no more than give them a little extra time, others felt that, after taking the cure, they could forget about their health for the rest of the year.

This place was a kind of melting-pot. Maigret's own case was typical. It had all started one evening when they were dining with the Pardons. Madame Pardon had served *canard au sang*, a dish that she made to perfection, and which the Chief Superintendent particularly relished.

'Is there anything wrong with it?' she had asked anxiously, seeing that Maigret had barely tasted it.

Surprised, Pardon had turned to his guest and subjected him to a searching look. Then, sounding really worried, he had asked:

'Aren't you feeling well?'

'Just a twinge . . . It's nothing. . . .'

The doctor, however, had not failed to notice his friend's unwonted pallor, and the beads of perspiration on his forehead.

The subject was not mentioned again during dinner. The Chief Superintendent had scarcely touched his wine, and when, over coffee, he was offered a glass of old Armagnac, he had waved it away:

'Not tonight, if you don't mind.'

It was not until some time later that Dr Pardon had said quietly:

'Let's go into my consulting-room, shall we?'

Maigret had agreed reluctantly. He had known for some time that this was bound to happen, but he had kept putting it off from one day to the next. Dr Pardon's consulting-room was small and by no means luxurious. His stethoscope lay on the desk amid a litter of bottles, jars and papers, and the couch on which he examined his patients sagged in the middle, as though the last one had left the imprint of his body on it.

'What seems to be the trouble, Maigret?'

'I don't know. It's my age, I daresay.'

'How old are you? Fifty-two?'

'Fifty-three . . . I've had a lot on my plate lately. Work. . . . Worry. . . . No sensational cases . . . nothing exciting. . . . Just the opposite. . . . On the one hand, a flood of paper-work arising out of the reorganization at the Palais de Justice. . . . On the other, an epidemic of assaults on young girls and women living alone, in some cases including rape, in some not. . . . The press is howling for blood, and I haven't the staff to lay on full-scale patrols without disrupting my whole department. . . .'

'Do you suffer from indigestion?'

'I do occasionally have stomach cramps . . . pains . . . as I did tonight . . . or rather a kind of constriction in the chest and abdomen . . . I feel leaden . . . tired.'

'Would you mind if I had a look at you?'

His wife, in the next room, must have guessed, Madame Pardon too, and this bothered Maigret. He had a horror of anything to do with illness.

As he stripped off his tie, jacket, shirt and vest, he recalled something he had said when he was still in his teens: 'I'd rather die young than live the life of an invalid, all pills and potions and diets, and being made to do this and not being allowed to do that.'

In his vocabulary, being an invalid meant listening to one's heart, worrying about one's stomach, liver and kidneys and, at more or less regular intervals, exposing one's naked body to a doctor.

He no longer talked glibly of dying young, but he still did not feel ready to enter the invalid state.

'My trousers too?'

'Just pull them down a little.'

Pardon took his blood pressure, listened to his chest, felt his diaphragm and stomach, pressing here and there with his finger.

'Am I hurting you?'

'No. . . . A little tenderness there, I think. . . . No . . . lower down. . . .'

Well, here he was, behaving just like anyone else, apprehensive, ashamed of his own cowardice, afraid to look his old friend in the face. Awkwardly, he began putting on his clothes again. When Pardon spoke, there was no change in his voice:

'When did you last take a holiday?'

'Last year, I managed to get away for a week, then I was recalled because. . . .'

'What about the year before last?'

'I couldn't leave Paris.'

'Having regard to the life you lead, you ought to be in very much worse shape than you are.'

'What about my liver?'

'It has stood up valiantly, considering the way you've treated it. . . . Admittedly, it's slightly enlarged, but it's in excellent working order.'

'What's wrong, then?'

'There's nothing precisely wrong . . . a little of everything. . . . You're over-tired, there's no doubt about that, and it will take more than a week's holiday to put that right. . . . How do you feel when you wake up in the morning?'

'Like a bear with a sore head.'

Pardon laughed.

'Do you sleep well?'

'According to my wife, I thrash about in bed, and occasion-ally talk in my sleep.'

'I see you're not smoking.'

'I'm trying to cut it down.'

'Why?'

'I don't know. . . . I'm trying to cut down on drink, too.'

'Sit down, won't you?'

Pardon sat in the chair behind his desk. Here, in his consulting-room, he was very much the medical man, quite different from the host entertaining in his drawing-room or dining-room.

'Just you listen to me. You're not ill. As a matter of fact, having regard to your age and the life you lead, you're quite remarkably fit. I'll thank you to get that into your head once and for all. Stop fretting about every little twinge and odd pain here and there, and don't start worrying every time you go up a flight of stairs. . . .'

'How did you know?'

'Tell me, when you're questioning a suspect, how do *you* know?'

They were both smiling.

'Here we are in June. Paris is sweltering. You'll oblige me by taking a holiday at once, if possible leaving no forwarding address. . . . At any rate, I'm sure you will have the good sense not to ring through to the Quai des Orfèvres every day. . . .'

'I daresay it could be managed,' Maigret said, not very graciously. 'There's our cottage at Meung-sur-Loire. . . .'

'You'll have plenty of time to enjoy that when you retire. . . . This year, I have other plans for you. . . . Do you know Vichy at all?'

'I've never set foot in the place, in spite of the fact that I was born within forty miles of it, near Moulins. . . . But in those days, of course, not everyone owned a car. . . .'

'That reminds me, has your wife passed her test?'

'We've actually got as far as buying a small car.'

'I don't think you could do better than take the waters at Vichy. It will do you a power of good. . . . A thorough clean-out of the system. . . .'

When he saw the look on the Chief Superintendent's face, he almost burst out laughing.

'You want me to take the cure?'

'It will only mean drinking a few pints of water every day. . . . I don't suppose the specialist will insist on your having all the trimmings: mud-baths, mineral baths, vibro-massage, and all that taradiddle. There's nothing seriously wrong with you. Three weeks of rest and regular exercise, no worry. . . .'

'No beer, no wine, nothing to eat but rabbit's food. . . .'

'You've had a good many years of eating and drinking whatever you fancied, haven't you?'

'That's true,' he had to admit.

'And you have many more ahead, even if you do have to be a little more moderate in future. . . . Are we agreed, then?'

Maigret got to his feet and, much to his own astonishment, heard himself saying, just as though he were any other patient of Pardon's:

'Agreed.'

'When will you go?'

'In a day or two, a week at the outside. Just long enough to catch up with my paper-work.'

'I'll have to hand you over to a man on the spot who will be able to tell you more than I can. . . . I could name half-a-dozen. Let me think. . . . There's Rian, a decent young fellow, not too full of himself . . . I'll give you his address and telephone number . . . and I'll drop him a line tomorrow, to put him in the picture. . . .'

'I'm much obliged, Pardon.'

'I wasn't too rough with you, I hope?'

'You couldn't have been more gentle.'

Returning to the drawing-room, he smiled at his wife, a reassuring smile. But nothing was said, illness not being considered a suitable topic of after-dinner conversation at the Pardons'.

It was not until they reached the Rue Popincourt, walking arm-in-arm, that Maigret remarked casually, as though it were a matter of no importance:

'We're going to Vichy for our holiday.'

'Will you be taking the cure?'

'I suppose I might as well while I'm there!' he said wryly. 'There's nothing wrong with me. In fact, I gather I'm exceptionally healthy, which is why I'm being packed off to take the waters, I daresay!'

That evening at the Pardons' had not really been the start of it. He had for some time been obsessed by the strange notion that everybody was younger than he was, from the Chief Commissioner and the examining magistrates to the prisoners brought in for questioning. And now there was Dr Rian, fair-haired and affable, and well on the right side of forty.

A kid, in other words, at any rate a young man, but none the less sober and self-assured for that. And this was the man who was to be the arbiter of his, Chief Superintendent Maigret's, fate. Well, more or less. . . .

Maigret was irritated and at the same time apprehensive, for he certainly did not feel old, nor even middle-aged.

For all his youth, Dr Rian lived in an elegant red-brick house in the Boulevard des Etats-Unis. Maybe it was rather too Edwardian in style, but it had a certain grandeur, with its marble staircase, its handsome carpets, its highly-polished furniture. There was even a maid in a lace-trimmed cap.

'I presume your parents are dead? What did your father die of?'

The doctor carefully wrote down his answers on a memo-pad, in a neat, clerical hand.

'And your mother? . . . Any brothers? . . . Sisters? . . . Childhood ailments? . . . Measles? . . . Chicken pox? . . .'

Chicken pox, no, measles, yes, when he was very small and his mother still living. It was, in fact, his warmest and most vivid memory of his mother, who died very shortly afterwards.

"How about games and sport? . . . Have you ever had an accident? . . . Are you subject to sore throats? . . . You're a heavy smoker, I take it? . . .'

The young doctor smiled, with a touch of mischief, by way of showing Maigret that he knew him by repute.

'No one could say that you lead a sedentary life, exactly.'

'It varies. Sometimes I don't set foot outside my office for two or three weeks at a time, and then, all of a sudden, I'm running round all over the place for days on end.'

'Regular meals?'

'No.'

'Do you watch your diet?'

He was forced to admit that he liked rich food, especially highly seasoned stews and sauces.

'Not just a gourmet, in fact, but a hearty eater?'

'You could say so, yes.'

'What about wine? A half-bottle, a bottle a day?'

'Yes. . . . No. . . . More. . . . As a rule I don't have more than two or three glasses with my dinner. . . . Occasionally I have a beer sent up to the office from the brasserie nearby.'

'Spirits?'

'I quite often have an aperitif with a colleague.'

In the Brasserie Dauphine. It wasn't the drink itself, but the clubbable atmosphere, the cooking smells, the aroma of aniseed and Calvados, with which, by this time, the very walls were impregnated. Why should he feel ashamed, all of a sudden, in the presence of this neat, well-set-up young man in his luxurious consulting-room?

'In other words, you don't drink to excess?'

He had no wish to conceal anything.

'It depends what you mean by excess. I'm not averse to a

157

glass or two of sloe gin after dinner. My sister-in-law sends it from Alsace. . . . And then often, when I'm working on a case, I'm in and out of cafés and bars a great deal. . . . How shall I put it? If, at the start of a case, I happen to be in a bistro where Vouvray is a speciality, as likely as not I'll go on drinking Vouvray right through to the end.'

'How much in a day?'

It reminded him of his boyhood, the confessional in the village church, smelling of mildew and the curé's snuff.

'A lot?'

'It would seem a lot to you, I daresay.'

'For how long at a stretch?'

'Anything from three to ten days, sometimes even longer. It's a matter of chance. . . .'

There were no reproaches, no penances, but he had a pretty shrewd idea what the doctor thought of him, as he sat, elbows on his handsome mahogany desk, with the sun shining on his fair hair.

'No severe indigestion? No heartburn or giddiness?'

Giddiness, yes. Nothing serious. From time to time, especially of late, the ground seemed to tilt slightly, and everything about him appeared a little unreal. He felt off balance, unsteady on his feet.

It was not bad enough to cause him any serious anxiety, but it was an unpleasant sensation. Fortunately, it never lasted more than a couple of minutes. On one occasion, he had just left the Palais de Justice and was about to cross the road. He had waited until it was over, before venturing to step off the pavement.

'I see . . . I see. . . .'

What did he see? That he was a sick man? That he smoked heavily and drank too much? That it was high time, at his age, that he learned to watch his diet?'

Maigret was not letting it get him down. He smiled in the way his wife had grown used to, since they had come to Vichy. It was a self-mocking smile, if a little morose.

'Come with me, please.'

This time, he was given the full treatment! He was made

to climb up and down a ladder repeatedly for three full minutes. He had his blood-pressure taken lying down, sitting up and standing. Then he was X-rayed.

'Breathe in . . . deeper. . . . Hold it. . . . Breathe out. . . . In. . . . Hold it. . . . Out. . . .'

It was comical yet somehow distressing, dramatic and at the same time slightly dotty. He had, perhaps, thirty years of life still to look forward to, and yet any minute now he might be tactfully informed that his life as a healthy, active man, was over and that henceforth he would be reduced to the status of an invalid.

They had all been through this experience, all the people one saw in the park, under the spreading trees, at the mineral springs, on the lake shore. Even the members of the Sporting Club across the river, whom one could watch sunbathing, or playing tennis or bowls in the shade, had been through it.

'Mademoiselle Jeanne.'

'Yes, sir.'

The receptionist knew what was wanted. It was all part of a familiar routine. Soon the Maigrets would be following a routine of their own.

First, the little needle or the prick on the finger tip, then the glass slides and phials for the blood smears.

'Relax. . . . Clench your fist.'

He felt the prick of a needle in the crook of his elbow.

'Right, that will do.'

He had had blood samples taken before, but this time, it seemed to him, there was something portentous about it.

'Thank you. You can get dressed now.'

A few minutes later they were back in the consulting-room, with its walls lined with books and bound volumes of medical journals.

'I don't think any very drastic treatment is needed in your case. Come and see me again at this time the day after tomorrow. By then I shall have the results of the tests. Meanwhile, I'm going to put you on a diet. I presume you're staying in a hotel? Here is a diet sheet. All you have to do is to hand it to the head waiter. He'll attend to it.'

It was a card, with forbidden foods printed in one column, and permitted ones in the other. It even went so far as to list sample menus on the back.

'I don't know if you are aware of the different chemical properties of the various springs? There is an excellent little handbook on the subject, written by one of my colleagues, but it may be out of print. For a start, I want you to alternate between two springs, Chomel and Grande Grille. You'll find them both in the park.'

Both men looked equally solemn. Maigret felt not the least inclination, as he watched the doctor scribbling notes on his pad, to shrug the whole thing off, or indulge in a little secret smile.

'Do you usually have an early breakfast? I see. . . . Is your wife here with you? . . . In that case, I don't want to send you half across the town on an empty stomach. Let's see. You'd better start at about 10.30 in the morning at the Grande Grille. There are plenty of chairs, so you won't have to stand about, and, if it rains, there's a vast glass enclosure for shelter. . . . I want you to have three half-pints of water at half-hourly intervals, and it should be drunk as hot as you can take it.

'I want you to repeat the process in the afternoons at about five, at the Chomel spring.

'Don't worry if you feel a bit languid the first day. It's a purely temporary side-effect of the treatment. . . . Anyway, I shall be seeing you. . . .'

Those early days, before his initiation into the mysteries of each individual spring, seemed very far away now. Now, as for thousands of others, as for tens of thousands of others, with whom he rubbed shoulders every hour of the day, the cure had become a part of his life.

Just as in the evening, when there was a concert, every one of the little yellow chairs round the bandstand was occupied, so, at certain times of day, there was not a chair to be had, so great was the crowd gathered round the springs, all waiting for a second, third or fourth glass of the waters.

Like everyone else, they had bought measuring glasses, Madame Maigret having insisted on getting one for herself.

'But *you're* not taking the waters!'

'Why shouldn't I? Where's the harm? It says in one of the pamphlets that the waters are slimming. . . .'

Each glass had its own case of plaited straw, and Madame Maigret carried both of theirs slung over one shoulder like binoculars at a race meeting.

They had never walked so much in their lives. Their hotel was in the France district, a quiet part of the town near the Célestins spring. They were out and about by nine every morning when, apart from the delivery men, they had the streets almost to themselves.

A few minutes' walk from their hotel, there was a children's playground with a paddling pool, swings, play apparatus of all sorts, even a puppet theatre, more elaborate than the one in the Champs-Elysées.

'Your tickets, sir?'

They had bought two one-franc tickets, and strolled among the trees, watching the half-naked children at play. Next day they had come again.

'We sell books of twenty tickets at a reduced rate.'

They were reluctant to commit themselves so far ahead. They had come upon the playground by chance and, for want of anything better to do, had fallen into the habit of returning there every day at the same hour.

Regularly, they went on from there to the bowling club, where they would watch two or three games being played, with Maigret attentively following every throw, especially those of the tall, thin, one-armed man, always to be found under the same tree, who was, in spite of his disability, the finest player of all. Another regular player was a dignified old gentleman with pink cheeks, snow-white hair and a southern accent, always addressed by his companions as 'Senator'.

It was not far from there to the life-guards' hut and the beach, with buoys bobbing in the water to mark the limits of the bathing area. Here, too, they would find the same familiar faces under the same familiar beach umbrellas.

'You're not bored, are you?' she had asked him on their second day.

'Why on earth should I be?' he had retorted in surprise.

For indeed he was not bored. Little by little, his habits, his tempo of living, were changing. For instance, he caught himself filling his pipe on the Pont de Bellerive and realized, to his amazement, that he always smoked a pipe just at this time and place. There was also the Yacht Club pipe, which he smoked while watching the young people skimming over the water on skis.

'It's a dangerous sport, wouldn't you say?'

'In what way?'

Finally, the park, the attendant filling their glasses from the spring, the two of them drinking the water in little sips. It was hot and salty. The water from the Chomel spring tasted strongly of sulphur, and after drinking it Maigret could hardly wait to light his pipe.

It amazed Madame Maigret that he should take it all so calmly. It was most unlike him to be so docile. It quite worried her at times, until it dawned on her that he was amusing himself by playing at detection. Almost in spite of himself he watched people, classifying them, taking note of everything about them, down to the smallest detail. He had, for instance, already discovered which of their fellow-guests in the Hôtel de la Bérézina—more a family pension than a hotel—had liver trouble and which diabetes, simply by observing what they had to eat.

What was this one's life history? What did that one do for a living? These were his preoccupations, in which he sometimes invited his wife to share.

Especially intriguing to them were the couple whom they called 'the happy pair,' the dumpy little man who seemed always on the verge of coming up to shake his hand, and his diminutive wife who looked like something out of a confectioner's shop. What was their station in life? They seemed to recognize the Chief Superintendent, but was this not perhaps merely because they had seen his picture in the papers?

Not many people here did, in fact, recognize him, many fewer than in Paris. Admittedly, his wife had insisted on buying him a light mohair jacket, almost white in fact, of the kind that

elderly men used to wear when he was a boy. But even allowing for this, it would probably not have occurred to most
people that the head of the Paris C.I.D. could be here, in
Vichy. When anyone peered at him with a puzzled frown, or
turned back to look at him, he felt almost sure that they
were thinking:

'Good heavens! That might almost be Maigret!'

But they did not think that it *was* Maigret. And no wonder.
He scarcely recognized himself!

Another person who intrigued them was the lady in lilac.
She too was taking the waters, but only at the Grande Grille,
where she could be seen every morning. She always sat a little
removed from the crowd, near the newspaper stand. She never
drank more than a mouthful of the water. Afterwards, with
her usual air of remote dignity, she would rinse out her glass
and put it away carefully in its straw case.

There were usually one or two people in the crowd who
seemed to know her well enough to greet her. The Maigrets
never saw her in the afternoon. Was she perhaps undergoing
hydrotherapy? Or had she been ordered by her doctor to
take an afternoon rest?

Dr. Rian had said:

'E.R.S., perfect. Average sedimentation rate: 6 mm per
hour. . . . Cholesterol, a little on the high side, but well within
the acceptable limits. . . . Urea normal. . . . You're a bit low
on iron, but there's no cause for anxiety. . . . No need to worry
about uric acid either . . . just keep off game, shellfish and
offal. As to your blood count, it could scarcely be better, with
98 per cent haemoglobin.

'There's nothing wrong with you that a thorough clean-out
won't cure. Any headaches or unusual fatigue? . . . Right
then, we'll carry on with the same treatment and diet for the
next few days. . . . Come and see me again on Saturday.'

There was an open-air band concert that night. They did
not see the lady in lilac leave, because, as usual, they themselves left early, well before the end. The Hôtel de la Bérézina,
in the France district of the town, gleamed with fresh paint, and
its double doors were flanked on either side by flowering

shrubs in urns. The Maigrets enjoyed walking back to it through the deserted streets.

They slept in a brass bed, and all the furniture in their room was in the style of the early 1900s—like the bath, which was raised on legs, and had old-fashioned goose-neck taps.

The hotel was well-kept and very quiet, except when the Gagnaire boys, who had rooms on the first floor, were let loose in the garden to play at Cowboys and Indians.

Everyone was asleep.

Was it the fifth day? Or the sixth? Of the two, it was Madame Maigret who was the more confused, waking up as she did every morning to the realization that she need not get up to make the coffee. Their breakfast was brought in on a tray at seven o'clock, coffee and fresh croissants, and the *Journal de Clermont-Ferrand*, which devoted two pages to news and features about life in Vichy.

Maigret had got into the habit of reading the paper from cover to cover, so that by now there was precious little he did not know about local affairs. He even read the death column and the small ads.

'Desirable residence, in excellent repair. Three rooms, bathroom, all mod cons. Uninterrupted view. . . .'

'Are you thinking of buying a house?'

'No, but this is interesting. I can't help wondering who will buy it. A family coming regularly for the cure, who won't live in it for more than a month each year? An elderly couple from Paris who want to retire here? Or . . .

They got dressed, taking turns in the bathroom, and went down the staircase, with its red carpet held in place by triangular brass clips. The proprietor was there in the hall, always ready with a friendly greeting. He was not a local man, as was obvious from his accent, but came from Montélimar.

They nibbled the hours away. . . . The children's playground. . . . The bowling greens. . . .

'I see, by the way, that Wednesdays and Saturdays are market days. It's a big market. We might go and have a look round. . . .'

They had always been attracted to markets, their stalls

164

laden with sides of beef, fish and live lobsters, and their all-pervading smell of fresh fruit and vegetables.

'Well, Rian did advise me to walk four miles a day,' he remarked with heavy irony, adding:

'Little does he know that, on average, we cover the best part of twelve!'

'Do you really think so?'

'Work it out. We spend at least five hours a day walking. . . . We may not be striding out like a couple of athletes, but all the same we can't be doing much less than three miles an hour.'

'I'd never have thought it!'

The glass of water. Sitting on one of the yellow chairs, reading the papers that had just come from Paris. Lunch in the white dining-room, where the only touch of colour was an opened bottle of wine on a table here and there, labelled with the name of the resident who had ordered it. There was no wine on the Maigrets' table.

'Did he say no wine?'

'Not in so many words. But while I'm about it . . .'

She could not get over the fact that, while scrupulously keeping to his diet, he was, at the same time, perfectly good-tempered about it.

They permitted themselves a short rest after lunch, before setting off again, this time for the opposite end of the town. Here, where most of the shops were, the pavements were so crowded that they were seldom able to walk abreast.

'Was there ever a town with so many osteopaths and chiropodists?'

'It's no wonder, if everyone walks as much as we do!'

That evening, the bandstand in the park was deserted. Instead, there was a concert in the gardens of the Grand Casino. Here, in place of the brass band, a string orchestra played. The music was of a more serious kind, matched by the expressions on the faces of the audience.

They did not see the lady in lilac. They had not seen her in the park either, though they had caught a glimpse of 'the happy pair,' who tonight were more formally dressed than usual, and seemed to be going to the Casino theatre, where a light comedy was showing.

The brass bedstead. It was astonishing how quickly the days went by, even when one was doing absolutely nothing. Croissants, coffee, cubes of sugar in greaseproof wrappings, the *Journal de Clermont-Ferrand*.

Maigret, in pyjamas, was sitting in an armchair next to the window, smoking his first pipe of the day. His coffee cup was still half-full. He enjoyed lingering over it as long as possible.

His sudden exclamation brought Madame Maigret from the bathroom, in a blue flower-printed dressing-gown, with her toothbrush still in her hand.

'What's the matter?'

'Look at this.'

There, on the first page devoted to Vichy, was a photograph, a photograph of the lady in lilac. It was not a very recent one. She looked several years younger in it, and, for the occasion, had managed to produce a tight-lipped semblance of a smile.

'What's happened to her?'

'She's been murdered.'

'Last night?'

'If it had happened last night, it wouldn't be in this morning's paper. No, it was the night before.'

'But we saw her at the band concert.'

'Yes, at nine o'clock. . . . She lived only a couple of streets from here, Rue du Bourbonnais. . . . I had a feeling that we were almost neighbours. . . . She went home. . . . She had time to take off her shawl and hat and go into the sitting-room, which leads off to the left from the passage. . . .'

'How was she killed?'

'She was strangled. Yesterday morning the lodgers were surprised not to hear her moving about downstairs as usual.'

'She wasn't just here for the cure then?'

'No, she lived in Vichy. . . . She owned the house, and let furnished rooms on the first floor. . . .'

Maigret was still in his armchair, and his wife well knew just how much self-control was needed to keep him there.

'Was it a sex maniac?'

'The place was ransacked from top to bottom, but nothing seems to have been taken. . . . In one of the drawers that had been broken into, they found jewellery and quite a lot o money. . . .'

'She wasn't . . . ?'

'Raped? No.'

He stared out of the window in silence.

'Who's in charge of the case, do you know?'

'Of course I don't! How could I?'

'The Chief C.I.D. Officer at Clermont-Ferrand is Lecœur, who used to work under me. . . . He's here. . . . Naturally, he has no idea that I'm here too. . . .'

'Will you be going to see him?'

To this he made no immediate answer.

CHAPTER TWO

IT WAS FIVE MINUTES TO NINE, and Maigret had not yet answered his wife's question. It seemed as though he had put himself on his honour to behave exactly as he would have done any other morning, to adhere, without the smallest deviation, to their established Vichy routine.

He had read the paper from beginning to end, while finishing his coffee. He had shaved and bathed, as usual, listening meanwhile to the news on the radio. At five minutes to nine he was ready, and together they went down the staircase, with its red carpet held in place by the triangular brass clips.

The proprietor, in white coat and chef's hat, was waiting for them below.

'Well, Monsieur Maigret, you can't say we don't look after you in Vichy, even to the extent of handing you a splendid murder on a plate. . . .'

He managed to force a non-committal smile.

'You will be attending to it, I trust?'

'This is not Paris. I have no authority here. . . .'

Madame Maigret was watching him. She thought he was unaware of this, but she was wrong. When they came to the Rue d'Auvergne, he composed his features in an expression of guileless innocence and, instead of going down it towards the Allier and the children's playground, turned right.

Admittedly, they did occasionally take a different route, but, up to now, only on the way back. Her husband's unerring sense of direction never failed to astonish Madame Maigret. He never looked at a map, and would wander off, apparently at random, into a maze of little side-streets. Often, just when it seemed to Madame Maigret that they must be lost, she would suddenly realize, with a start, that there in front of them was the door of their hotel, flanked on either side by the flowering shrubs in their green-painted urns.

On this occasion he turned right again, and then again, until they came to a house where a small crowd was gathered, hoping to catch a glimpse inside.

There was a twinkle in Madame Maigret's eye. The Chief Superintendent, after a moment's hesitation, crossed the road, stopped, gave his pipe a sharp tap against his heel to knock out the ash, and then slowly filled it with fresh tobacco. At times like these, he seemed to her just a great baby, and a wave of tenderness swept over her.

He was having a struggle with himself. At last, trying to look as though he had no idea where he was, he joined the group of spectators, and stood gaping like the rest at the house across the street, where a police constable was standing guard and, nearby, a car was parked.

It was an attractive house, like most of the others in the street. It had recently had a fresh coat of warm-white paint, and the shutters and balcony were almond green.

On a marble plaque, in Gothic lettering, was inscribed the name: *Les Iris.*

Madame Maigret had been following every move in this little private drama, from his decision not to call at the Police Station to his present determination *not* to cross the road, make himself known to the constable on duty, and gain admission to the house.

There was no cloud in the sky. The air was fresh, clear, invigorating, here in this clean little street. A few doors along, a woman, standing at her window shaking the dust out of her rugs, looked with disapproval at the people down below. But had she not herself been among the first yesterday, when the murder was discovered and the police arrived in force, to join with her neighbours in gaping at a house that she had seen every day of her life for years?

Someone in the crowd remarked:

'They say it was a *crime passionnel.*'

This suggestion was received with derision:

'Oh! Come! She can't have been a day under fifty.'

A face could be dimly seen at one o the upstairs windows, a pointed nose, dark hair, and from time to time, behind it, the shadowy figure of a youngish man.

The door was painted white. A milk float was moving slowly along the street, leaving bottles on doorsteps behind it. The milkman, with a bottle of milk in his hand, went up to the white door. The constable spoke to him, no doubt telling him that there was no point in leaving it, but the milkman shrugged, and left the bottle just the same.

Wasn't anyone going to notice that Maigret . . . ? He couldn't hang about here indefinitely. . . .

He was just about to move off, when there appeared in the doorway a tall young man with an unruly mop of hair. He crossed the road, making straight for the Chief Superintendent.

'The Divisional Superintendent would very much like to see you, sir.'

His wife, suppressing a smile, asked:

'Where shall I wait for you?'

'At the usual place, the spring. . . .'

Had they seen and recognized him from the window? With dignity, he crossed the road, assuming a grumpy expression to hide his gratification. It was cool in the entrance. There was a hatstand on the right, with two hats hanging from its branches. He added his own, a straw hat which his wife had made him buy at the same time as the mohair jacket, and in which he felt slightly foolish.

'Come on in, chief.'

A voice full of warm pleasure, a face and figure Maigret instantly recognized.

'Lecœur!'

They had not met for fifteen years, not since the days when Désiré Lecœur had been an inspector on Maigret's staff at the Quai des Orfèvres.

'Oh! yes, chief, here I am, longer in the tooth, wider in girth and higher up the ladder. Here I am, as I say, Divisional Superintendent at Clermont-Ferrand, which is why I'm landed with this ghastly business. . . . Come on in.'

He led him into a little parlour painted a bluish-grey,

and sat at a table covered with papers, which he was using as an improvised desk.

Maigret lowered himself cautiously into a fragile, reproduction Louis XVI chair. Lecœur must have noticed his puzzled expression, because he said at once:

'I daresay you're wondering how I knew you were here. In the first place, Moinet—you haven't met him, he's the head of the Vichy police—noticed the name on your registration form. . . . Naturally, he didn't want to intrude, but his men have seen you out and about every day. . . . It seems, in fact, that the chaps doing duty on the beach have been laying bets as to when you would make up your mind to try your hand at bowls. Your interest in the game, according to them, was visibly growing, day by day. So much so that . . .'

'Have you been here since yesterday?'

'Yes, of course, with two of my men from Clermont-Ferrand. One of them is the young chap, Dicelle, whom I sent out to fetch you when I saw you out there in the street. I was reluctant to send you a message at your hotel. I reckoned you were here for the cure, not for the purpose of giving us a helping hand. Besides I knew that, in the end, if you were interested, you would. . . .'

By now, Maigret really was looking grumpy.

'A sex maniac?' he mumbled.

'No, that's one thing we can say for sure.'

'A jealous lover?'

'Unlikely. Mind you, I could be wrong. I've been at it for twenty-four hours, but I'm not much wiser than when I got here yesterday morning.'

Referring from time to time to the papers on his desk, he went on:

'The murdered woman's name was Hélène Lange. She was forty-seven years old, born at Marsilly, about ten miles from La Rochelle. I rang the town hall at Marsilly and was told that her mother, who was widowed very young, had for many years kept a small draper's shop in the Place de l'Eglise.

'There were two daughters. Hélène, the elder, took a course in shorthand and typing at La Rochelle. After that she worked for a time in a shipping office, and later went to Paris, after which nothing more was heard of her.

'No request for a copy of her birth certificate was ever received, from which one must infer that she never married, besides which her identity card is made out in her maiden name.

'There was a sister, six or seven years younger, who also began her working life in La Rochelle, as a manicurist.

'Like her elder sister, she subsequently migrated to Paris, but returned home about ten years ago.

'She must have had substantial savings, because she bought a hairdressing establishment in the Place des Armes, which she still owns. I tried to get her on the phone, but was told by the assistant in charge that she was on holiday in Majorca. I cabled to her hotel, asking her to return immediately, and she should be here some time today.

'This sister—her name is Francine—is also unmarried. . . . The mother has been dead eight years. . . . There's no other family, as far as anyone knows.'

Quite unwittingly, Maigret had slipped back into his familiar professional role. To all appearances, he was in charge of the case, and Lecœur was a subordinate reporting to him in his office.

But there was no pipe-rack for him to fidget with as he listened, no sturdy armchair for him to lean back in, and no view of the Seine from the window.

As Lecœur talked, Maigret was struck by one or two unusual features of this little parlour, which had obviously been used as a living-room, in particular the fact that there were no photographs of anyone but Hélène Lange herself. There she was on a little bow-fronted chest, aged about six, in a dress that was too long for her, with tight plaits hanging down on either side of her face.

A larger photograph, obviously taken by a skilled photographer, hung on the wall. In this she was older, about twenty, and her pose was romantic, her expression ethereal.

A third photograph showed her on a beach, wearing not a bathing suit but a white dress, the wide skirt of which, blown to one side by the breeze, streamed out like a flag, and holding in both hands a light, wide-brimmed hat.

'Do you know how and when the murder was committed?'

'We're having difficulty in finding out what exactly did happen that evening. . . . We've been working on it since yesterday morning, but we haven't made much headway.

'The night before last—Monday night, that is—Hélène Lange had supper alone in her kitchen. She washed up—or at any rate we didn't find any dirty dishes in the sink—got dressed, switched off all the lights, and went out. If you want to know, she ate two boiled eggs. She wore a mauve dress, a white woollen shawl and a hat, also white. . . .'

Maigret, after an internal struggle, couldn't in the end resist saying:

'I know.'

'Have you been making enquiries, then?'

'No, but I saw her on Monday evening, sitting near the bandstand, listening to the concert.'

'Do you know what time she left?'

'She was still there just before half-past nine, when my wife and I went for our walk, as we do every evening.'

'Was she alone?'

'She was always alone.'

Lecœur made no attempt to hide his astonishment.

'So you'd noticed her on other occasions?'

Maigret, now looking much more good-humoured, nodded.

'What was it about her?'

'Nothing in particular. One spends one's time here just walking about, and, almost unconsciously, one registers a face here and there in the crowd. You know how it is . . . one is always running into the same people in the same places at certain times of day. . . .'

'Have you any ideas?'

'What about?'

'What sort of woman she was.'

'She was no ordinary woman, I'm sure of that, but that's all I can say.'

'Well, to proceed. . . . Two of the three bedrooms on

173

the first floor are let, the largest to the Maleskis, a couple from Grenoble. He's an engineer. They were out at the cinema. They left the house a few minutes after Mademoiselle Lange, and didn't get back till half-past eleven. All the shutters were closed as usual, but they could see through the slats that the lights were still on downstairs. When they got inside, they noticed strips of light under the doors of Mademoiselle Lange's living-room and bedroom. That's the room on the right. . . .'

'Did they hear anything?'

'Maleski heard nothing, but his wife said, with some hesitation, that she thought she had heard a murmur of voices. . . . They went straight up to bed, and slept undisturbed until morning. . . .

'The other lodger is a Madame Vireveau, a widow from Paris, Rue Lamarck. She's rather an overbearing woman, aged about sixty. She comes to Vichy every year to lose weight. . . . This is the first time she's taken a room in Mademoiselle Lange's house. In former years, she always stayed at a hotel.

'She's seen better days, apparently. Her husband was a rich man, but over-lavish, and, when he died, she found herself in financial difficulties. . . . To put it briefly, she's loaded with imitation jewellery, and she booms like a dowager in a bad play. . . . She left the house at nine. She saw no one, and claims that, when she went out, the house was in total darkness.'

'Do the lodgers have their own keys?'

'Yes. Madame Vireveau spent the evening at the Carlton Bridge Club, and left just before midnight. She hasn't a car. The Maleskis have a Mini, but they seldom use it in Vichy. Most of the time, it's left in a garage nearby. . . .'

'Were the lights still on?'

'I'm coming to that, chief. Naturally, I saw the old girl only after the crime had been discovered, and by then the whole street was in a turmoil. . . . Maybe all that fancy jewellery goes with a vivid imagination. . . . I really can't say. . . . Anyway, according to her story, she almost bumped into a man as she turned the corner, the corner of the Boulevard de La-Salle and the Rue du Bourbonnais, that is. He couldn't possibly have seen her coming, and she swears that he was visibly startled, and shielded his face with his hand to avoid being recognized.'

'Did she, in fact, recognize him?'

'No, but she swears nevertheless that she would recognize him if she saw him again face to face. He was very tall and heavily built—with a great bulging chest like a gorilla, she says. He was hunched up and walking fast. He gave her a proper fright, she says, but all the same she turned back to watch him striding away towards the town centre.'

'Had she any idea of his age?'

'Not young. . . . Not old either. . . . Very heavily built. . . . Frightening. . . . She almost ran the rest of the way. . . . She didn't feel safe until her key was in the lock. . . .'

'Were the lights still showing on the ground floor?'

'That's just it, they weren't, that is, if one can accept that she's a reliable witness. She didn't hear a thing. She went up to bed, so shaken that she had to take a teaspoonful of peppermint essence on a lump of sugar. . . .'

'Who discovered the body?'

'All in good time, chief. Mademoiselle Lange, while quite willing to let her rooms to respectable people, was not prepared to serve meals. No cooking was allowed. She wouldn't even let them have a spirit stove for a cup of morning coffee.

'Yesterday morning, at about eight, Madame Maleski came downstairs with her thermos flask, as she always did, to get it filled and buy some croissants at a nearby coffee bar. She didn't notice anything amiss, then or when she got back. What did surprise her, though, was the absolute quiet downstairs, especially the second time, because Mademoiselle Lange was an early riser, and could usually be heard moving about from one room to another.

' "Perhaps she's not well," she remarked to her husband over breakfast.

'Because it seems that the landlady often complained of poor health. At nine o'clock—Madame Vireveau was still in her room—the Maleskis went downstairs, where they found Charlotte looking worried. . . .'

'Charlotte?'

'The girl who comes in every morning from nine to twelve to clean the rooms. She cycles in from a village about ten miles away. She's a bit simple.

' "All the doors are locked," she said to the Maleskis.

'Usually she arrived to find all the doors and windows on the ground floor wide open; Mademoiselle Lange was a great one for fresh air.

' "Haven't you got a key?"

' "No, if she's not in, I might as well go home."

'Maleski tried to open the door with the key of his room, but it didn't fit, so in the end he went to the coffee bar where his wife gets their breakfast, and rang the police from there.

'And that's about all. An inspector from Vichy Police Headquarters arrived within minutes with a locksmith. The key to the living-room door was missing, and the kitchen and bedroom doors were locked from inside, with the keys in the locks.

'Here, in this room, they found Hélène Lange. She was lying stretched out, or rather doubled up, on the edge of the carpet, here on this exact spot. She had been strangled. . . . It wasn't a pretty sight. . . .

'She was still wearing her mauve dress, but had taken off her hat and shawl, which were both found hanging on the hatstand in the hall. All the drawers were open, and there were papers and cardboard boxes scattered all over the floor.'

'Had she been raped?'

'No, nothing of that sort was even attempted. And as far as we know, nothing was stolen. The report in this morning's *Journal* is reasonably accurate. . . . In one of the drawers we found five hundred-franc notes. . . . The assailant had been through the dead woman's handbag, and the contents were scattered about the room. These included four hundred francs in small notes, some silver, and a season ticket for the Grand Casino Theatre. . . .'

'Had she lived here long?'

176

'Nine years. . . . Before that she lived for some years in Nice. . . .'

'Did she work there?'

'No. She lived in rather a shabby lodging house in the Boulevard Albert I. Presumably she had a small private income.'

'Did she travel at all?'

'She was in the habit of going away about once a month, for a day or two at a time.'

'Do you know where she went?'

'She was very secretive about her comings and goings.'

'And after she came here?'

'For the first two years, she had the whole house to herself. Then she advertised three rooms to let during the season, but the house was not always full. Just now, for instance, the blue room isn't let. . . . I should perhaps mention that each bedroom has a different colour scheme. Besides the blue room, there is a white room and a pink room.'

At this point, Maigret suddenly noticed another odd thing. Nowhere in the living-room was there the smallest touch of green, not a single ornament or cushion, not even a trimming.

'Was she superstitious?'

'How did you guess? One day, she got into quite a state because Madame Maleski had brought home a bunch of carnations. She said they were flowers of ill-omen, and she wouldn't have them in the house.

'On another occasion, she warned Madame Vireveau against wearing a green dress, prophesying that she would pay dearly for it. . . .'

'Did she ever have visitors?'

'According to the neighbours, never.'

'Any mail?'

'We've spoken to the postman. There was an occasional letter from La Rochelle, but apart from that, nothing but circulars and bills from local shops.'

'Did she have a bank account?'

'With the Crédit Lyonnais, on the corner of the Rue Georges-Clemenceau.'

'You've made enquiries there, of course?'

'She paid in regularly, round about 5,000 francs a month, but not always on the same day of the month.'

'In cash?'

'Yes. During the season, she paid in more, because of the money coming in from the lodgers.'

'Did she ever sign cheques?'

'There were a number of cheques made out to shops in Vichy and Moulins, where she sometimes went to do her shopping. Occasionally she would order something from Paris—something she had seen in a mail order catalogue: look, there's a pile of them over there—and for these things, too, she would pay by cheque.'

Lecœur was watching the Chief Superintendent, and thinking how different he looked, in his off-white jacket, from the man he had worked for in the Quai des Orfèvres.

'What do you make of it, chief?'

'I'll have to be going. My wife is waiting for me.'

'Not to mention your first glass of water!'

'So the Vichy police know about that too, do they?' grumbled Maigret.

'But you'll be back, won't you? The C.I.D. hasn't a branch in Vichy. I drive back to Clermont-Ferrand every night. It's only fifty miles. The Chief of the Vichy Police has offered me the use of an office with a telephone, but I'd sooner have my headquarters here on the spot. My men are trying to trace any neighbours or passers-by who may have seen Mademoiselle Lange returning home on Monday night, because we still don't know whether the murderer came with her or was waiting for her in the house. . . .'

'Forgive me, my dear fellow. . . . My wife. . . .'

'Of course, chief.'

Maigret was still determined to stick to his routine, though curiosity very nearly got the better of him. He felt he really ought not to have turned right instead of left when setting out from the Hôtel de la Bérézina. Had he not done so, he would have lingered, as always up till now, in the children's playground, and then, further on, stopped to watch a game or two of bowls.

He wondered whether Madame Maigret, all on her own, had followed the familiar route, stopping at all the places where they usually stopped together.

'Would you care for a lift? My car is at the door, and I'm sure there's nothing young Dicelle would like better than to . . .'

'No, thank you, I shall walk. That's what I'm here for.'

And walk he did, alone, striding along at a brisk pace to make up for lost time.

He had drunk his first glass of water and returned to his seat, midway between the great glass hall built round the spring and the nearest tree. Although his wife asked no questions, he could feel her watching his every movement, trying to interpret his expression.

With the newspapers spread out on his lap, he sat gazing at the sky through the trees. There was scarcely any movement among the leaves, and the sky was still the same clear blue, with one small solitary cloud, dazzlingly white, drifting across it.

Sometimes in Paris he would feel a twinge of nostalgia for half-forgotten sensory experiences: a puff of wind, warmed by the sun, against his cheek, the play of light among leaves or on a gravel path, the crunch of gravel under running feet, even the taste of dust.

And here, miraculously, they all were. While reflecting on his meeting with Lecœur, he was at the same time basking in his surroundings, savouring every little thing.

Was he really deep in thought, or just daydreaming? There were small family groups to be seen here and there, as there are everywhere, but in this place the proportion of elderly couples was greater.

And what about the solitary figures in the crowd? Were there more men than women? Women, especially old women, tend to be gregarious. They could be seen arranging their chairs in little groups of six or eight, leaning forward as though to exchange confidences, although they had probably known one another not more than a few days.

Were they really exchanging confidences? Who could say? No doubt they discussed their illnesses, their doctors, their treatment, and went on to talk about their married sons and daughters, and to display the photographs of their grand-children, which they carried about in their handbags.

It was uncommon to see one of them remaining aloof, keeping herself to herself, like the lady in lilac, to whom he could now attach a name.

Solitary men were more numerous. Often these showed signs of exhaustion and pain, and it was an obvious effort for them to move with dignity among the crowd. Their drawn features and sad eyes bespoke a vague, distressed apprehension that they might crumple to the ground, and lie there in a patch of sunlight or shade, in among the legs of the people passing by.

Hélène Lange was one of the solitary ones, and everything about her, her expression, her bearing, told that she was a proud woman. She would not allow herself to be treated as an old maid, she would not accept pity. She went her way, very erect, chin held high, walking with a firm tread.

She consorted with no one, having no need of the relief of facile confidences.

Was it by choice that she had lived alone?

This was the question uppermost in his mind, as he tried to conjure up an image of her as he had seen her, sitting, standing, in motion, still.

'Have they any clue?'

Madame Maigret was beginning to feel a little aggrieved at his day-dreaming. In Paris, she would never have dared question her husband while he was working on a case. But here it was different. Here, walking side by side for hours on end, they had got into the habit of thinking aloud.

They did not converse exactly, exchanging question and answer, but rather one or the other would occasionally let fall the odd, disjointed phrase, to indicate what he or she was thinking.

'No. They can't do much until the sister gets here.'

'Had she no other family?'

'Apparently not.'

'It's time for your second glass.'

They went into the hall. The heads of the girl attendants showed above the sides of the well in which they stood. Hélène Lange came here every day to take the waters. Was this on medical advice, or was it just to give some point to her morning walk?

'What's bothering you?'

'I'm wondering why Vichy.'

It was almost ten years since she had come to settle in the town, and bought her house. She was therefore thirty-seven at the time, and must have had independent means, since it was not until she had had the house to herself for two years that she started letting rooms.

'Why not Vichy?' retorted Madame Maigret.

'There are hundreds of towns in France, small towns, larger towns, where she might have gone to settle, not to mention La Rochelle, where she grew up. . . . Her sister, having spent some time in Paris, went back to La Rochelle and stayed there. . . .'

'Perhaps the two sisters didn't get on.'

It wasn't as simple as that. Maigret was still watching the people strolling about. The tempo of the moving crowds reminded him of something, of a constant stream of people, ebbing and flowing in hot sunshine. In Nice, on the Promenade des Anglais.

For Hélène Lange, before coming to Vichy, had lived five years in Nice.

'She lived five years in Nice,' he said, speaking his thoughts aloud.

'Like a lot of other people on small fixed incomes.'

'Just so. . . . People on small fixed incomes, but also people from all walks of life, the same as here. . . . Only the day before yesterday I was trying to remember what I was reminded of by the crowds strolling in the park and sitting on the chairs. . . . They're just like the crowds on the sea-front at Nice . . . an agglomeration of elements so diverse that they cancel each other out. Vichy, like Nice, must surely have its share of superannuated sirens, former stars of stage and screen. . . . You've seen for yourself the streets of opulent private villas, where there are actually footmen in striped waistcoats still.

'And up in the hills, well away from the public gaze, there are villas even more opulent.

'As in Nice. . . .'

'And what do you deduce from that?'

'Nothing. She was thirty-two when she went to live in Nice, and she was as much on her own there as she was here. Solitude doesn't as a rule, come so early in life.'

'There are such things as unhappy love-affairs.'

'Yes, but the sufferers don't look as she did.'

'Broken marriages are not unknown.'

'Ninety-five per cent of those women remarry.'

'What about the men?'

With a broad grin, he retorted:

'A hundred per cent!'

She could not be sure whether he was teasing her or not.

Nice has a floating population, several casinos, and branches of nearly all the main Paris shops. Vichy virtually changes its population every three weeks, as the hundreds of thousands taking the cure come and go. It has branches of the same shops, three casinos and a dozen cinemas.

Anywhere else, she would have been known. People would have taken an interest in her, they would have pried into her mode of life, her comings and goings.

Not in Nice. Not in Vichy. Was it that she had something to hide?

'Are you going back to see Lecœur?'

'He said to come whenever I felt like it. He calls me "chief," just as though he were still working under me.'

'They all do.'

'That's true. It's just habit, I daresay.'

'You don't think it could be affection?'

He shrugged, and suggested that it was time they were on their way. This time, they went through the old town, stopping to look in the windows of the antique shops, where so many old and some touchingly pathetic objects were displayed.

In the dining-room, they were conscious of being stared at by their fellow guests. Oh! Well, they would just have to get used to it.

Maigret had conscientiously modified his eating habits in accordance with the doctor's instructions: chew everything thoroughly before swallowing, even mashed potatoes; never replenish your fork until you have swallowed the previous mouthful; do not drink more than a couple of sips of water with your meals, flavoured with a drop of wine, if you must.

He preferred to do without wine altogether.

On the way upstairs, he permitted himself a couple of puffs at his pipe, before stretching out, fully dressed, for his afternoon rest. His wife sat in the armchair by the window. There was just enough light coming in through the slats in the blinds to enable her to read the paper, as he had done earlier. From time to time, as he lay dozing, he could hear the rustle of a page being turned.

He had been resting for barely twenty minutes, when there was a knock at the door. Madame Maigret got up hastily, and went out, shutting the door behind her. After a whispered consultation, she went downstairs. She was back within minutes.

'It was Lecœur.'

'Any fresh news?'

'The sister has just arrived in Vichy. She went straight to the police station. She's about to be taken to the mortuary, to make a formal identification. Lecœur will be waiting to see her in the Rue du Bourbonnais. He thought you might like to be present when he questioned her.'

Maigret, grumbling to himself, was already on his feet. For a start, he would have the shutters open, to let a little light and life into the place.

'Shall we meet at the spring?'

Five o'clock in the afternoon: the spring, the first glass of water, the iron chair.

183

'It won't take that long. You'd better wait for me on one of the benches near the bowling greens.'

He was looking dubiously at his straw hat.

'What's the matter? Are you afraid of being laughed at?'

Well, let them laugh. He was on holiday, wasn't he? Defiantly, he put it on.

The same constable was on guard outside the house. There were still a good many people about, drawn there by curiosity, but when they found that there was nothing to be seen through the closed windows, most of them moved off, shaking their heads.

'Take a seat, chief. If you move your chair into that corner over there by the window, you'll be able to see her with the light full on her.'

'Have you seen her yet?'

'I was in a restaurant having lunch—and a very good lunch it was, I may say—when I got a message that she was at the police station. They said they'd see to it that she was taken to the mortuary, and brought on here afterwards.'

And at that moment they saw, through the net curtains, a black car with a policeman in uniform at the wheel and, following behind, a long red, open sports car. It was plain from their dishevelled hair and tanned faces that the man and woman in the front seats had just got back from holiday.

The couple talked for a minute or two, their heads close together. They exchanged a hurried kiss, and she got out of the car and slammed the door. Her companion, still sitting at the wheel, lit a cigarette.

He was dark, with strong features and athletic shoulders, which were clearly outlined under his close-fitting, yellow, polo-neck sweater. He was surveying the house with a bored expression, when the constable ushered the young woman into the living-room.

'I am Superintendent Lecœur. . . . You are Francine Lange, I presume?'

'That's right.'

She glanced briefly at Maigret, whose face was in shadow, and to whom she had not been introduced.

'Madame or Mademoiselle?'

'I'm not married, if that's what you mean. I have a friend with me; he's in the car. But I know too much about men to marry one of them. It's the devil's own job to get rid of them afterwards. . . .'

She was a fine-looking woman, who appeared much younger than her forty years, and her provocative curves seemed out of place in this conventional little room. She was wearing a flame-coloured dress of material so thin that her bare flesh showed through it, and the salt tang of the sea seemed still to cling about her.

'I got your telegram last night. Lucien managed to get seats on the first plane to Paris. . . . We had left our car at Orly so we drove the rest of the way from there. . . .'

'I take it she was, in fact, your sister?'

Showing no sign of emotion, she nodded.

'Won't you sit down?'

'Thank you. Do you mind if I smoke?'

She looked meaningfully at the smoke rising up from Maigret's pipe, as if to say:

'If he can smoke, what's to stop me?'

'Please do. . . . I take it you were no more prepared for this murder than we were?'

'Well, naturally, I wasn't expecting it!'

'Do you know of anyone who might have had a grudge against your sister?'

'Why should anyone have had a grudge against Hélène?'

'When did you see her last?'

'Six or seven years ago, I can't say exactly. . . . It was winter, I remember, and there was a storm raging. . . . She hadn't let me know she was coming, so I was taken by surprise when she coolly walked into my hairdressing salon.'

'Did you get on well together?'

'As well as most sisters. . . . We never saw much of one another, because of the difference in our ages. . . . When I started school, she had just left. . . . Then she went to the Secretarial College in La Rochelle. . . . I didn't train as a manicurist till years after. . . . Later, she left the town.'

'How old was she then?'

'Let me think. . . . I was in the second year of my training
. . . so I must have been sixteen. . . . She was seven years
older. . . . That would make her twenty-three. . . .'

'Used you to correspond?'

'Very rarely. . . . We don't go in much for letter-writing
in our family.'

'Was your mother still alive then?'

'Yes . . . she died two years later, and Hélène came to
Marsilly for the share-out of her property. . . . Not that there
was much to share. . . . The shop was almost worthless. . . .'

'What was your sister doing in Paris?'

Maigret never took his eyes off her, making a mental
comparison, line by line, between her face and figure and
those of the dead woman. There was very little resemblance
between the two women, the dark-eyed, long-jawed Hélène
and the blue-eyed Francine, who was almost certainly not a
natural blonde, with that bizarre streak of fiery red dangling
over her forehead.

At first sight, she seemed a good sort, hail-fellow-well-met
with her clientele, no doubt, exuberantly cheerful, if a little
coarse.

She made no pretence of refinement, indeed she seemed
bent on accentuating her natural vulgarity, almost as if
she relished it.

It was not half an hour since she had viewed her sister's
body in the mortuary, yet here she was answering Lecœur's
questions good-humouredly, almost gaily, and—probably just
from habit—attempting to make a conquest of him.

'What was she doing in Paris? Working as a shorthand-
typist in an office presumably, though I never went there to
find out. . . . We had very little in common. I was just fifteen
when I had my first boy-friend—a taxi driver, he was—and I've
had a good many since. . . . I don't fancy that was Hélène's
style at all, unless she was a very dark horse. . . .'

'What address did you write to?'

'At the beginning, as far as I remember, it was a hotel in
the Avenue de Clichy. . . . I forget the name. . . . She moved

several times. . . . Later she took a flat in the Rue Notre-Dame-de-Lorette. . . . I can't remember the number. . . .'

'You yourself went to live in Paris after a time. . . . Did you never go and see her?'

'Yes, I did. She was living in the Rue Notre-Dame-de-Lorette by then. A very nice little flat it was. . . . I was amazed. . . . I remember remarking on it. . . . She had a large bedroom looking out on the street, a living-room, a kitchenette and a real bathroom. . . .'

'Was there a man in her life?'

'I never found out. I wanted to stay a few days with her, while I looked for a suitable room. She said she knew of a very clean, modestly priced hotel where I could stay, but she couldn't bear to have anyone living with her.'

'Not even for three or four days?'

'Apparently not.'

'Did it surprise you?'

'Not all that much. . . . I may say, it takes a lot to surprise me. . . . I don't like other people to meddle in my affairs, and I don't interfere in theirs.'

'How long were you in Paris?'

'Eleven years.'

'Working as a manicurist?'

'To begin with. I worked in several salons in the neighbourhood, and then moved to a beauty parlour in the Champs-Elysées. That was where I trained as a beauty specialist.'

'Were you living alone?'

'Sometimes alone, sometimes not.'

'Did you see anything of your sister?'

'To all intents and purposes, nothing.'

'So you can't really tell us anything about her life in Paris?'

'All I know is that she had a job. . . .'

'When you returned to La Rochelle to open your own salon, had you much in the way of savings?'

'A fair amount.'

He did not ask how she had earned this money, nor did she volunteer the information, but she probably took it for granted that he understood.

'You never married?'

'I've answered that already. I'm not such a fool as to. . . .'

And, turning to the window, from which they could see her companion lounging at the wheel of the red sports car:

'He looks a nasty bit of work, don't you think?'

'And yet you're living with him. . . .'

'He works for me, and what's more, he's a first-class hair-dresser. We don't live together in La Rochelle; I wouldn't want him around all night as well as all day. . . . On holiday, it's different. . . .'

'Is the car yours?'

'Of course.'

'But he chose it?'

'How did you guess?'

'Did your sister ever have a child?'

'Why do you ask?'

'I don't know . . . she was a woman. . . .'

'Not to my knowledge, she didn't. . . . I shouldn't have thought it was the kind of thing you could hide. . . .'

'What about you?'

'I had a child while I was living in Paris. . . . Fifteen years ago. . . . My first thought was to get rid of it. . . . It would have been better if I had. . . . It was my sister who urged me not to. . . .'

'So you were in touch with her then?'

'It was because of it that I went to see her. . . . I needed someone to talk to—a member of my own family. . . . You may think it silly, but there are times when one instinctively turns to one's family. . . . Anyway, I had a son, Philippe. . . . I put him out to foster-parents in the Vosges. . . .'

'Why the Vosges? Had you any ties there?'

'None whatever. Hélène saw an advertisement somewhere or other. . . . I used to go and see him. . . . I suppose I went about ten times in two years. . . . He was well cared for. . . . The foster-parents were very kind. . . . They had a small farm, beautifully kept. . . . Then one day I heard from them that the child was dead, drowned in a pond. . . .'

She was silent and thoughtful for a moment or two, then she shrugged:

'All things considered, it was probably for the best. . . .'

'Did you know of no one who was close to your sister, man or woman?'

'I doubt if she had many friends. Even in the old days in Marsilly she looked down her nose at the other girls. They used to call her the Princess. . . . It was no different, I imagine, at the Secretarial College in La Rochelle. . . .'

'Was it pride?'

She thought this over, then said uncertainly:

'I don't know. . . . That's not the word I would choose. . . . She didn't like people. . . . She didn't like the company of other people. . . . That's it! She was happiest on her own.'

'Did she ever attempt suicide?'

'Why should she? You don't think . . . ?'

Lecœur smiled.

'No, no one commits suicide by strangulation. . . . I just wondered whether, at any time in the past, she had been tempted to put an end to her life.'

'I'm sure it never entered her head. . . . She had a good opinion of herself. Basically, she was very self-satisfied.'

Yes, thought Maigret, that was it, self-satisfied. In his mind's eye he saw once again the lady in lilac sitting facing the bandstand. At the time, he had tried to interpret her expression, and failed.

Francine had put her finger on it: self-satisfaction.

She was so self-absorbed that she kept no less than three photographs of herself in her living-room, and no doubt there were others in the dining-room and bedroom, which he had not yet seen.

She had no photograph of anyone else. None of her mother, none of her sister, none of any friend, man or woman. Even on the beach, she had been photographed alone, against a background of waves.

'I take it that, as far as you know, you are her sole heir? . . . We found no will among her papers. Admittedly, the murderer scattered them all over the place, but I can't imagine any reason why he should have made off with her will. . . . So far, we have heard nothing from any lawyer. . . .'

'When is the funeral to be?'

'That's up to you. The forensic laboratory have completed their work so you can claim your sister's body whenever you wish.'

'Where do you think she should be buried?'

'I haven't the least idea.'

'I don't know a soul here. . . . If I took her back to Marsilly the whole village would turn out for the funeral—to gape. . . . I wonder if it really would have been her wish to end up in Marsilly. . . . Look, if you don't need me any more, I'd like to go and book into a hotel. I'm longing for a good hot bath. . . . Let me think it over, and tomorrow morning . . .'

'Very well. I shall expect to see you tomorrow morning.'

Just as she was leaving, having shaken hands with Lecœur, she turned to glance briefly at Maigret. She was frowning, as though puzzled by the presence of this silent man sitting in shadow.

Did she recognize him?

'Till tomorrow, then. You have been most kind.'

They saw her get into the car and lean over to say something to her companion at the wheel, and then the car drove off.

In the living-room the two men looked at one another. Lecœur was the first to speak:

'Well?' he said. It was almost comical.

And Maigret, puffing at his pipe, retorted:

'Well, what?'

He didn't feel like discussing the case. Besides, he hadn't forgotten that he had promised to meet his wife near the bowling greens.

'I must be going, my dear fellow. I'll see you tomorrow.'

'Till tomorrow, then.'

The constable's military salute was no more than was due to him. All the same, he felt a glow of pride.

CHAPTER THREE

HE WAS BACK in his old place, sitting in the green arm-chair near the open window. The weather had not changed since the day they arrived, warm sunshine in abundance, yet with a cool breeze at the start of the day, when the municipal sprinkler-carts made their rounds of the streets. And later on it would be pleasantly cool in the shade of the thickly wooded park, the many tree-lined boulevards, and the Allier promenade.

He had eaten his three croissants. His coffee cup was still half-full. His wife was having her bath next door, and, on the floor below, he could hear the sounds of people moving about their rooms, getting ready to go downstairs.

It was not without a touch of wry amusement that he noted how quickly he had formed new habits. That was always his way. Wherever he was, he would almost instinctively establish a routine, and then adhere to it, as though subject to some immutable law.

It would be true to say that, when he was in Paris, each separate enquiry had a tempo of its own, which included periods of rest in one particular bistro or brasserie, with its own characteristic smells and quality of light.

Here, in Vichy, he felt much more like a man on holiday than a man taking the cure, and even the death of the lady in lilac had failed to shatter his indolent mood.

The night before, they had gone for their customary walk in the park, where several hundred others like themselves appeared as dark shadows, except when they moved through a pool of light cast by one of the frosted globes of the lamp standards. At this hour, most people were at the theatre, the cinema or the casino. Everywhere, after a light meal of cold ham, people were coming out of their hotels, pensions and lodgings, in search of their own chosen form of entertainment.

Many were quite happy just to sit and relax on the florid little yellow chairs, and Maigret, without thinking, had caught himself searching in the crowd for an erect and dignified figure, a face with a long jaw-line, a chin held high, and an expression that was at once wistful and hard.

Hélène Lange was dead, and Francine, no doubt, was consulting with her gigolo as to where she should have her sister buried.

Somewhere in this town, there was a man who could solve the mystery of the lonely woman who owned a house called *Les Iris*, the man who had strangled her.

Was he taking his customary walk in the park, or was he, at this minute, on his way to the theatre or the cinema?

Maigret and his wife had undressed and gone to bed in silence, but each had known what the other was thinking.

He lit his pipe, and opened his paper at the section devoted to local news.

A photograph of himself spread over two columns caused him to draw in his breath sharply. It was a recent photograph, showing him drinking one of his daily glasses of water. He couldn't imagine when it had been taken. His wife had been sitting beside him at this time—they had left in about a third of her—and in the background were several blurred, anonymous faces.

'*Maigret to the rescue?*

'Out of consideration for his privacy, we have not hitherto informed our readers of the presence among us of Chief Superintendent Maigret. He is in Vichy in a private capacity, having come, like so many other distinguished public figures, to take advantage of the beneficial properties of our mineral springs.

'The question now arises, will the Chief Superintendent be able to resist the temptation to try his hand at solving the mystery of the Rue du Bourbonnais?

'He has been seen in the neighbourhood of the house where the murder was committed, and rumour has it that he is in touch with Superintendent Lecœur, the popular head of C.I.D., Clermont-Ferrand, who is in charge of the case.

'With loyalties divided between the cure and the case, which will he choose?'

He dropped the paper with a shrug. He was used to personal gossip of this sort, and it no longer angered him. He turned, and stared absent-mindedly out of the window.

Up to now—it was nine o'clock—he had behaved exactly as he did every morning, and when Madame Maigret reappeared, wearing her pink suit, they went downstairs as usual.

'Monsieur, Madame, good morning. . . .' As usual, the proprietor was there to greet them. Maigret had already seen the two men outside, and the glint of their camera lens.

'They've been waiting for you for the past hour. They're from the Saint-Etienne *Tribune*, not the local paper.'

The photographer was tall, with red hair. The man with him, small and dark, had one shoulder higher than the other. They ran up to the door.

'May we take a picture? Just one?'

What was the use of saying no? He stood quite still for a moment on the doorstep, between the two flowering shrubs, Madame Maigret having retreated into the shadows.

'Look up, please, sir. Your hat . . .'

He could not remember when he had last been photographed wearing a straw hat. The only other he now possessed was the one he kept at Meung-sur-Loire for gardening.

'One more. . . . It won't take a second. . . . Thank you.'

'Just one question, Monsieur Maigret, is it true that you are taking part in the investigation?'

'As Chief of the Criminal Investigation Department at the Quai des Orfèvres, I have no authority here.'

'All the same, you must be taking an interest?'

'No more than all your other readers.'

'It has one or two peculiar features, don't you think?'

'What do you mean?'

'The victim was a recluse. . . . She had no friends. . . . There is no obvious motive. . . .'

'When we know more about her, the motive, no doubt, will become apparent.'

It was not a particularly profound remark, and it committed him to nothing, but, all the same, it contained a germ of essential truth. For a long time now, others besides Maigret have seen the importance of studying the character of the victim. Increasingly, the attention of criminologists has centred upon the dead person, even to the extent of laying a large share of the blame at the victim's door.

Might there not have been something in Hélène Lange's manner and way of life which had, in a sense, doomed her to death by violence? From the very first, when he had seen her under the trees in the park, the Chief Superintendent had fixed upon her as an object of interest.

True, she was not the only one. The two whom he and his wife always referred to as 'the happy pair' had also aroused his interest.

'Isn't it a fact that Superintendent Lecœur used to be on your staff?'

'He did work for a time in the Palais de Justice in Paris.'

'Have you seen him?'

'I paid him a friendly call.'

'Will you be seeing him again?'

'Very likely.'

'Will you be discussing the murder with him?'

'Very likely. Unless we confine ourselves to the weather, and the strange quality of the light in your charming town.'

'What's so strange about it?'

'It's soft and shimmering at one and the same time.'

'Do you intend to come back to Vichy next year?'

'That depends on my doctor.'

'Many thanks. . . .'

As the two men leapt into their battered motor car, Maigret and his wife walked slowly away from the hotel.

'Where shall I wait for you?'

She took it for granted that her husband was going to the Rue du Bourbonnais.

'At the spring?'

'At the bowling greens.'

In other words, he didn't intend to stay long with Lecœur.

He found him in the tiny parlour, talking on the telephone.

'Take a seat, chief. . . . Hello! . . . Yes. . . . It's a bit of luck finding the same concierge there after all these years. . . . Yes. . . . She doesn't know where? . . . She went by métro. . . . From Saint-Georges? . . . Don't cut us off, miss. . . . Carry on, mate. . . .'

The call lasted for another two or three minutes.

'Thanks. . . . I'll see you get a formal authorization, just for the record. You can send us your report then. . . . How's the wife? . . . Of course. . . . There's always something to worry about with kids. . . . I should know, with four boys of my own. . . .'

He hung up, and turned to Maigret.

'That was Julien. He's an inspector in the IXth *Arrondissement* now. . . . You must have known him. . . . I rang him yesterday, and he agreed to look through his departmental files. . . . He's located the place in the Rue Notre-Dame-de-Lorette where Hélène Lange lived for four years.'

'From the age of twenty-eight to thirty-two, in fact. . . .'

'Roughly. . . . The concierge is still there. . . . Mademoiselle Lange, it seems, was a nice, quiet young woman. . . . She went out and came back at regular hours, as one would expect of a working girl. . . . It seems that she seldom went out in the evenings, except occasionally to the theatre or cinema.

'Her place of work must have been some distance away, as she used the métro. . . . She always went out early to do her shopping, and she had no domestic help. . . . She usually got home for lunch at about twenty-past twelve, and left again at half-past one. After that she wasn't seen again until she got back from work at half-past six.'

'Did she have any visitors?'

'Only one, a man. Always the same man.'

'Did you get his name from the concierge?'

'She knew nothing about him, except that he used to call once or twice a week at about half-past eight at night, and always left before ten.'

'What sort of man?'

'Very respectable, according to her. He drove his own car.

It never occurred to the concierge to make a note of the number. It was a large black car, American, I imagine.'

'What age?'

'In his forties. . . . On the heavy side. . . . Very well groomed. . . . Expensive clothes. . . .'

'Was he paying the rent?'

'He never set foot in the concierge's lodge.'

'Did they go away together for week-ends?'

'Only once.'

'What about holidays?'

'No. . . . At that time, Hélène Lange only got two weeks' holiday, and she nearly always went to Etretat, staying in a family pension, to which her mail was forwarded.'

'Did she get many letters?'

'Very few. . . . One from her sister occasionally. . . . She subscribed to a lending library nearby. She was a great reader.'

'Do you mind if I take a look round the flat?'

'Of course not. Make yourself at home, chief.'

He noted that the television set was not in the little parlour, but in the dining-room, which was furnished in rustic style, with the inevitable brass ornaments much in evidence. On the sideboard was a photograph of Hélène Lange bowling a hoop, and another of her in a bathing suit, with a cliff in the background, probably taken at Etretat. She had a well-proportioned figure, the long slender lines of the face being carried through to the body, though she was by no means thin or desiccated. She was one of those women to whom clothes are unflattering.

In the kitchen, which was modern and bright, there was a washing-up machine, not to mention every other labour-saving appliance.

Across the hall was a bathroom, also modern and well-equipped, and the dead woman's bedroom.

Maigret was amused to find that it was almost a replica of his own hotel bedroom, with the same style of brass bedstead and the same elaborately carved furniture. The wall-paper was striped, lavender blue and pale pink, and here too hung a photograph of Hélène Lange, taken when she was about thirty.

But he scarcely recognized, behind that wide, spontaneous, joyous smile, the secretive face he had come to know.

It was an enlarged snapshot, probably taken in a wood, if the foliage in the background was anything to go by. She was looking straight into the lens, her features softened in an expression almost of tenderness.

'It would be interesting to know who it was holding the camera,' mumbled Maigret to Lecœur, who had just come into the room.

'A bit of a mystery, isn't she?'

'I take it you've checked up on the lodgers?'

'It was my first idea, too, that it might be an inside job. The widow is in the clear, and anyway, in spite of her bulk, she wouldn't have the strength to strangle anyone who put up a fight like Mademoiselle Lange. . . . The Carlton staff confirm that she was there playing bridge until twenty-past eleven. . . . And, according to the police surgeon, the murder was committed between ten and eleven. . . .'

'In other words, by the time Madame Vireveau got home, Hélène Lange was dead.'

'Almost certainly.

'The Maleskis saw a light under the living-room door. . . . It follows, since the lights were later turned off, that the murderer was still in the flat. . . .

'That's what I keep telling myself. . . . Either he came in with his victim and strangled her before searching the flat, or she found him at it, and had to be silenced. . . .'

'What about the man Madame Vireveau claims to have seen on the corner?'

'We're working on that. Just about that time, as the proprietor of a nearby bar was pulling down his iron shutter, he saw a heavily built man walking rapidly past. He seemed out of breath, he says. . . .'

'Which way was he going?'

'Towards the Célestins.'

'Did he describe him?'

197

'He wasn't paying much attention. . . . All he could say was that he was wearing a dark suit and no hat. . . . He thinks he remembers noticing that he had receding hair.'

'Any anonymous letters?'

'Not so far.'

There would be. There had never been a crime with a bit of mystery to it that did not produce its crop of anonymous letters and cryptic telephone calls.

'Have you seen the sister again?'

'I'm still waiting to hear from her what she wants done with the body. . . .'

And, after a brief pause, he added:

'You could scarcely find two sisters more unlike, could you? The one so reserved, so introverted, so superior, and the other a thoroughgoing extrovert, overflowing with health and vitality. . . . And yet . . .'

Maigret looked at Lecœur with an indulgent smile, noting that he had put on weight round the middle, and that there were one or two white hairs among the bristles of his red moustache. His blue eyes were innocent, almost childlike, and yet, Maigret remembered, he had been one of his ablest assistants.

'What are you smiling at?'

'Because I saw her alive, and yet you, who know her only from photographs and hearsay, have reached the same conclusions as I have.'

'You mean that Hélène Lange was a prey to sentimental and romantic delusions?'

'I believe she was playing a part, deceiving even herself perhaps, but she couldn't hide the look in her eyes, which was hard and shrewd.'

'Like her sister. . . .'

'Francine Lange has cast herself in the role of the emancipated woman, who doesn't give a damn for anyone or anything. . . . If you were to ask in La Rochelle, I'm sure you'd find that she had a wide circle of friends, all of whom would regale you with colourful details of her conversations and escapades. . . .'

'Which is not to say . . .'

There was no need for either of them to spell things out.

'That, underneath it all, she doesn't know how many beans make five!'

'And what's more, gigolos or no gigolos, she knows what she wants. . . . Starting with a miserable little shop in Marsilly, she now owns, at the age of forty, one of the smartest hair-dressing salons in La Rochelle. I know the town. Place des Armes. . . .'

He took out his pocket-watch.

'My wife will be waiting. . . .'

'At the spring?'

'No. I'm going to watch a game or two of bowls first. It will give me something else to think about. . . . I used to play a bit years ago, at Porquerolles. If only some of those chaps would twist my arm. . . .'

He went on his way, filling a fresh pipe. It was warmer than it had been. By the time he got there, he was glad of the shade of the great trees.

'Anything new?'

'Nothing of any interest.'

'Haven't they found out about her life in Paris yet?'

His wife was eyeing him warily, not wishing to overstep the mark, but he answered with perfect good humour:

'Nothing definite. . . . Only that she had at least one lover.'

Madame Maigret grew bolder.

'Anyone would think you were pleased!'

'In a way, perhaps. It shows that, for a time at least, she got a bit of fun out of life, that she wasn't always shut up inside herself, chewing over God knows what obsessions and fantasies. . . .'

'What do you know about him?'

'Practically nothing, except that he drove a big black car, and went to see her once or twice a week in the evening, and always left before ten. They never went away together for a holiday, or even a week-end. . . .'

'A married man. . . .'

'Probably. . . . Aged about forty, ten years older than she was. . . .'

'What about the neighbours in the Rue du Bourbonnais? Did none of them ever see him?'

'Well, for one thing, he's not a man of forty now. More like sixty. . . .'

'Do you think . . . ?'

'I don't think anything. I'd like to know what sort of life she lived in Nice. Was it a period of transition, or had she already acquired the habits of an old maid? . . . Watch out, he's going to bowl. . . .'

The one-armed player, bowling with great deliberation, sent the jack spinning.

Involuntarily, he exclaimed:

'I envy them.'

'Why?'

Her skin, dappled with sunlight and shade, was smooth. She's looking younger, he thought. His holiday mood was coming back. With a twinkle he said:

'Haven't you noticed how completely engrossed they are? To them, bowling a good ball is the supreme fulfilment. It really is important to them. But when we come to the end of an enquiry . . .'

He left the sentence in the air, but his wry little grimace was eloquent. In this job, when they had finished with a man, he was abandoned, left to stand alone at the bar of Justice. . . . The end was prison, sometimes death. . . .

Shaking himself out of it, he emptied his pipe, and then said:

'What about our walk?'

Well, that was what they were here for, wasn't it?

Lecœur's assistants had questioned all the neighbours.

Not only had no one heard or seen anything on the night of the murder, but all were agreed that Hélène Lange had no friends of either sex, and that she had never been known to have a visitor.

From time to time she was seen to leave the house carrying

a small overnight bag, and, on these occasions, the shutters would remain closed for two or three days.

She never took any heavy luggage. She never ordered a taxi, and she had no car.

Nor had she ever been seen in the street with a companion, man or woman.

Every morning of the week she went out to do her shopping in the local shops. Although she was not exactly mean, she knew the value of money, and on Saturdays always did her week-end shopping in the market. Invariably, she wore a hat, white in summer, dark in winter.

As to her present lodgers, they were completely in the clear. Madame Vireveau had come on the recommendation of a friend in Montmartre, who had stayed at Mademoiselle Lange's during the season, for several years in succession. A bit showy she might be, with her ample figure and flamboyant paste jewels, but she was not the woman to commit a murder, especially without motive. Her husband had been a florist in Paris, and, up to the time of his death, she had worked in the shop in the Boulevard des Batignolles. Afterwards, she had moved to a little flat in the Rue Lamarck.

'I had nothing against her,' she said of Hélène Lange, 'except that she had very little to say for herself.'

The Maleskis had been coming to Vichy for the cure for the past four years. The first year, they had gone to a hotel, and had discovered Mademoiselle Lange quite by chance, through a card in a shop window advertising rooms to let, which they had noticed one day when they were out for a walk. They had enquired about her charges, and had at once booked a room for the following season. This was their third summer at *Les Iris*.

Maleski suffered from a disease of the liver, which meant that he had to take care of himself and keep to a very strict diet. Although only forty-two, he was already burnt out, a shadow of a man with a sad smile. Enquiries made over the telephone to Grenoble, however, revealed that he was at the top of his profession, and highly regarded as a man of scrupulous honesty.

It had been made clear to him and his wife from the first that Mademoiselle Lange preferred to keep her distance with the lodgers. The only room they had ever been into on the ground floor was the little parlour, and then not more than two or three times. They had never been asked in for a drink, or even a cup of coffee.

Occasionally, when they stayed in on wet evenings, they could hear the television, but it was always turned off quite early.

All this information was buzzing in Maigret's head as he lay on the bed dozing, as he did every afternoon, while Madame Maigret sat at the window reading. Through half-closed eyes, he could see the lines of light thrown on the wall opposite the window by the slats of the venetian blind, and was conscious of a golden afternoon outside.

Ideas swirled round and round in his head, broke up and reassembled, and suddenly he was asking himself, as though it were the key question: 'Why that night in particular?'

Why had she not been murdered the night before, or the night after, or last month, or two months ago?

On the face of it, it was a pointless question, and yet, half-asleep as he was, he felt it to be of the utmost significance.

For ten years, ten long years, she had lived alone in that quiet Vichy street. No one had ever visited her. She, as far as anyone could tell, had never visited anyone, except perhaps when she was away on one of her brief monthly trips.

The neighbours had seen her as she came and went. She was also to be seen, sitting on one of the yellow chairs in the park, sipping her glass of water, or, in the evening near the bandstand, listening to the music.

Had Maigret personally questioned the shopkeepers, they would probably have been amazed at the things he wanted to know.

'Did she ever indulge in small talk? . . . Did you ever see her bend down and stroke your dog? Did she talk to the other housewives in the queue, or exchange greetings with those whom she regularly met at the same time, more or less every day? . . .'

And finally:

'Have you ever known her to laugh? . . . Only smile?'

It was necessary to go back fifteen years to find evidence of any kind of personal relationship with another human being, the man who used to visit her once or twice a week in her flat in the Rue Notre-Dame-de-Lorette.

Was it possible that she could have lived all these years without ever feeling the need to unburden herself to anyone, to speak her thoughts aloud?

Someone had strangled her.

'But why that night in particular?'

To Maigret, half-asleep as he was, this question was assuming obsessional proportions. He was still seeking an answer, when his wife's voice broke in with the announcement that it was three o'clock.

'Were you asleep?'

'Dozing.'

'Are we going out?'

'Of course we're going out! Don't we always go out? Why do you ask?'

'I thought you might be meeting Lecœur.'

'I'm not meeting anyone.'

And, to prove it, he took her on a grand tour of the town, starting with the children's playground, and going on via the bowling greens and the beach, across the Pont de Bellerive, to walk the length of the boulevard leading to the Yacht Club, where they stopped for a while to watch the antics of the water-skiers.

Then on much further, as far as the new buildings, twelve storeys high, towering white blocks that were, in themselves, a town on the outskirts of the town.

Across the Allier, they could see the horses cantering alongside the white fence posts of the racecourse, and the heads and shoulders of the people in the stands, and, on the lawns, groups of figures in sunlight and in shadow.

'The proprietor of the hotel says that, every year, more and more retired people are coming to live in Vichy.'

Teasingly, he asked:

'Is that what you're softening me up for?'

'We've got our house at Meung. . . .'

They came upon a street of older houses. Each district had its own style, representing its own period. The houses had their own individuality, and one could envisage the kind of people who had built them.

It amused Maigret to stop outside every one of the innumerable little restaurants they passed, and read the menu.

'Room to let. Room with kitchen. Luxurious furnished rooms.'

That explained the restaurants, and also the tens of thousands of people streaming through the streets and along the promenades.

At five o'clock, at the spring, they were both glad to take the weight off their aching feet. They smiled understandingly at one another. Maybe they had overdone it a bit. What were they trying to prove? That they were both young still?

In the crowd, they recognized two faces, those of 'the happy pair', but there was something different about the way the man was looking at Maigret. What was more, instead of walking past, he was coming straight up to the Chief Superintendent, with his hand held out.

What could Maigret do, but take it?

'Don't you remember me?'

'I know I've seen you before, but I can't for the life of me recall . . .'

'Does the name Bébert mean anything to you?'

Nicknames like Bébert, P'tit Louis and Grand Jules were common enough in his experience.

'The métro.'

Smiling more broadly than ever, he turned to his wife, as if seeking confirmation.

'The first time you arrested me, it was during a procession in the Boulevard des Capucines. . . . And, would you believe it, I can't even remember which Head of State it was in honour of, only the horseguards on either side of his carriage. . . . The second time was outside the entrance to the métro at the Bastille. You'd been following me for some time. . . . All this didn't happen yesterday. . . . I was a young man then. . . . So, if I may say so, were you. . . .'

All Maigret could remember about the métro affair was that he had lost his hat while chasing the culprit across the Place de la Bastille, and good lord, now he came to think of it, it had been a straw boater of the kind fashionable at the time—so this wasn't the first time he had worn a straw hat.

'How long were you sent down for?'

'Two years. . . . It taught me a lesson. . . . Made me pull myself together. . . . To begin with, I worked for a junk dealer, mending vast quantities of old glass—I always was good with my hands.'

He gave a knowing wink, intended, no doubt, to convey that this had been very useful to him in the days when he was a pickpocket.

'Then I met Madame.'

He laid great emphasis on the 'Madame', and quite glowed with pride as he spoke.

'No police record. She's always been straight. She was fresh from Brittany, working in a dairy. . . . It was never anything but serious with her, so we were married. . . . She even insisted on our going back home to her village for a real white wedding in church. . . .'

He exuded *joie de vivre* at every pore.

'I was almost sure it was you. . . . Every time I saw you. . . . But I couldn't be quite certain . . . until this morning, when I opened my paper, and there was your photograph. . . .'

He pointed to the glasses in their little straw cases.

'Nothing serious, I hope?'

'I'm in excellent health.'

'Me too, or so all the doctors say, but here I am all the same, on account of pains in the knee-joints. . . . Hydrotherapy, massage under water, ultra-violet rays, the lot. . . . And you?'

'A few glasses of water.'

'Oh! well, there can't be much wrong then. . . . But I mustn't keep you and your good lady. . . . You played very fair with me in the old days. . . . Lovely weather, isn't it? . . . Good-day to you, sir. . . . Say goodbye, Bobonne. . . .'

As he watched them disappear into the distance, Maigret was still smiling at the resolute little ex-pickpocket's success story. Then his wife saw the smile fade, and a worried frown take its place. At length, with a sigh of relief, he said:

'I think I now know why. . . .'

'Why the woman was murdered?'

'No, why she was murdered on that particular day. . . . Why she wasn't murdered last month or last year. . . .'

'What do you mean?'

'Ever since we got here, we've been meeting the same people two or three times a day, and have come to know them quite well by sight. . . . Take that nut case. . . . He's never spoken to me until today, because he couldn't be sure about me until he saw my picture in the paper. . . .

'But then, this is the first time we've come for the cure, and it will probably be the last. But if we were to come back next year, we'd very likely see quite a few familiar faces about the place. . . .

'What I'm trying to say is this: There is someone else in Vichy who, like ourselves, is here for the first time . . . going through the same routine: medical examination, tests, prescribed course of treatment, visits to the springs, measured doses of the waters to be taken at fixed hours. . . .'

'He must have seen Hélène Lange somewhere, and thought he recognized her. . . .

'Then he saw her again, and again. . . . Maybe he was not far from where she was sitting the other night, when she was listening to the music.'

It all sounded so simple: Madame Maigret was surprised he should be making such a song and dance about it.

The Chief Superintendent, sensing this, hastened to add, not without a touch of self-mockery:

'According to the brochures, some two hundred thousand people come to Vichy every year for the cure. The season lasts six months, so presumably they pour in at the rate of more than thirty thousand a month. Assuming a third of them are newcomers like ourselves, that leaves us with about two thousand suspects. . . . No! wait a bit . . . we can exclude the women and children. . . . What's the proportion of women and children, would you say?'

'There are more women than men. As to children. . . .'

'No, wait! What about the people in wheel chairs, and those on crutches or walking with a stick? None of them, not to mention the very old, would be capable of strangling a healthy woman still in her prime. . . .'

Was he teasing her, or did he really mean it, she wondered?

'Let's say we're left with a thousand men capable of committing this murder. But, according to the evidence of Madame Vireveau and the proprietor of the bar, the murderer was unusually tall and thick-set, so we can ignore the skinny and undersized . . . which leaves us with about five hundred.'

It was a relief to hear him laugh.

'What's the joke?'

'The policeman's lot. Our job. I shall shortly inform the good Lecœur that I have narrowed the field down to five hundred suspects, unless we are able to eliminate a few more, those who were at the theatre that night, for instance, or who can prove that they spent the whole evening at the bridge tables, or what have you. . . . And to think that, more often than not, that's how criminals are caught! In one case, Scotland Yard questioned every single inhabitant of a town with a population of two hundred thousand. . . . It took months. . . .'

'Did they find their man?'

Wryly, Maigret had to admit:

'Quite by chance, in some other town. The fellow was drunk, and opened his mouth too wide.'

It was probably too late to see Lecœur today. There were still two glasses of water to be drunk, with a half-hour interval between.

He tried to concentrate on the evening paper, which was full of gossip about visiting celebrities. It was an odd thing, but even those well-known for the dissolute lives they led liked to be photographed surrounded by their children or grandchildren, asserting that they wanted nothing better than to spend all their time with them.

By the time they reached the corner of the Rue d'Auvergne, there was a fresh breeze blowing. A van was parked outside Mademoiselle Lange's house.

As they drew near, they could hear the sound of hammering.

'Shall I go back to the hotel?' murmured Madame Maigret.

'Yes. This won't take long.'

The living-room door was open, and men in buff overalls were hanging black draperies on the walls.

Lecœur came forward to meet him.

'I thought you might be coming. . . . We'll go in here. . . .'

He led the way into the bedroom, where it was quieter.

'Is she to be buried in Vichy?' Maigret asked. 'Is that what her sister has decided?'

'Yes, she was here just before lunch.'

'With the gigolo?'

'No, she came alone in a taxi.'

'When is the funeral?'

'The day after tomorrow, to give time for the neighbours to pay their last respects.'

'Will there be prayers?'

'Apparently not.'

'Are the Langes not Catholics?'

'The old people were. The children were baptized, and took their First Communion. After that . . .'

'I was wondering if she was divorced.'

'To find the answer to that, we should need to know whether she was ever married.'

Lecœur, twiddling the ends of his red moustache, looked enquiringly at Maigret.

'You yourself had never set eyes on either of them before, I take it?'

'Never.'

'But you did spend some time in La Rochelle?'

'I've been there twice. . . . Each time, for about ten days. Why do you ask?'

'Because I noticed a change in Francine Lange this morning. She was a good deal less lively . . . less forthright. I had the feeling that she had something on her mind . . . that there was something she wanted to tell me, but she was in two minds about it. . . .

'At one point she said:

' "Wasn't that Chief Superintendent Maigret who was here yesterday?"

'I asked her if she had ever seen you before, and she said no, but she had recognized your picture in the morning paper.'

'She's not the only one. I suppose there must be about fifty others among the thousands I meet in the street every day. . . . Only today, an old customer of mine bore down on me with his hand outstretched. I was lucky to escape a hearty slap on the back.'

'I think there's more to it than that,' said Lecœur, still following his own train of thought.

'You mean you think I may have had dealings with her when she was living in Paris?'

'Considering her mode of life, it's not all that far-fetched. . . . No! It's something less obvious, more subtle. . . . As far as she's concerned, I'm just a country cop, doing his best, asking the standard questions, noting the answers, and moving on to the next. . . . Do you see what I'm getting at? It would explain why, when she came here the first time, she was very much at her ease, as she was yesterday afternoon. . . . I caught her looking at you once or twice sitting there in the corner, but I could see she hadn't recognized you. . . .

'Then she booked in at the Hôtel de la Gare. There, as in most other hotels here, the local newspaper is sent up on the breakfast trays. . . . And when she saw your photograph, no doubt, she began to wonder what you were doing sitting in on our interview.'

'And what are your conclusions?'

'Aren't you forgetting your reputation, your public image?'

He flushed suddenly, fearful that he might have given offence.

'Besides, it's not only the public. . . . We in the Force are the first to . . .'

'Skip it. . . .'

'No, it's important. . . . It would never have crossed her

mind that your presence—sitting in that armchair—might be fortuitous. . . . And even if it was, the very fact that you were interested in the case . . .'

'Did she seem at all frightened?'

'I wouldn't go as far as that. Her manner was different, more guarded. I only asked a few harmless questions, but even so, she weighed every word before answering. . . .'

'Has she traced the notary?'

'I wondered about that too. I did ask her. Apparently, the boy-friend got a list of all the notaries in town, and rang every single one. . . . Hélène Lange, it seems, had never consulted any of them, though there was one who remembered that, ten years ago, when he was still an articled clerk, his firm had drawn up the deed of conveyance for her house.'

'Do you know his name?'

'Maître Rambaud.'

'What about giving him a ring?'

'At this hour?'

'Surely most lawyers outside Paris practise from their homes. . . .'

'What do you want me to ask him?'

'Whether she paid by cheque or banker's order.'

'I'll have to stop those chaps hammering first.'

In the meantime, Maigret prowled back and forth from the bathroom to the kitchen, though not with anything particular in mind.

'Well?'

'You guessed, didn't you?'

'What?'

'That she paid in cash. It's the only time Rambaud has ever known it happen, which is why he still remembers it. There were enough notes to fill a small suitcase.'

'Have you taken statements from the booking clerks at the railway station?'

'Good lord! I never thought of that!'

'It would be interesting to find out whether she always went to the same place on her monthly trips, or to a different place each time. . . .'

'I'll let you know tomorrow. . . . It's time you were off to your dinner. . . . Enjoy yourself! . . .'

There was a band concert in the park that night, and the Maigrets permitted themselves the luxury of sitting down to listen to it. They had walked far enough for one day.

CHAPTER FOUR

FOR SOME MYSTERIOUS REASON, he was ten minutes ahead of schedule. Maybe there was less news than usual in this morning's *Journal de Clermont-Ferrand*? Madame Maigret, who always waited until he had finished before going into the bathroom, was still in there. He called to her through the half-open door:

'I'm going out. . . . Wait for me downstairs.'

There was a green wooden seat on the pavement outside the hotel, for the convenience of residents. The sky was as cloudless as ever. During the whole of their stay in Vichy, it had not rained once.

Needless to say, the proprietor was waiting for him at the foot of the stairs.

'Well, what news of the murder?'

'It's no concern of mine,' he answered with a smile.

'Do you think that these Clermont-Ferrand people are really up to the job? It's very bad, in a place like this, to have a strangler on the loose. Quite a number of old ladies have left already, I hear. . . .'

With a non-committal smile, he set off for the Rue du Bourbonnais. He saw, from the far end of the street, that the front door of *Les Iris* was draped in black, with a large letter 'L' embroidered in silver on the pelmet. There was no longer a policeman on guard outside. Had there been one last night? He had not noticed. After all, it was none of his business. He was here to take the waters, and his only interest in the case was as a bystander, an amateur.

He was about to ring the bell, when he noticed that the white door was ajar. He pushed it open and went in. A very young girl, barely sixteen, he judged, was mopping the floor of the entrance with a damp cloth. Her dress was so short that, when she bent forward, he could see her pink bloomers. She had plump, shapeless legs, as girls so often do at the awkward age. They reminded him of the crudely painted legs of a cheap doll.

She turned to look at him, a pair of expressionless eyes staring at him out of a round face. She did not ask his name, nor what he was doing there.

'In there,' was all she said, pointing to the living-room.

The room, all draped in black, was dark, with the coffin resting on what must have been the dining-room table. There were unlit candles, holy water in a glass bowl, and a sprig of rosemary.

The kitchen and dining-room doors were open. The living-room furniture and ornaments had been stacked in the dining-room. The young constable, Dicelle, was sitting in the kitchen reading a comic, with a cup of coffee on the table in front of him.

'Will you join me in a cup of coffee? I've made a full pot.'

On Hélène Lange's gas cooker, which would scarcely have met with her approval!

'Hasn't Superintendent Lecœur arrived yet?'

'He was called back urgently to Clermont-Ferrand late last night. . . . A hold-up at the Savings Bank. . . . One man killed . . . a passer-by, who noticed the door ajar and went in to investigate, just as the thieves were coming out. . . . One of them shot him at point-blank range. . . .'

'Nothing new here?'

'Not that I know of.'

'Have you questioned the station staff?'

'Trigaud—one of my colleagues—is looking into it. He's not back yet.'

'I presume the little servant-girl out there has been questioned? What has she to say?'

'That half-wit! It's a wonder she can talk at all! She doesn't know a thing. She was only taken on for the season, to see to the lodgers' rooms. She didn't do the ground floor; Mademoiselle Lange saw to her own housework.'

'Did she ever see any visitors?'

213

'Only the man who reads the gas meter, and the delivery boys. She came to work at nine, and left at twelve. . . . The Maleskis upstairs are a bit worried. . . . They've paid in advance to the end of the month, and they want to know whether they'll be able to stay on. . . . It isn't easy to find rooms in the middle of the season, and they don't want to move to a hotel.'

'What does the Superintendent say?'

'I think, as far as he's concerned, they can stay. . . . They're up there now, at any rate. . . . The other one, the fat one, has gone to the masseur for her daily pummelling.'

'Have you seen Francine Lange?'

'I'm expecting her any time. . . . No one seems to know what's happening. . . . She insisted on the lying-in-state, but it wouldn't surprise me if no one turned up. . . . My instructions are to stay here, and keep a discreet eye on the callers, if any.'

'I wish you joy of it,' mumbled Maigret, going out of the kitchen.

The books, like everything else from the living-room, had been moved into the dining-room. Mechanically, he picked one up off the top of a pile stacked on a small occasional table. It was *Lucien Leuwen*. The yellowing pages had the distinctive smell of well-thumbed books from lending libraries, public or private.

The name and address of the library was stamped in violet ink on the flyleaf.

He put the book back on top of the pile, and slipped quietly out into the street. A ground floor window opened, and a woman in a dressing-gown and hair-rollers looked out.

'Excuse me, Superintendent, can you tell me if one can call and pay one's respects?'

It seemed to him rather an odd way of putting it, and, for a moment, he was nonplussed.

'I imagine so. The door is open, and they've turned the living-room into a little chapel.'

'Can one see her?'

'As far as I know, the coffin is closed.'

She sighed:

'I prefer it that way. . . . It's less distressing.'

He found Madame Maigret waiting for him on the green seat. She seemed surprised to see him back so soon.

They set off on their usual morning walk. They were only a couple of minutes behind schedule, a schedule that they had never planned, but now adhered to as though their lives depended on it.

'Were there many people?'

'Not a soul. They're waiting. . . .'

This time, they went straight to the children's playground, where they strolled for a time in the shade of the trees, some of which—like those along the banks of the Allier—were very rare specimens, from America, India and Japan. These were distinguished by little metal plates, bearing their botanical names in Latin and French. Many were tokens of gratitude from long-forgotten heads of state who had benefited from the cure at Vichy, obscure maharajahs, and other Eastern princelings.

They did not stop more than a minute or two at the bowling greens. Madame Maigret never asked her husband where they were making for. He always walked purposefully, as though he knew exactly where he was going, but more often than not he would turn down this street rather than that, just for a change of scene, because he enjoyed savouring new sights and sounds.

They still had a little time in hand before the first glass of water, when he turned into the Rue Georges-Clemenceau. Was there something he wanted from the shops, she wondered? But he turned left into one of the little side alleys, the one leading to the theatre, and stopped at a bookshop, where there were some second-hand books in trays on the pavement, and more books inside on revolving shelves.

'Come on,' he said to his wife, who was looking at him enquiringly.

The proprietor, in a long grey overall, was tidying the shelves. He obviously recognized Maigret, but waited for him to speak.

'Can you spare me a few minutes?'

'With pleasure, Monsieur Maigret. It's about Mademoiselle Lange, I daresay.'

'She was one of your subscribers, wasn't she?'

'She came in at least once a week, twice more often than not, to change her books. Her subscription allowed her to have two books out at a time.'

'How long have you known her?'

'I took over here six years ago. I'm not a local man. I came here from Paris, Montparnasse. She was already a subscriber in my predecessor's time.'

'Did she ever stop for a chat?'

'Well, you know, she wasn't very forthcoming. . . .'

'Didn't she ever ask your advice, when she was choosing new books?'

'She had very decided views of her own. Come with me. . . .'

He led the way to a room at the back of the shop, lined from floor to ceiling with books in black cloth bindings.

'She would often spend half an hour to an hour browsing in here, reading a paragraph here and a page there. . . .'

'Her last book was Stendhal's *Lucien Leuwen*.'

'Stendhal was her latest discovery. Before that, she had read all Chateaubriand, Alfred de Vigny, Jules Sandeau, Benjamin Constant, Musset and Georges Sand. It was always the romantics. On one occasion, she took one of Balzac's novels —I can't remember which—but she brought it back the next day. Apparently it didn't appeal to her. I asked her why. She said: "It's too coarse . . ." or words to that effect. . . . Balzac coarse, I ask you!'

'No contemporary writers?'

'She never gave them a chance. On the other hand, she read the letters of Georges Sand and Musset over and over again.'

'I'm much obliged to you. . . .'

He was almost at the door when the bookseller called him back.

'Just one more thing that might interest you. I discovered,

to my astonishment, that someone had been marking passages in pencil, underlining words and phrases and, here and there, putting a cross in the margin. I wondered who on earth it could be. It turned out in the end to be Mademoiselle Lange.'

'Did you mention it to her?'

'I had to. . . . My assistant was having to spend all his time rubbing out the marks. . . .'

'How did she react?'

'She looked very prim and said "I'm sorry. . . . When I'm reading, I forget that the books don't belong to me." '

Everything looked just the same, the people taking the waters, the pale trunks of the plane trees, the patches of sun and shade, the thousands of yellow chairs.

She had not been able to stomach Balzac. . . . His realism had been too much for her, no doubt. She had restricted herself to the first half of the nineteenth century, grandly dismissing Flaubert, Hugo, Zola, Maupassant. . . . At the same time, Maigret had noticed, that very first day, a pile of glossy magazines in a corner of the living-room. . . .

It was as though he could not help himself, he must forever be adding fresh touches to the picture of her that he was building up. Her reading was confined to the romantic, the sentimental, and yet he had more than once seen her eyes narrow in a hard, shrewd look.

'Did you see Lecœur?'

'No. He's been called back to Clermont-Ferrand because of a bank hold-up.'

'Do you think he'll find the murderer?'

Maigret started. He was the one who needed bringing down to earth! The truth was that he had not been thinking about the case in terms of murder. He had almost forgotten that the woman who owned the house with the green shutters had been strangled, and that the first priority was to find the killer.

True, he was looking for someone, more intensely, indeed, than he himself would have wished, almost to the point where it was becoming an obsession.

The really intriguing figure, as far as he was concerned, was the man who, at a given moment, had broken into the life of this solitary woman.

There was no trace of him in the Rue du Bourbonnais, no photograph, not a single letter, not even a note.

Nothing! Nothing from anyone else either, apart from bills and receipts.

One had to go back twelve years, to Paris, to the Rue Notre-Dame-de-Lorette, to find anyone who remembered a shadowy figure who called once or twice a week, and spent an hour in the flat of Mademoiselle Lange, then still a comparatively young woman.

Even Francine, her own sister, who was living in the same city at the time, claimed to know nothing about him.

She read voraciously, watched television, did her shopping and her housework, walked under the trees in the park like the summer visitors, sat and listened to the band, staring straight in front of her, and never addressing a word to anyone.

This was what puzzled him. Often, in the course of his career, he had met individuals, both men and women, who clung fiercely to their independence. He had also met eccentrics, who, having renounced the world, had taken refuge in the most unlikely, sometimes the most sordid, surroundings.

But even men and women such as these, in his experience, kept some link with the outside world. The old ones, for instance, often had a favourite bench in a square, where they would meet some other old crone to talk to, or they were members of a church, going to confession, exchanging greetings with the priest. Some had a favourite bistro, where they were known, and welcomed as old friends.

But here was a case, Maigret realized—the first he had ever known—of stark, unrelieved isolation.

There was not even an element of aggression. Mademoiselle Lange had been civil enough to the neighbours and shopkeepers. She had not been high-handed with them nor, in spite of her somewhat formal style of dress and her preference for old-world colours, had she put on superior airs.

It was rather that she did not concern herself with other people. She had no need of them. She took in lodgers because the spare bedrooms were there, and they provided a small income. Between the flat on the ground floor and the bedrooms upstairs, she had erected an invisible barrier, and, to clean the guest rooms, she had engaged a servant girl, who was little better than a moron.

'Can you spare a moment, sir?'

A shadow fell across Maigret. He looked up to see a tall man holding a chair by its back. The Chief Superintendent recognized him as one of the men he had seen with Dicelle in the Rue du Bourbonnais, Trigaud presumably.

'How did you find me?' Maigret asked.

'Dicelle said you would be here.'

'And how did Dicelle . . . ?'

'There isn't a man in the local Force, sir, who doesn't know you by sight, so that wherever you go. . . .'

'Any fresh news?'

'I was at the station for an hour last night, interviewing the night-staff, and this morning I went back to question the day-staff. . . . Then I rang Superintendent Lecœur, who is still at Clermont-Ferrand. . . .'

'Won't he be back today?'

'He's not sure yet. But whatever happens, he'll be coming early tomorrow for the funeral. I presume you'll be there, too. . . .'

'Have you seen Francine?'

'She called in at the undertaker's. The hearse will be leaving the house at nine o'clock. . . . Some flowers were delivered at the house. . . . They must have come from her, I imagine. . . .'

'How many wreaths?'

'Just the one.'

'Check that it did come from her . . . I beg your pardon . . . I was forgetting . . . it's really none of my business. . . .'

'I don't think the Super would agree with you there. He told me to be sure and let you know what I'd found out. He made a special point of it. I fancy that there are a good many

in the Force, including your humble servant, who would go
along with that. . . .'

'On these monthly trips of hers, did she go far?'

Trigaud pulled a bundle of papers out of his pocket, and,
after some searching, found what he was looking for.

'They couldn't remember all the details, of course, but one
or two places stuck in their minds, because they are by no
means easy to get to from here; Strasbourg, for instance, and
the following month, Brest. Some of her trips involved changing trains two or three times: Carcassonne . . . Dieppe . . .
Lyons . . . not quite so far. . . . Lyons was, in fact, exceptional.
. . . Mostly, she went much further afield: Nancy, Montélimar.'

'Never to a small town or a village?'

'No, she always seemed to choose a fairly large town, though,
of course, she may have gone on somewhere by bus.'

'Did she never take a ticket to Paris?'

'Never.'

'How long has this been going on?'

'The last man I spoke to has been working at the same
window for nine years.

' "I ought to know my regular customers by now," he said.

'She was well known to the station staff. They looked
forward to her coming, and even laid bets as to where she
would choose to go next.'

'Did she always go on the same day of the month?'

'No, that's the odd thing. Sometimes there would be an
interval of six weeks, usually in the summer. I daresay it was
on account of the lodgers. It wasn't always the end of the
month, or any fixed date.'

'Did Lecœur tell you what he intends to do next?'

'He's having copies made of her photographs. . . . For a
start, he'll send a couple of men to the nearest towns, and
copies of the photographs to the various local police stations. . . .'

'You don't happen to know why Lecœur wanted me put
in the picture?'

'He didn't say. . . . No doubt he thought you had formed
your own view. . . . That's what I think, too. . . .'

Everyone always credited him with knowing more than

he let on. It was no good protesting. They would only think it was the old fox up to his usual tricks.

'Has anyone turned up at the house?'

'According to Dicelle, things started livening up round about ten. . . . A woman in an apron put her head round the door, and then, rather hesitantly, went in to see the coffin. She took a rosary out of her pocket and muttered a prayer. Then she crossed herself with holy water and left. . . .

'She must have told the neighbours, because they all came after that, in ones and twos. . . .'

'Any men?'

'A few . . . the butcher, and a carpenter who lives at the end of the street . . . all local people. . . .'

Why assume that the murderer wasn't a local man? They were searching up and down the country, in all the widely separated towns visited by the lady in lilac, in Nice, in Paris, trying to unravel the mystery of her life. But no one had given a thought to the thousands of people who lived in the France district of Vichy.

Maigret himself had not.

'Can you suggest anything further I should do?'

Trigaud wasn't saying this off his own bat. That cunning devil Lecœur must have put him up to it. After all, here was Maigret on the spot. Why not make use of him?

'I was wondering whether the booking clerks could remember any precise dates. We wouldn't need very many. Two or three would do.'

'I have one already . . . June 11. . . . The chap remembered it, because she took a ticket for Rheims, and his wife comes from there, and, as it happened, June 11 was her birthday.'

'If I were you, I'd find out from her bank manager whether she paid in any money on the 13th or 14th. . . .'

'I think I see what you're driving at . . . blackmail.'

'Or an allowance. . . .'

'Why should anyone pay out an allowance at irregular intervals?'

'Just what I was wondering myself.'

221

Trigaud stole a sideways glance at Maigret, convinced that he was either keeping something from him or making fun of him.

'I'd much rather they'd put me on the hold-up,' he grumbled. 'At least you know where you stand with pros. . . . I'm sorry to have bothered you. . . . My best respects, madame.'

He got up awkwardly, not quite knowing how to make his escape, blinking, with the sun full in his eyes.

'It's too late now for the bank. I'll call in there after lunch. Then, if necessary, I'll go back to the railway station.'

Maigret had been through it all in his time. Pounding the beat for hours at a stretch, on pavements scorching hot or slippery with rain, questioning wary witnesses, whose words had to be coaxed out of them, one by one.

'We'd better go and have our glass of water.'

While Trigaud, no doubt, would be regaling himself with a long, cool glass of beer.

'You'd better be at the spring at about eleven . . . I hope I'll be able to get there.'

He sounded a little out of temper. Madame Maigret had been afraid that he would get bored in Vichy, with nothing to do, and no one but herself for company, from morning to night.

The good-humoured contentment that he had shown in the first few days had not wholly reassured her. She could not help wondering how long it would last.

However, in the past two or three days, he had been thoroughly put out every time they had had to miss one of their regular walks.

Today, there was the funeral. He had promised Lecœur to be there. The sun was still shining, and, as usual in the morning, the streets were damp, and a fresh breeze was blowing.

The Rue du Bourbonnais was unusually crowded. Apart from the neighbours who could be seen leaning out of their windows, like spectators at a public procession, there were people all along the pavement, several deep outside the house itself.

The motor hearse was already there. Behind it was a black car, supplied, no doubt, by the undertaker, and behind that another, which Maigret had not seen before.

Lecœur came out to meet him.

'I've had to drop the bank robbery for the time being,' he explained. 'There's a hold-up practically every day of the week. The public are used to them, and they don't get het up about them any more. But a woman strangled in her own house, in a law-abiding town like Vichy, and for no apparent reason. . . .'

Maigret recognized the scruffy mop of red hair belonging to the *Tribune* photographer. There were two or three other photographers there as well. One of them took a shot of the two police officers crossing the road.

The fact was that there was nothing to see, and, from the expressions on their faces, some of the bystanders were wondering whether it had really been worth their while to come.

'Have you got men on watch in the street?'

'Three. . . . I can't see Dicelle, but he's somewhere around. . . . He thought it would be a good idea to have the butcher's boy with him. . . . He knows everyone hereabouts, and will be able to point out any strangers. . . .'

There was no feeling of sadness, no sense of horror. Everyone, Maigret included, was waiting.

'Will you be going to the cemetery?' he asked Lecœur.

'I'd be glad if you'd come with me, chief. I've brought my own car. I felt a police car wouldn't be quite the thing. . . .'

'What about Francine?'

'She got here a few minutes ago, with the boy-friend. . . . They're in the house.'

'I don't see their car.'

'I daresay the undertakers, who know what's what, dropped a hint that an open red sports job would look just as much out of place in a funeral procession as a police car. . . . Those two will go in the black car.'

'Have you spoken to her?'

'She gave me a nod when she arrived, I thought she looked

223

nervous . . . anxious. . . . She stood for a moment, before coming into the house, scanning the crowd as though she was looking for someone. . . .'

'I still can't see young Dicelle.'

'That's because he's wangled a seat in someone's window, for himself and the butcher's boy.'

Several people came out of the house, two more went in and reappeared almost at once. Then the driver of the hearse took his seat at the wheel.

As though in response to a signal, four men, not without difficulty, manoeuvred the coffin through the door, and slid it into the hearse. One of them went back into the house, and returned carrying a wreath and a small spray of flowers.

'The spray is from the lodgers.'

Francine Lange stood at the door, in a black dress that did not suit her. She must have bought it for the occasion in the Rue Georges-Clemenceau. Her companion was behind her, a shadowy figure in the darkness of the entrance hall.

The hearse moved forward a few feet. Francine and her lover got into the black car.

'Let's go, chief.'

All along the street there were people, standing very still. Only the photographers were darting hither and thither.

'Is that the lot?' Maigret asked, looking over his shoulder.

'She had no other relations . . . no friends. . . .'

'What about the lodgers?'

'Maleski is seeing his doctor at ten, and the fat woman, Madame Vireveau, has her massage. . . .'

They drove through streets that Maigret recognized from his exploration of the town. He filled his pipe, and watched the houses go by. Soon, to his surprise, they were at the railway station.

The cemetery was nearby, just on the other side of the track. It was deserted. The hearse stopped at the end of the drive.

So here they were, just the four of them, except for the undertaker's men, standing on the gravel path. Lecœur and Maigret went up to the other two. The gigolo was wearing sunglasses.

'Will you be staying long?' Maigret asked the young woman.

Maigret had spoken idly, just for something to say, but it did not escape him that she was looking penetratingly at him, as though searching for some hidden meaning in his words.

'Probably another two or three days, just to get things sorted out.'

'What about the lodgers?'

'They can stay till the end of the month. There's no reason why not. I'll just have to lock up the ground floor flat.'

'Will you be selling the house?'

Before she could answer, one of the men in black came up to her. They wheeled the coffin, on a handcart, down a narrow side turning to the edge of an open grave.

A photographer—not the tall, red-headed man, but another whom Maigret had not seen before—appeared, apparently from nowhere, and took a few shots while the coffin was being lowered into the grave, then another as Francine, at a sign from the master of ceremonies, threw a handful of earth on to the coffin.

The grave was at the far end of the cemetery, a few yards from the low surrounding wall which divided it from a patch of waste ground, where derelict cars lay rotting. Beyond, in the background, were one or two white villas.

The hearse drove away, then the photographer. Lecœur looked enquiringly at Maigret who, however, did not respond, and seemed to be lost in thought. What precisely was he thinking of? Of La Rochelle, a town he had always liked, of the Rue Notre-Dame-de-Lorette, as it was in the very early days when he was personal assistant to the Superintendent of Police in the IXth *Arrondissement*, of the bowling greens, and the men he had seen there. . . .

Francine, clutching a crumpled handkerchief, was coming towards them. She had not used the handkerchief to dry her tears. She had not shed a tear. She had been no more moved than the undertaker's men or the gravedigger. Indeed, there had been nothing in the least moving about the ceremony. It could not have been more matter-of-fact.

The crumpled handkerchief was just for the sake of appearances.

'I don't know the form. . . . It's usual, isn't it, to provide refreshments of some sort after a funeral? But I'm sure you wouldn't want to have lunch with us. . . .'

'There's so much to be done. . . .' murmured Lecœur.

'At least allow me to buy you a drink.'

Maigret was astonished at the change in her. Even here, in this desert of a cemetery, from which even the photographer had fled, she was still looking about her anxiously, as though she felt some danger threatening her.

'I'm sure there will be other opportunities,' replied Lecœur diplomatically.

'Haven't you got a lead yet?'

It was not at Lecœur that she looked as she spoke, but at Chief Superintendent Maigret, as though he were the one she was afraid of.

'We're still making enquiries.'

Maigret filled his pipe, and pressed down the tobacco with his forefinger. He was puzzled. This was a woman who had certainly had a few knocks in her time, and was quite capable of taking things in her stride. It was not her sister's death that had changed her. She had been cheerful and ebullient enough when she had first heard of it.

'In that case, gentlemen. . . . I don't know how to put it. . . . Oh! well, I daresay I'll be seeing you. . . . Thanks for coming!

If she had waited a minute or two longer, Maigret might have asked point-blank whether she had received any threats. But she went, teetering on her high heels, impatient to get back to her hotel room, where she could shut the door and change out of the black dress, bought especially for the occasion.

Maigret turned to his colleague from Clermont-Ferrand.

'What do you make of her?' he asked.

'So you noticed it, too? I'd very much like a private chat with her in my office. But I'd have to find a plausible excuse. It wouldn't be decent today, somehow. . . . She looked scared to me.'

226

'That was what I thought.'

'Do you think she's been threatened? What would you do, if you were me?'

'What do you mean?'

'We don't know why her sister was strangled. . . . It might, after all, turn out to be a family affair. . . . We know precious little about these people. . . . Maybe it was some business in which both women were concerned. . . . Didn't I hear her tell you she'd be staying on in Vichy for another two or three days? I'm short-handed, of course, but the hold-up can wait. . . . The pros always get caught in the end. . . .'

They had returned to their car, and were driving towards the cemetery gates.

'I shall have her followed, discreetly, though in a hotel that's almost impossible. . . . Where would you like me to drop you?'

'Anywhere near the park.'

'Ah! yes, I'd almost forgotten you were here for the cure. . . . I don't know why I've never got around to taking it myself. . . .'

At first, he thought his wife had not yet arrived. She wasn't sitting in her usual place. He was so used to seeing her there that it gave him quite a start when he found her sitting in the shade, under a different tree.

For a moment he watched her, unseen. Sitting there placidly, with her hands folded in the lap of her light dress, she was looking at the people passing by, with a contented little smile, as though she were quite prepared to wait for him forever.

'Oh! there you are!' she exclaimed, then, without pausing, 'Our chairs were taken. . . . I heard them talking. . . . They're Dutch, I think. . . . I hope they're not staying . . . otherwise we've probably lost our seats for good. . . . I didn't think it would be over so soon. . . .'

'It's not far to the cemetery.'

'Were there many people?'

'In the street outside the house. There were only the four of us at the funeral.'

227

'So the boy-friend went too, did he? Come on, it's time for our glass of water. . . .'

They had to wait in a queue for a time. Afterwards, Maigret bought the Paris newspapers, but there was scarcely a mention of the Vichy strangler. One paper only, the evening paper of the previous day, had a photograph of Maigret under a headline in those very words: 'The Vichy Strangler.'

He was anxious to hear what, if anything, had been discovered as a result of the enquiries made in several of the many towns visited at various times by the lady in lilac.

Nevertheless, he allowed his mind to wander. With half an eye on the news, he could see the people walking past, over the top of his paper. After a time, they had to push their chairs back into the receding shade.

That was why they had chosen the place now occupied by the Dutch couple. The sun never reached it at the times they were in the park.

'Don't you want a paper?'

'No. . . . Those two comics have just gone by, and he swept you a tremendous bow.'

They were already lost in the crowd.

'Did the sister cry?'

'No.'

He was still puzzled by her. If he had been in charge of the case, he too would have wanted to have her in his office for a private chat.

Several times, in the course of the morning, his thoughts returned to her. They walked back to the Hôtel de la Bérézina, and after going upstairs for a wash, sat down at their table in the dining-room. As usual, at every table except theirs, there were open wine bottles beside the little trumpet-shaped vases, each holding one or two fresh flowers.

'There's escalope Milanaise and calves' liver *à la bourgeoise*. . . .'

'I'll have escalope,' he said with a sigh. 'It will be grilled as usual, of course. I'll be gone by the end of the season, but Rian will still be here next year and the year after. What he says goes. . . .'

'Don't you feel the better for it?'

'Only because I'm away from Paris. Besides, I never felt really ill. A bit weighed down . . . giddiness from time to time. . . . These things happen to most people at some time or other, I imagine.'

'Still, you do have faith in Pardon. . . .'

'I haven't much choice.'

They had had noodles as a first course, and were just starting on their escalopes when Maigret was called to the telephone.

The call-box was in one of the smaller reception rooms, with a window overlooking the street.

'Hello! I'm not disturbing you, I hope? Had you started your lunch?'

Recognizing Lecœur's voice, he replied crossly:

'For all they give me to eat!'

'I have news for you. . . . I sent one of my men to keep watch on the Hôtel de la Gare. . . . But first he thought he'd better find out the number of Francine Lange's room. The receptionist looked surprised, and told him she'd checked out.'

'When?'

'Barely half an hour after they left us. It seems that, when they got back to the hotel, the man stopped at the desk before going up to their room, and asked them to get their bill ready. They must have packed in a great hurry, because, ten minutes later, they rang down for a porter. They flung everything into the back of the red car, and off they went.'

Maigret said nothing, and Lecœur did not prompt him. After an appreciable pause, Lecœur said:

'What do you make of it, chief?'

'She's a frightened woman. . . .'

'Agreed, but so she was this morning, anyone could see that. . . . But that didn't prevent her from saying she intended staying another two or three days in Vichy.'

'That might have been just to prevent you from detaining her.'

'How could I detain her, not having anything against her?'

'You know the law, but she may not.'

'Anyway, we shall know tomorrow morning, if not tonight, whether she's gone back to La Rochelle.'

'It's the most likely explanation.'

'I agree. I'm livid, all the same. I'd quite made up my mind that we were going to have a long chat. . . . Admittedly I may find out more, as a result of this. . . . Could you be here at two?'

It would mean missing his afternoon rest. He said, rather grudgingly:

'I'm not doing anything in particular, as you very well know.'

'This morning, while I was out, someone rang the local police station asking to speak to me. . . . That's where I am now. . . . I decided, after all, to take them up on their offer of a room here. . . . The caller was a young woman, apparently by the name of Madeleine Dubois, and guess what she does for a living . . . ?'

Maigret said nothing.

'She's a switchboard operator on the night shift at the Hôtel de la Gare. My colleague here told her that I would probably be here at the station—it's in the Avenue Victoria— at two o'clock. . . . He suggested that she should leave a message, but she said she'd prefer to see me personally. . . . So I'm here, waiting for her. . . .'

'I'll be there.'

He missed his rest but, by way of compensation, had the pleasure of seeing for the first time the exquisite, white turreted villa set in extensive grounds, which did duty as a police station in Vichy. He was taken up to the first floor by a constable and, at the end of a corridor, found Lecœur ensconced in an office almost entirely devoid of furniture.

'It's just five to two,' remarked Lecœur. 'I hope she hasn't changed her mind. Which reminds me, I'd better try and find another chair.'

Maigret could hear him in the corridor, opening and shutting doors. Eventually he found what he wanted, and came back carrying it.

On the dot of two, the constable on duty knocked at the door and announced:

'Madame Dubois.'

She was a lively little woman, with dark hair and very expressive eyes. She stood there, looking from one to the other.

'Which of you is the officer I have come to see?'

Lecœur introduced himself but not Maigret, who was sitting unobtrusively in a corner of the room.

'I don't know whether what I have to tell you is important. . . . It didn't seem so at the time. . . . The hotel is full, and I was kept very busy until one in the morning. . . . After that I dozed off, as I usually do. . . . It's about one of the hotel guests, Madame Lange. . . .'

'I presume you mean Mademoiselle Francine Lange?'

'I thought she was married. I know her sister is dead, and that her funeral was this morning. . . . Yesterday evening, at about half-past eight, someone asked to speak to her. . . .'

'A man?'

'Yes, a man. He had an odd sort of voice. . . . Asthmatic, I think. . . . I'm almost sure. . . . I had an uncle who suffered from asthma, and he sounded just like that. . . .'

'Did he give his name?'

'No.'

'Did he ask for her room number?'

'No. I rang, and there was no reply . . . so I told him that the person he wanted to speak to was out. . . . He rang again at about nine, but there was still no reply from Room 406. . . .'

'Did Mademoiselle Lange and her companion share a double room?'

'Yes. . . . The man rang for the third time at eleven, and this time Mademoiselle Lange answered. . . . I put him through. . . .'

She seemed embarrassed, and glanced quickly at Maigret, as though trying to gauge his reactions. Presumably she, like everyone else, had recognized him.

'Did you listen?' murmured Lecœur, with an encouraging smile.

'I'm afraid I did. . . . I don't make a habit of it. . . . I know

231

everyone imagines switchboard girls are always listening to people's conversations . . . if they only knew how boring they were, they'd think differently. . . . Perhaps it was because of the murder of her sister. . . . Or because the man had such a peculiar voice. . . .

' "Who's speaking?" she said.

' "Is that Mademoiselle Francine Lange?"

' "Yes. . . ."

' "Are you alone?"

'She hesitated. . . . I'm almost sure the man was in there with her.

' "Yes," she said, "but what business is it of yours?"

' "I have something very private to tell you. . . . Listen carefully. . . . If I'm interrupted, I shall ring back in half an hour. . . ."

'He had difficulty with his breathing, and every now and again he wheezed, just like my uncle.

' "I'm listening . . . you still haven't told me who you are. . . ."

' "It's of no importance. . . . What is of the utmost importance—what is essential—is that you should stay on in Vichy for a few days. . . . It's in your own interest. . . . I'll be in touch with you again. . . . I can't say when exactly. . . . There may be a great deal in it for you . . . a large sum of money. . . . Do you understand?"

'Then suddenly, he stopped speaking, and hung up. A few minutes later, a call came through from Room 406.

' "Mademoiselle Lange here. . . . I've just had a phone call . . . could you tell me whether it was a local or a trunk call?"

' "Local."

' "Thank you!"

'Well, that's it! At first I thought it wasn't any business of mine. But, when I came off duty this morning, I just couldn't get to sleep, so I rang here and asked to speak to the officer in charge of the case.'

She was fidgeting nervously with her handbag, her glance shifting from one man to the other.

'Do you think it's important?'

'You haven't been back to the hotel?'

'I don't go on duty until eight o'clock in the evening.'

'Mademoiselle Lange has left.'

'Wasn't she at her sister's funeral?'

'She left almost immediately after the funeral.'

'Oh!'

Then, after a pause for thought:

'You think the man was setting a trap for her, don't you? Could it, by any chance, have been the strangler?'

The colour drained from her face at the thought that she had actually heard the voice of the lady in lilac's murderer.

Maigret was no longer regretting having missed his afternoon rest.

CHAPTER FIVE

THE TWO MEN stayed where they were after the telephone girl had left, Maigret puffing reflectively at his pipe, and Lecœur smoking a cigarette that looked as if it were going to set fire to his moustache at any minute. The smoke rose, spread out, and hung above their heads. Down below, in the yard, they could hear a squad of constables drilling.

For a time, neither spoke. They were both old stagers, and there was little anyone could teach them about their trade. They had had dealings with every sort of criminal, every sort of witness.

'There's no doubt that it was him ringing her. . . .' Lecœur said at last, with a sigh.

Maigret did not reply at once. His reaction was different. It wasn't so much a question of method—a term they both disliked—as of approach to a problem.

Thus, since the strangling of the lady in lilac, Maigret had given very little thought to the murderer. It was not deliberate, but simply because he was haunted by the recollection of this woman, sitting on her yellow chair near the bandstand, haunted by the memory of her long jawline, and of her gentle smile, which belied the hard expression of her eyes.

Little details had been added to his picture of her as a result of his visits to her house in the Rue du Bourbonnais. He had learnt something, though not much, of her stay in Nice, her life in Paris, and a great deal about her taste in literature.

The strangler was still a very shadowy figure, a tall, heavily built man, whom Madame Vireveau claimed to have seen, walking very rapidly, at the corner of the street, and who had been glimpsed by the proprietor of a bar, who could not describe his features.

Almost without realizing it, he began thinking about him.

'I wonder how he found out that Francine Lange was staying at the Hôtel de la Gare.'

The newspapers, which had announced the arrival in Vichy of the victim's sister, had given no address.

Maigret was feeling his way forward cautiously, one step at a time.

'Come to think of it, there was nothing to prevent him from ringing one hotel after another, and asking for Mademoiselle Lange.'

He could picture him poring over a classified directory. The list of hotels in a place like this would be a long one. Had he gone through it in alphabetical order?

'You might try one of the hotels beginning with the letters A or B.'

With a twinkle in his eye, Lecœur picked up the receiver.

'Get me the Hôtel d'Angleterre, will you? No, not the manager or the desk—I want the switchboard operator. . . . Hello! Is that the switchboard of the Hôtel d'Angleterre? I'm a police officer. . . . Can you tell me if anyone has been asking to speak to Mademoiselle Lange? . . . No, not the murdered woman. . . . Her sister, Francine Lange. . . . That's right. . . . Perhaps your colleague would know. . . .'

He turned to Maigret.

'There are two girls on the switchboard. . . . It's a huge place. . . . Five or six hundred rooms. . . . Hello, yes. . . . Hello! You say you took the call yourself? . . . Anything strike you as odd? . . . A hoarse voice, did you say? . . . As though the man. . . . Yes, I see. . . . Thank you. . . .'

And to Maigret:

'Yesterday morning at about ten. A man with a hoarse voice, or rather one who seemed to have trouble with his breathing. . . .'

Someone who was here for the cure, as Maigret had suspected from the very first, and who, quite by chance, had run into Hélène Lange. No doubt he had discovered where she lived by the simple expedient of following her home. . . .

The telephone rang. It was the inspector whom Lecœur had despatched to Lyons. There was no record of the dead woman having stayed in any of the hotels in the town, but he had found a post office clerk who remembered her. She had been into the post office twice, on each occasion to collect a large manila envelope. The first time, the envelope had lain there a week. On the last occasion, it had just arrived when she called.

'Have you got the dates?'

Thoughtfully, still puffing lingeringly at his pipe, Maigret watched his colleague at work.

'Hello! . . . Is that the Crédit Lyonnais? . . . Have you got that list of deposits I asked for? . . . No. . . . I'll send for it later today. . . . Can you tell me if she paid in on January 14 or 15, and February 23 or 24? . . . Yes, I'll hang on.'

It didn't take long.

'8,000 francs on January 15, and 5,000 on February 23 of this year. . . .'

'Usually about 5,000 francs, you say?'

'Almost always, with a few exceptions. . . . I have the figures here. . . . I see that, five years ago, the sum of 25,000 francs was credited to her account. . . . That's the only time such a large sum was ever paid in.'

'In notes, as usual?'

'Yes.'

'How does the account stand at the moment?'

'In credit to the tune of four hundred and fifty-two thousand, six hundred and fifty. . . .'

Lecœur repeated the figure to Maigret.

'She was a rich woman,' he murmured, 'and still she let furnished rooms during the season. . . .'

The Chief Superintendent's reply surprised him:

'He's a very rich man.'

'You're right. . . . It does look as though she was getting all the money from a single source. A man who can lay out five thousand francs a month, sometimes more. . . .'

Yet this man had been kept in ignorance of the fact that Hélène Lange was the owner of a little white villa with pale green shutters in the France district of Vichy. Each payment had been made to a different address.

The money had been paid every month, but not on any fixed date. Presumably, it was no accident that Mademoiselle Lange had generally allowed a few days to elapse before collecting it, no doubt as a precaution against being seen going into the post office by anyone who might be looking out for her.

A rich man, or at any rate comfortably off. When he had finally tracked down the sister, he had not attempted to arrange a meeting, but had merely asked her to stay on in Vichy for a day or two, until she heard from him again. . . . Why?

'He must be a married man. . . . Here with his wife, and possibly his children too. . . . Obviously, he's not master of his own time. . . .'

Lecœur, in his turn, was obviously enjoying seeing Maigret's mind at work. But was it really *his* mind at work? He was making every effort to get inside the mind of the murderer. . . .

'He couldn't find what he was looking for in the Rue du Bourbonnais. . . . And he could get nothing out of Hélène Lange. . . . If he had done, she would probably still be alive today. . . . He tried to frighten her into telling him whatever it was he wanted to know. . . .'

'Whether his wife is with him or not, we know that he was able to get away that night.'

Maigret was silent, pondering this objection.

'What was on at the theatre on Monday night?'

Lecœur took up the receiver to find out.

'*Tosca*. . . . It was sold out.'

Moving towards a conclusion, Maigret was not exactly reasoning it out, but rather progressing by leaps of the imagination. Here was this man, a person of some social standing, staying, no doubt, at one of the best hotels in Vichy, with his wife and, very probably, a party of friends.

The night before the performance, or possibly the night before that, he had seen Hélène Lange, and followed her, to find out where she lived.

On the night of the murder, *Tosca* was being performed in the theatre of the Grand Casino. Is it not a well-known

fact that women are generally more partial than men to
Italian grand opera?

'Why don't you go without me? . . . I feel rather tired at
the end of the day . . . the treatment. . . . I'd be glad of the
chance of an early night. . . .'

What was it he wanted to find out from Hélène Lange, that
she had so stubbornly refused to tell him?

Had he reached the house before her, forcing the flimsy
lock, and searching through drawers and cupboards, while
she was still at the concert?

Or had he followed her home, strangled her, and searched
the flat afterwards, throwing everything in confusion on the
floor?

'What are you smiling at, chief?'

'Because something quite absurd has just occurred to me.
. . . Before he struck lucky with the Hôtel de la Gare, the
murderer, if he really did ring all the hotels in alphabetical
order, must have made about thirty telephone calls. . . . What
does that suggest to you . . . ?'

He refilled his pipe, thoughtfully.

'The entire police force is searching for him. . . . Almost
certainly he shares a double room in the hotel with his wife.
. . . But, he's faced with the necessity of repeating the name of
his victim aloud, over and over again.

'In a hotel, all phone calls go through the switchboard.
. . . Besides, there's his wife. . . . It's reasonable, therefore,
to suppose . . .

'Too chancy to make the calls from a café or bar, with the
risk of being overheard. . . .

'If I were you, Lecoeur, I should detail as many men as I
could spare to watch the public telephone boxes.'

'But, since he did get through to Francine Lange in the
end! . . .'

'He'd said he'd ring her back. . . .'

'But she's left Vichy. . . .'

'He doesn't know that.'

In Paris, Maigret, in common with most married men, saw
his wife three times a day, on waking in the morning, at

midday, and at night. And often, when he wasn't able to get home for lunch, only twice.

For the rest of the day, for all she knew, he might have been up to anything.

But in Vichy? They, like most other married couples there for the cure, were in each other's company almost twenty-four hours a day.

'He wouldn't have been able to risk a long absence, even to use a public call box,' he said with a sigh.

More than likely he had made some excuse—he was out of cigarettes or wanted a breath of air—while his wife was dressing. . . . One or two quick calls. . . . If she too was taking the cure, perhaps having hydrotherapy, that would give him a little more time to himself. . . .

He could imagine him, taking advantage of every opportunity, making opportunities whenever he could, lying to his wife like a naughty child to its mother.

A heavily built man, elderly, rich, of some standing, having come to Vichy in the hope of finding relief from chronic asthma.

'Doesn't it surprise you that the sister has decamped?'

Francine Lange liked money. Heaven knows what depths she had sunk to when she was living in Paris, in order to get it. And now she was the owner of a flourishing business and her sister's sole heir.

Surely she was not the sort of woman to turn up her nose at the offer of a further substantial sum?

Was it the police she was afraid of? Unlikely, unless she intended to make a clean break, and leave the country.

No! She had gone back to La Rochelle, where she was just as accessible to police questioning as in Vichy. For the moment, she was still on the road with her gigolo at the wheel, in the open, red sports car, which must surely be the envy of every young person who saw it.

For a car like that would eat up the miles. She would probably reach La Rochelle some time in the middle of the afternoon.

'Did any of the papers mention that she lived in La Rochelle?'

'No, they just announced her arrival.'

'She was a frightened woman already, this morning in the house, and at the cemetery. . . .'

'I wonder why it was you she kept peering at, when she thought we weren't looking. . . .'

'I think I know why. . . .'

Maigret, smiling, went on, though not without some embarrassment:

'I've been built up in the newspapers as a sort of father-confessor . . . she must have been tempted to confide in me, to ask my advice. . . . But then, on reflection, she decided the stakes were too high.'

Lecœur frowned.

'I don't quite see . . .'

'The man tried to get some information out of Hélène Lange. It must have been important, because her refusal to give it drove him berserk. A man doesn't strangle a woman in cold blood. . . . He came unarmed to the Rue du Bourbonnais. He never meant to kill her. . . . And then he went away empty-handed. . . .'

Brooding over the manner of her death, Maigret went on:

'If I may venture to say so . . .'

'You mean, he thinks the sister knows what she knew?'

'No doubt about it. . . . Otherwise, he'd never have taken so much trouble and run so many risks to find out where she was staying. . . . He would never have rung her, and dropped that hint of a large bribe. . . .'

'And what about her? Does she know what he wants from her?'

'It's possible,' murmured Maigret, looking at his watch.

'She must do, surely? . . . Unless she was scared out of her wits, why should she have run off without a word to us . . . ?'

'I must be off to meet my wife. . . .'

He might have added:

'Just like that other fellow!'

Just like that broad-shouldered, corpulent man, who had been forced to resort to every kind of childish trick in order to slip out to a public telephone box to make his calls.

In the course of their daily walks, the Maigrets might well have passed that particular couple more than once. Who could tell? It was possible that they had sat side by side, drinking their glasses of water, that their chairs . . .

'Don't forget the telephone boxes. . . .'

'It would take as many men as you have in Paris. . . .'

'There are never enough. . . . When will you be ringing La Rochelle?'

'Round about six, before I leave for Clermont-Ferrand, where I have an appointment with the examining magistrate. I'm seeing him at his house. . . . This business is worrying him. He's very well in with the *Compagnie Fermière*, and they don't much care for publicity of this sort. . . . If you want to be present . . .'

He found Madame Maigret waiting for him on a bench. Never in all their lives had the Maigrets spent so much time sitting on park benches and garden chairs. He was late, but, quick to note that his mood had changed since the morning, she made no mention of it.

How well she knew that preoccupied frown.

'Where are we going?'

'For a walk.'

Just as on any other day. Just like that other couple. The wife, surely, could have suspected nothing. How could she guess, as she walked at his side, that he blenched inwardly at the sight of every policeman in uniform?

He was a murderer. He could not cut short his cure and leave, without arousing suspicion. He would have to carry on with the daily round like the Maigrets.

Was he staying at one of the two or three luxury hotels in the town? It wasn't Maigret's business, but if he were in Lecœur's place. . . .

'Lecœur is a first-class man,' he murmured, by which he really meant: 'He's sure to think of it. There aren't so many people staying in that class of hotel that . . .'

All the same, he would have liked to have ferreted about a bit for himself.

'We mustn't forget your appointment with Rian.'

'Is it today?'

'No, tomorrow at four. . . .'

He would have to go through it all again, undressing, allowing himself to be prodded and then weighed, listening to the fair-haired young doctor solemnly laying down the law about how many glasses of water he should drink from then on. Perhaps he would prescribe water from one or more of the other springs this time.

He thought of Janvier, who had taken over his office, as Lucas was also away on holiday. He had gone to the mountains, somewhere around Chamonix.

Little boats in single file sailed gently into the wind and, one by one, heeled over. Occasionally they saw a couple in a pedal boat. There was a wall all along the Allier, and beyond it, every fifty yards or so, was a miniature golf course.

Maigret caught himself looking back over his shoulder every time they passed a heavily-built, elderly man.

To him, Hélène Lange's murderer was no longer a shadowy figure. He was beginning to take shape and assume a personality.

He was somewhere in this town, possibly on one of the promenades where the Maigrets so often walked. He was going through more or less the same motions as themselves, seeing the same sights, the sailing boats, the pedal boats, the yellow chairs in the park, and the constant ebb and flow of the crowds in the streets and gardens.

Rightly or wrongly, Maigret saw him with a woman at his side, perhaps, like himself, rather overweight, complaining of sore feet.

What did they talk about as they walked? What, for that matter, did all the other couples like them talk about?

He had killed Hélène Lange. . . . He was a wanted man. It needed only a careless word or an unguarded action to bring the police about his ears.

A ruined life. His name on the front page of every newspaper. His friends shocked and incredulous. The security of his home and family threatened.

From a luxurious hotel suite to a police cell.

It could all happen in a matter of minutes, or even seconds. At any time, he might feel a strange hand on his shoulder and, turning, see the glint of a police badge.

'You are Monsieur . . . if I am not mistaken?'

Monsieur what? It was immaterial. His wife's astonished indignation.

'It's all a mistake, officer! . . . I know him so well. . . . I should do. . . . I'm his wife. . . . Anyone will tell you. . . . Say something, Jean! . . .'

Jean or Pierre or Gaston. . . .

Maigret was looking about him blankly, as though he had no idea where he was.

'And even so, he persists. . . .'

'What does he persist in . . . ?'

'In trying to get at the truth.'

'What are you talking about?'

'You know very well who I'm talking about. . . . He telephoned Francine Lange. . . . He wants to meet her. . . .'

'Surely he won't run the risk of being caught?'

'If only she'd warned Lecœur in time, he could have set a trap. . . . It's still not too late. . . . He's only heard her voice that once. . . . Lecœur must have thought of it. . . . One would only need to plant a woman of about her age in Room 406. . . . Then when he rang . . .'

Maigret stopped short where he stood, clenched his fists, and uttered a grunt of fury.

'What the devil can he be at, taking that sort of risk?'

A man's voice answered:

'Hello! Who do you wish to speak to?'

'Mademoiselle Francine Lange.'

'Who is that?'

'Divisional Superintendent Lecœur.'

'Hold on, please.'

Maigret was sitting opposite Lecœur in the bare little office, listening on an extension.

'Hello! Can't it wait till the morning?'

'No.'

'Can you ring back in half an hour?'

'I shall have left by then.'

'We've only just got here. . . . Francine, Mademoiselle Lange, that is to say, is in the bath.'

'Be good enough to ask her, from me, to get out of it. . . .'

Lecœur winked at his colleague from Paris. Once again, they heard the voice of Lucien Romanel:

'She won't keep you a moment. She's just rubbing down with a towel. . . .'

'You don't seem to have made very good time. . . .'

'We had a puncture. . . . We wasted an hour trying to get a spare tyre. . . . Here she is!'

'Hello!'

Her voice came across more faintly than the gigolo's.

'Mademoiselle Lange? . . . I understood from you this morning that you were planning to spend two or three more days in Vichy. . . .'

'I had intended to, but I changed my mind.'

'May I ask why?'

'I could say: "I just did, that's all." There's no law against it, is there?'

'No, and there's no law against my taking out a summons to compel you to answer my questions. . . .'

'What difference does it make whether I'm in Vichy or La Rochelle?'

'It makes a great deal of difference to me. . . . I will repeat my question: What made you change your mind?'

'I was frightened. . . .'

'What of?'

'You know the answer to that. . . . I was frightened this morning, but I kept saying to myself that he wouldn't dare. . . .'

'Could you be more explicit, please. Who were you afraid of?'

'Of my sister's murderer. . . . I said to myself, if he attacked her, he's quite capable of attacking me. . . .'

'For what reason?'

'I don't know. . . .'

'Is it someone you know?'

244

'No. . . .'

'Haven't you the least idea who it could be?'

'No. . . .'

'And yet, having told me that you were staying on in Vichy, you suddenly decided, early this afternoon, that you couldn't get away fast enough. . . .'

'I was frightened. . . .'

'You're lying, or rather prevaricating. . . . You had a very particular reason for being frightened. . . .'

'I told you. . . . He killed my sister. . . . He might equally well . . .'

'For what reason?'

'I don't know. . . .'

'Are you telling me that you don't know why your sister was killed?'

'If I had known, I should have told you. . . .'

'In that case, why didn't you tell me about the phone call?'

He could imagine her wrapped in a bath-robe, with her hair still damp, surrounded by suitcases which she had not yet had time to unpack. Was there an extension in the flat, he wondered. If not, Romanel must be straining his ears, trying to hear what he was saying.

'What telephone call?'

'The one you received last night at your hotel.'

'I don't see what you . . .'

'Do you wish me to repeat what he said? Did he not, in fact, advise you to stay on in Vichy for a day or two longer? Did he not say that he would be getting in touch with you again, and that there could be big money in it for you?'

'I was scarcely listening. . . .'

'Why not?'

'Because I thought it was some sort of leg-pull. . . . Isn't that how it struck you?'

'No.'

A very emphatic 'no', followed by a menacing silence. She was badly shaken, standing there, all those miles away, holding the receiver, and trying to think of something to say.

'I'm not a policeman. . . . I tell you I thought it was a leg-pull. . . .'

'Have you ever known it happen before?'

'Not quite like that. . . .'

'Is it not a fact that you were so badly shaken by this telephone call that you felt you must get away from Vichy as soon as you possibly could?'

'Well, since you obviously don't believe me . . .'

'If you tell me the truth, I'll believe you. . . .'

'It was frightening. . . .'

'What?'

'The realization that the man was still at large in Vichy. . . . It's enough to frighten any woman, the thought of a strangler roaming the streets. . . .'

'Nevertheless, I haven't noticed any mass exodus from the hotels. . . . Had you ever heard that voice before . . . ?'

'I don't think so. . . .'

'A very distinctive voice . . . ?'

'I didn't notice. . . . I was taken by surprise. . . .'

'Just now you were talking in terms of a leg-pull. . . .'

'I'm tired. . . . The day before yesterday, I was still on holiday in Majorca. I've scarcely had an hour's sleep since then.'

'That's no reason for lying to me.'

'I'm not used to being harried in this way. And now you have me out of my bath, and subject me to an inquisition over the telephone. . . .'

'If you wish, I can arrange for my colleague in La Rochelle to call on you officially in an hour's time, and take down your statement in writing.'

'I'm doing my best to answer your questions.'

Maigret's eyes sparkled with pleasure. Lecœur was doing splendidly. He himself would not have set about it in precisely that way, but it would come to the same thing in the end.

'You knew yesterday that the police were looking for your sister's murderer. . . . You must also have known that the smallest clue might prove invaluable. . . .'

'I suppose so, yes.'

246

'Now, there was every reason to believe that your anonymous caller was the murderer. . . . You thought so yourself. . . . In fact, you were sure of it. . . . That's why you were so frightened . . . though I wouldn't have thought you were the type to be easily scared. . . .'

'Maybe I did think it might be the murderer, but I couldn't be sure. . . .'

'Anyone else in your place would have informed the police immediately. . . . Why didn't you?'

'Aren't you forgetting that I had just lost my sister—my only relative? . . . She was not even buried. . . .'

'I was at the funeral, remember? You didn't turn a hair.'

'What do you know about my feelings?'

'Answer my questions. . . .'

'You might have prevented me from leaving.'

'There can't be anything very urgent for you to attend to in La Rochelle. In the ordinary way, you would still have been on holiday in Majorca.'

'I found the atmosphere oppressive. . . . The thought that that man . . .'

'Or the thought that, if you mentioned the telephone call, you might have to answer some awkward questions?'

'You might have wanted to use me as a decoy. . . . When he rang back to suggest a meeting, you might have insisted on my going, and . . .'

'And?'

'Nothing. . . . I was frightened, that's all. . . .'

'Why was your sister murdered?'

'How should I know?'

'Someone whom she hadn't seen for years recognized her, followed her and forced his way into her house. . . .'

'I thought perhaps she had come upon a burglar unexpectedly. . . .'

'You're not as naive as all that. . . . There was something he wanted from her, the answer to a question, a vital question. . . .'

'What question?'

'That is precisely what I'm trying to find out. . . . Your sister came into some money, Mademoiselle Lange. . . .'

'Who from?'

'You tell me.'

'She and I jointly inherited my mother's estate. . . . She wasn't a rich woman. . . . There was just a little draper's shop in Marsilly, and a few thousand francs in a savings bank. . . .'

'Was her lover a rich man?'

'What lover?'

'The one who used to call at her flat in the Rue Notre-Dame-de-Lorette once or twice a week, when she was living in Paris.'

'I know nothing about that.'

'Did you never meet him?'

'No.'

'Don't ring off, Mademoiselle, I haven't nearly finished with you yet. . . . Hello!'

'I'm still here. . . .'

'Your sister was a shorthand typist. . . . You were a manicurist. . . .'

'Later, I trained as a beauty specialist.'

'Quite so. . . . Two young girls from a humble home in Marsilly. . . . You both went to Paris. . . . You didn't go together, but, for several years, you were both living there at the same time. . . .'

'So what?'

'You claim to know nothing about your sister's life at that time. . . . You can't even tell me where she worked. . . .'

'In the first place, there was a very big difference in our ages. . . . And besides, we never got on, even as children. . . .'

'Let me finish. . . . Not so very long after, you turn up again in La Rochelle—a young woman still—as proprietress of a hairdressing salon, and that must have cost you a pretty penny. . . .'

'I paid a lump sum down, and the rest in yearly instalments. . . .'

'We may have to go further into that later. . . . As for your sister, she—if I may put it that way—went out of circulation. . . . To begin with, she moved to Nice, where she spent five years. . . . Did you ever visit her there?'

248

'No.'

'Did you know her address?'

'I got three or four postcards from her. . . .'

'In five years?'

'We had nothing to say to one another.'

'And when she came to live in Vichy?'

'She said nothing to me about it.'

'You never heard from her that she had moved here permanently, and bought a house?'

'I heard about it from friends.'

'Who were these friends?'

'I don't remember. . . . Just some people who had run into her in Vichy. . . .'

'Did they speak to her?'

'They may have done. . . . You're confusing me. . . .'

Lecœur, very pleased with himself, once more winked at Maigret, who was struggling to re-light his pipe, which had gone out, without putting down the receiver.

'Did you go to the Crédit Lyonnais?'

'Where?'

'In Vichy.'

'No.'

'Didn't it occur to you to wonder how much your sister had left you?'

'I shall leave all that to my lawyer here in La Rochelle. I don't understand these things. . . .'

'Indeed? You're a business woman, aren't you? Haven't you any idea how much money your sister had in the bank?'

Another long silence.

'I'm waiting. . . .'

'I can't answer that. . . .'

'Why not?'

'Because I don't know. . . .'

'Would it surprise you to learn that it was something approaching five hundred thousand francs?'

'That's a great deal of money.'

She sounded rather matter-of-fact about it.

'A lot, I mean, for a girl coming from a little village like

249

Marsilly, who worked as a shorthand typist in Paris for barely ten years.'

'I wasn't in her confidence. . . .'

'Is it not a fact that when you took over the hairdressing business in La Rochelle, it was your sister who provided the money in the first instance? Think carefully before you answer, and remember that we have ways and means of getting at the truth.'

Another long silence.

Between two people who are face to face, silence is less alarming than in the course of a telephone conversation, when all contact is temporarily broken.

'It's surely not a thing you could forget!'

'She did lend me a little money. . . .'

'How much?'

'I'd have to ask my lawyer.'

'At that time your sister was still living in Nice, was she not?'

'Possibly. . . . Yes. . . .'

'So you were in touch with her, not just through the exchange of postcards. . . . It seems more than likely that you went to see her, to explain the details of your project. . . .'

'I must have done. . . .'

'A moment ago, you denied it.'

'All these questions. . . . I'm confused. . . . I don't know what I'm saying. . . .'

'It's not my questions that are confusing. . . . It's your answers.'

'Have you done with me?'

'Not quite. . . . And I must impress upon you once again that you would be well advised to stay on the line, otherwise I should be forced into taking more drastic measures. . . . This time I want a straight answer, yes or no. . . . In whose name was the deed of sale drawn up, yours or your sister's? In other words was your sister, in fact, the owner?'

'No.'

'Then you were?'

'No.'

'Who, then?'

'We owned it jointly.'

'In other words, you and she were partners, and yet you've been trying to make me believe that there was no contact between you. . . .'

'It's a family matter, and nobody's business but our own. . . .'

'May I remind you that this is a case of murder?'

'That has nothing to do with it.'

'Are you so sure?'

'I hardly think . . .'

'You hardly think. . . . In that case why did you rush away from Vichy like a mad woman?'

'Have you any more questions to ask me?'

Maigret nodded, took a pencil from the desk, and scribbled a few words on the pad.

'One moment. . . . Don't hang up. . . .'

'Will you be long?'

'Here it is. . . . You had a child, did you not?'

'I told you so.'

'Was it born in Paris?'

'No.'

'Why not?'

All Maigret's note said was: 'Where was the child born. Where was the birth registered?'

Lecœur was spinning it out, possibly in order to impress his famous colleague from Paris.

'I didn't want it generally known. . . .'

'Where did you go?'

'Burgundy.'

'Where exactly?'

'Mesnil-le-Mont.'

'Is that a village?'

'Scarcely more than a hamlet, really.'

'Is there a resident doctor?'

'There wasn't then.'

'And you chose to have your child in this remote hamlet, out of reach of a doctor?'

'How do you suppose our mothers managed?'

'Was it you who chose the place? Had you been there before?'

'No, I found it on the map.'

'Did you go alone?'

'I can't help wondering how you treat criminals, if you can torture innocent people in this way. . . . I haven't done anything. . . . In fact . . .'

'I asked you whether you were alone.'

'No.'

'That's better. It's much simpler, you know, to tell the truth than to lie. Who went with you?'

'My sister.'

'Do you mean your sister Hélène?'

'I have no other.'

'This was when you were both living in Paris, and never met except by chance. . . . You had no idea where she worked. . . . For all you knew, she might have been a kept woman. . . .'

'It was no business of mine. . . .'

'You didn't get on. . . . You saw as little as possible of one another, and yet, all of a sudden, she dropped everything, gave up her job, and went with you to some godforsaken hamlet in Burgundy. . . .'

There was nothing she could say.

'How long were you there?'

'A month.'

'In the local hotel?'

'It was just an inn, really.'

'Did you have a midwife?'

'I don't know whether she was qualified, but she acted as midwife to all the women in the district.'

'What was her name?'

'She was about sixty-five at the time. She must be dead by now.'

'Don't you remember her name?'

'Madame Radèche.'

'Did you register the birth?'

'Of course.'

252

'You, personally?'

'I was still in bed. . . . My sister went with the inn-keeper. He witnessed her signature.'

'Did you go yourself later to look at the entry?'

'Why on earth should I?'

'Have you a copy of the birth certificate?'

'It was so long ago. . . .'

'Where did you go next?'

'Look here, I can't take any more of this. . . . If you must put me through hours of questioning, come and see me here. . . .'

Unmoved, Lecœur asked:

'Where did you take the child?'

'To Saint-André. Saint-André-du-Lavion in the Vosges.'

'By car?'

'I didn't have a car then. . . .'

'And your sister?'

'She never learnt to drive. . . .'

'Did she go with you?'

'Yes! Yes! Yes! I'm sick of all this, do you hear me? Sick of it! Sick of it! Sick of it!'

Whereupon she hung up.

CHAPTER SIX

'WHAT'S ON YOUR MIND?'

In every marriage where husband and wife have been together for years, each observing the actions and emotions of the other, there are times when one partner, baffled by the expression on the other's face, asks diffidently:

'What's on your mind?'

Madame Maigret, it must be said, needed to be very sure that her husband was not under strain before she would ask this question, for, in their relationship, there were certain boundaries which she felt she had no right to overstep.

Following the long telephone call to La Rochelle, they had dined quietly in the relaxing atmosphere of the white dining-room of their hotel, with its potted palms in the alcoves, and wine bottles and flowers on the tables.

Ostensibly, no one paid any attention to the Maigrets, though they were in fact the focus of discreet interest, admiration and affection.

They were now taking their evening walk. From time to time, there was a rumble of thunder in the sky, and the still evening air was churned up every few minutes by little flurries of wind.

They had come, almost as if by accident, to the Rue du Bourbonnais. There was a light showing in one of the first floor windows, in the room occupied by the stout widow, Madame Vireveau. The Maleskis were out, walking, possibly, or at the cinema.

On the ground floor, all was darkness and silence. The furniture had been put back in place. Hélène Lange had been blotted out.

Sooner or later, no doubt, the contents of the house would be carted into the street, and the props and chattels which had once been part of a human life would fall under the hammer of some wise-cracking auctioneer.

Had Francine taken away the photographs? It seemed unlikely. Probably she would not even bother to send for them. They, too, would be sold.

They had reached the park where, inevitably it seemed, they always ended up, when Madame Maigret ventured to put her question.

'I'm thinking about Lecœur. He really is first-class at his job,' replied her husband.

The manner in which the Superintendent from Clermont-Ferrand had hammered away at Francine, giving her no time to collect herself, was a good example. He had made the fullest use of the facts at his disposal, to get the fuller information he needed to carry the enquiry a stage further.

Why then was Maigret not entirely satisfied? No doubt, he would have set about it differently. But then what two men, even working to the same end, go about it in precisely the same way?

It was not a question of method. Maigret was, if anything, a little envious of his ebullient colleague's assurance and self-confidence.

No, it was something else. To Maigret, the lady in lilac was not just a murder victim. He was not primarily concerned with the kind of life she had led, nor with what had happened to her. He was beginning to know her as an individual and, almost without realizing it, to penetrate the mystery of her personality.

And while he was walking back to his hotel, pondering, to the exclusion of all else, the relationship between the two sisters, Lecœur was bounding off, without a care in the world, to keep his appointment with the examining magistrate.

What could the examining magistrate really know about a case like this one, closeted in his office, and seeing nothing of life but what was laid before him, encapsulated in the official reports?

Two sisters in a village on the Atlantic coast, a little shop next door to the church. Maigret knew the village, whose

255

people reaped a harvest from both land and sea. A village dominated by four or five big landowners, who were also the owners of oyster beds and mussel farms.

He recalled the women, old women, young women and little girls, setting out at daybreak, sometimes even at night, depending on the tides, dressed in gumboots, thick fishermen's jerseys and shabby men's jackets.

Down on the shore, they gathered the oysters which lay exposed at low tide, while the men scraped the mussels off the hurdles, which were pegged down by stakes.

Few of these girls were ever educated beyond the most elementary stage, and even the boys fared little better, at least at the time when the Lange girls were growing up.

Hélène was the exception. She had gone to school in the town, and had reached a sufficiently high standard to go to work in an office.

Cycling to work in the morning and returning at night, she was quite the young lady.

And later, her sister too had somehow contrived to better herself.

They are both living in Paris. . . . They are never to be seen in the village now . . . they think themselves too good for us. . . .

The girls who had once been their playmates were still going out every morning to gather oysters and mussels. They had married and borne children, who, in their turn, had romped in the square outside the church.

It was cold-blooded determination that had got Hélène Lange what she wanted. Even as a child, she had turned her back on the life that should have been hers. She had mapped out for herself a different life, and retreated into a world of her own, peopled only by the characters in her favourite romantic novels.

She had been unable to stomach Balzac. His world had reminded her too much of Marsilly, her mother's shop, the freezing oyster beds, and the roughened hands of the women.

Francine, too, had managed to escape, in her own fashion.

At fifteen she had had her eyes opened by a taxi-driver. She was plump and seductive. Men were attracted by her saucy smile. And why not, she thought, why not turn her charms to good account?

And had she not, in the end, succeeded?

The elder sister had acquired a house in Vichy, and amassed a small fortune. The younger had chosen to return home, and flaunt her wealth in the most elegant beauty salon in town.

Lecœur did not feel the need to enter into their lives, to understand them. He uncovered facts, from which he drew conclusions, and, in consequence, was spared the discomfort of an uneasy conscience.

Intimately concerned with the lives of these two women there was a man. Unidentified, he was nevertheless here in Vichy, in a hotel bedroom, in the park, in one of the gaming rooms of the Grand Casino, somewhere, anywhere.

This man was a killer. And he was caught in a trap. He must know that the police, with their formidable resources, were closing in on him, that the invisible cordon was tightening about him, and that, very soon, the impartial hand of the law would be laid on his shoulder.

He too had a whole life behind him. He had been a child, a youth, he had fallen in love, almost certainly married, or else why should he, the nameless man who had called once or twice a week at the Rue Notre-Dame-de-Lorette, not have been able to stay more than an hour at a time?

Hélène had disappeared from Paris. When next heard of, she was living a solitary life in Nice, deliberately shunning attention, it seemed, in that town crowded with people who were all strangers to one another.

Now they knew that, before settling in Nice, she had gone to a tiny village in Burgundy, lived in the local inn for a month, to be with her sister when she gave birth to a child.

Maigret was beginning to understand the two women, but he needed to know more about the man. He was tall and heavily built. He had a distinctive voice, because he suffered from asthma, which was no doubt what had brought him to Vichy in the first place.

He had committed a murder, and gained nothing by it. He had gone to the Rue du Bourbonnais, not to take a life, but to ask a question.

Hélène Lange had brought about her own death. She had refused to answer. Even when he had seized her by the throat —probably just to frighten her—she had not spoken, and her silence had cost her her life.

He could have abandoned his quest. It would have been the sensible thing to do. Any further step he took was bound to entail grave risks. The machinery of the law had already been set in motion.

Had he known previously of the existence of the sister, Francine Lange? She claimed that he had not, and she could be telling the truth.

He could have learnt from the newspapers that Hélène Lange had a sister, and that she had just arrived in Vichy. He had got it into his head that he must speak to her, and, with astonishing thoroughness and guile, had managed to track her down to her hotel.

Hélène had refused to speak, but would the younger sister prove equally stubborn, if faced with the added inducement of a substantial bribe?

The man was rich, a person of some standing. It must be so, or he could not have afforded to part with more than five hundred thousand francs over a period of a few years.

Five hundred thousand francs in return for what? In return for nothing? He did not even know the address of the woman to whom he sent the money, Poste Restante, at the various towns designated by her up and down the country.

Had he been able to find her, would Hélène Lange have died sooner?

'Stay on in Vichy for another two or three days. . . .'

It was his last chance. He had to take it, even if it meant getting caught. He would ring her again. It wouldn't be easy, but he would find a way. He would do it as soon as he could escape from his wife without arousing suspicion.

But, by now, there was scarcely a public call-box in the town which was not being watched by one of Lecœur's men.

Had Maigret been right in believing that he would not risk telephoning from a bar, a café, or his hotel bedroom?

He and his wife walked past one of these public call-boxes. Through the glass panes, they could see a teenage girl chattering away with cheerful animation.

'Do you think he'll be caught?'

'Any time now, yes.'

Because here was a man with an over-riding obsession. Very likely he had lived with it for years. Probably ever since the very first monthly payment, he had been waiting and hoping for the chance meeting which had occurred at last, after fifteen years.

It might well be that he was a sound businessman, very level-headed as far as his everyday life was concerned.

Fifteen years of brooding . . .

He had squeezed too hard. He never meant to kill her. Or else . . .

Maigret stopped dead in his tracks, right in the middle of a busy boulevard. His wife, with a quick, sidelong glance at his face, stopped too.

Or else, he came face to face with something so monstrous, so unforeseen, so shocking . . .

'I wonder how Lecœur will set about it. . . .' he murmured.

'Set about what?'

'Getting him to make a clean breast of it. . . .'

'He'll have to find him and arrest him first. . . .'

'He'll give himself up. . . .'

It would be a relief to him to surrender . . . an end to lying and contriving. . . .

'I hope he's not armed.'

Because there was a wife in the case, Maigret could envisage an alternative outcome. Instead of giving himself up, the man might decide to end it, once for all. . . .

Had Lecœur warned his subordinates to proceed with caution? It wasn't for Maigret to interfere. In this instance he was merely a passive spectator, keeping well in the background, as far as was possible.

Even if he did not resist arrest, was there any reason why

he should talk? It would not mitigate his crime, nor carry any weight with a jury. To them, he would be just another strangler, and, whatever the provocation, in such a case leniency was not to be hoped for, still less pity.

'What you really mean is, you wish you were handling it yourself!'

She found that in Vichy she could say things to him that, in Paris, she would never have dared to utter. Was it because they were on holiday?

Because, as a result of being together all day and every day, a new intimacy had grown up between them?

She could almost hear his thoughts.

'I wonder . . . no . . . I don't think so. . . .'

Why should he worry? He was here for a rest, for a thorough clean-out of the system, to use Dr. Rian's phrase. In fact, he had an appointment with the doctor for tomorrow, and then, for half an hour at least, he would be just another patient, preoccupied with his digestion, his liver, his pulse-rate, his blood-pressure and his fits of giddiness.

How old was Lecœur? Barely five years younger than himself. In five years' time, Lecœur too would be thinking about retirement, and wondering what on earth he would find to do with himself when the time came.

They were behind the Casino now, walking past the town's two most luxurious hotels. Long, sleek cars slumbered along the kerb. In the garden, to one side of the revolving door, a man in a dinner-jacket was leaning back in a deck-chair, enjoying the cool of the evening.

A crystal chandelier filled the entrance hall with a blaze of light. They could see oriental carpets, marble pillars, and the liveried hall porter bending forward to answer an enquiry from an old lady in evening dress.

This hotel, or the one next to it, was perhaps where the man was staying. If not, then he was probably at the Pavillon Sévigné, near the Pont Bellerive. Beside the lift stood a very young page-boy, but not too young to be looking about him with a very supercilious air.

Lecœur had concentrated his attention on the weakest link,

in other words, Francine Lange, and she, taken by surprise, had revealed a good deal.

Presumably he would take the first opportunity of questioning her further. Was there anything more to be got out of her, or had she told all she knew?

'I won't be a minute. . . . I must get some tobacco. . . .'

He went into a noisy bar, where a great many people were looking at a television screen set up on a pedestal above eye-level. There was a strong smell of wine and beer. The bald barman was filling glasses without a moment's pause, and a waitress in black dress and white apron was going to and from the tables with laden trays of drinks.

Without thinking, he glanced at the telephone box, at the far end near the washrooms. It had a glass door. There was no one in it.

'Three ounces of shag.'

They were not far from the Hôtel de la Bérézina, and, as they approached, they saw young Dicelle waiting on the steps.

'Could I have a word with you, sir?'

Madame Maigret, leaving them to it, went in to collect her key from the desk.

'Let's walk, shall we?'

Their footsteps echoed in the deserted street.

'Did Lecœur send you?'

'Yes, he's been on the phone to me. He'd gone home to Clermont, to his wife and kids. . . .'

'How many children has he?'

'Four. The eldest is eighteen. He's shaping up to be a swimming champion. . . .'

'What's been happening?'

'There are ten of us watching the telephone boxes. The Super can't spare enough men for all of them, so we're concentrating on those in the centre, especially the ones closest to the big hotels.'

'Have you made an arrest?'

'Not yet. . . . I'm waiting for the Super. . . . He should be on his way by now. . . . There's been a slip up, I'm afraid. . . . My fault entirely. . . . I was on watch near the call-box in the Boulevard Kennedy. . . . It wasn't too difficult to keep out of sight, with all those trees. . . .'

'And you saw a man go in to use the telephone?'

'Yes. . . . A big, heavily built man, answering to the description. . . . He was behaving suspiciously. . . . He kept peering through the door . . . but he didn't see me. . . .

'He began dialling a number, and then, all of a sudden, changed his mind. Maybe I poked my head out too far. . . . I don't know. . . . At any rate, he dialled the first three figures, then thought better of it and came out. . . .'

'And you made no attempt to stop him?'

'My instructions were not to interfere with him in any way, but to follow him. To my surprise, there was a woman waiting for him in the shadows, not twenty yards away. . . .'

'What was she like?'

'Distinguished-looking, well-dressed, fiftyish. . . .'

'Did you get the impression that there was any collusion between them?'

'No. She just took his arm, and they walked back to the Hôtel des Ambassadeurs.'

The hotel with the sumptuous entrance hall and the crystal chandelier, that Maigret had stood and gazed at barely an hour earlier.

'What next?'

'Nothing. The man went up to the desk, and got his key from the hall porter, who wished him goodnight.'

'Did you get a good look at him?'

'Enough to know him again. I got the impression that he was older than his wife. . . . Nearer sixty, I'd say. They got into the lift, and I didn't see them again. . . .'

'Was he wearing a dinner-jacket?'

'No . . . a very well-cut dark suit. . . . He has greying hair brushed back, a healthy complexion and, I think a small white moustache. . . .'

'Did you make enquiries at the desk?'

'Of course. He and his wife have a suite—a large bedroom with adjoining sitting-room—on the first floor, number 105. This is their first visit to Vichy, but they are friends of the proprietor of the hotel, who also owns a hotel in La Baule. The man's name is Louis Pélardeau. He's an industrialist, and lives in Paris, Boulevard Suchet. . . .'

'Is he here for the cure?'

'Yes. . . . I asked the hall porter whether he had an unusually distinctive voice. He said yes, he suffered from asthma. . . . They're both being treated by Dr. Rian.'

'Is Madame Pélardeau taking the cure as well?'

'Yes. . . . It seems they have no children. . . . They've joined up with some friends from Paris who are staying in the same hotel, and they share a table with them at meals. . . . Occasionally, they all go to the theatre together.'

'Have you got someone watching the hotel?'

'I've put a local man on to it, until one of our people gets there, which should be about now. The local chap, though he had every right to tell me to go to hell, was most co-operative. . . .'

Dicelle was obviously thrilled by the whole business.

'He must be the man we're looking for, don't you think?'

Maigret did not answer at once. He lit his pipe with great deliberation. They were less than a hundred yards from the house of the lady in lilac.

'I think he is,' he said with a sigh.

The young detective stared at him in amazement. From the way the Chief Superintendent said it, one would really think he regretted it!

'I'm to meet my chief outside the hotel. He'll be there in twenty minutes at the outside.'

'Did he say whether he wanted me there?'

'He said you'd be sure to come.'

'I'll have to let my wife know first.'

In the interval, crowds of people poured out of the Grand Casino theatre into the street. Most of the women were wearing sleeveless dresses, cut very low. They and their escorts looked up apprehensively into the sky, which was streaked with intermittent lightning flashes.

Low clouds swirled past, and, worse, to the west, the stars

were blotted out by a dense, threatening blanket of cloud, moving slowly towards the town.

Outside the Hotel des Ambassadeurs, Maigret and Dicelle waited in silence, watched by the hall porter who, behind his counter of polished wood, stood guard over his nest of pigeon-holes and panel of dangling keys.

Just as the first few heavy drops of cold rain were falling, Lecœur arrived, and, at the same moment, a bell rang, signalling the end of the interval. It took him some minutes of careful steering and manoeuvring to park his car, and, when he finally joined them, he asked, with a worried frown:

'Is he in his room?'

Dicelle quickly reassured him:

'Number 105 on the first floor. His windows overlook the street. . . .'

'Is his wife with him?'

'Yes. They went up together.'

A figure, a uniformed constable whom Maigret did not recognize, loomed up out of the shadows.

'Am I to stay on watch?' he whispered.

'Yes.'

Lecœur, taking shelter in the doorway, lit a cigarette.

'I am not empowered to make an arrest during the hours between sunset and sunrise, unless a breach of the law is actually committed in my presence.'

There was more than a hint of irony in his voice as he cited this section of the Code of Criminal Procedure, adding thoughtfully:

'What's more, there isn't enough evidence to justify a warrant for his arrest.'

It sounded like an appeal to Maigret to help him out of his difficulty, but Maigret did not rise to the bait.

'I don't like leaving him to stew all night. . . . He must have guessed that he's a marked man . . . why else should he have changed his mind about telephoning? . . . and I'm puzzled by the presence of his wife, so close to the call-box. . . .'
Almost reproachfully, he added:

'What do you say, chief?'

'I have nothing to say. . . .'

'What would you do, in my place?'

'I shouldn't be inclined to wait, either. . . . I daresay, by now, they're undressing for bed. . . . I should try and avoid going up to their suite. . . . A discreet little note, sent up by hand, should meet the case. . . .'

'Saying what, for instance?'

'That there's someone downstairs who wishes to speak to him on a personal matter. . . .'

'Do you think he'll come?'

'I'm sure of it.'

'You'd better wait out here, Dicelle. It wouldn't do for us all to be seen going in together.'

Lecœur went up to the enquiry desk, leaving Maigret standing in the middle of the vast entrance hall, looking about him vaguely. The hall, brilliantly lit by chandeliers, was almost empty, except for an elderly foursome, two men and two women, a long way off—in another world almost—who were playing bridge. Distance and the deliberation of their movements made them seem unreal, like characters in a film sequence played in slow motion.

The page-boy, with an envelope in his hand, went briskly up to the lift.

He heard Lecœur's voice, muffled:

'Well, we'll soon see. . . .'

Then, as though struck by the solemnity of the occasion, he removed his hat. Maigret, too, was bareheaded, holding his straw hat in his hand. Outside, the storm had broken and the rain was pelting down. They could see a little group of people, huddled for shelter on the hotel steps.

In a very short time, the page-boy was back.

'Monsieur Pélardeau will be down directly,' he announced.

They were both watching the lift. They could not help themselves. Lecœur was smoothing his moustache with his forefinger, and Maigret could sense his excitement.

Somewhere up there, a bell was ringing. The lift went up, stopped for a moment, and then reappeared.

Out of it stepped a man in a dark suit, with a florid complexion and greying hair. He looked enquiringly round the hall, and then, somewhat hesitantly, came up to the two men.

Lecœur, who was holding his superintendent's badge discreetly in the palm of his hand, allowed the man to catch a glimpse of it.

'I should be obliged if I could have a few words with you, Monsieur Pélardeau.'

'Now?'

Yes, there was the hoarse voice, just as it had been described to them. The man did not lose his head. There was no doubt that he recognized Maigret, and seemed surprised to find him playing a passive role.

'Yes, now. My car is at the door, if you will be so good as to accompany mc to my office.'

The florid cheeks turned a shade paler. Pélardeau was a man of about sixty, but his carriage was remarkably upright, and there was great dignity in his bearing and expression.

'I don't suppose it would do any good to refuse.'

'None. It would only make matters worse.'

A glance at the hall porter, then another at the little far-off alcove, where the four bridge players were still to be seen. A quick look outside at the pouring rain.

'I don't suppose it would be possible for me to get my hat and raincoat from my suite?'

Maigret, meeting Lecœur's enquiring glance, looked up at the ceiling. It would be cruel, as well as pointless, to leave the wife in suspense up there. It looked like being a long night, and there was little hope of the husband's returning to reassure her.

Lecœur murmured:

'If you would care to write Madame a note . . . unless she already knows?'

'No. . . . What shall I say?'

'I don't know. . . . That you have been detained longer than you expected?'

The man went up to the desk.

'Can you let me have a sheet of writing paper, Marcel?'

He seemed saddened, rather than shocked or frightened. Using the ball-point pen chained to the desk, he scribbled a few words, declining the envelope that the hall porter held out to him.

'Send this up in five or ten minutes' time, will you?'

'Certainly, sir.'

The hall porter looked as though he would have liked to say something more, but, unable to find the right words, merely bowed his head.

'This way.'

As Dicelle, by this time sopping wet, opened the rear door, Lecœur stood by, murmuring instructions in a low voice.

'Get in, please.'

The industrialist bent down, and got into the car first.

'You too, chief.'

Maigret, aware that his colleague would not wish their prisoner to be left alone in the back of the car, obeyed. In no time, they were driving through the streets crowded with people hurrying for shelter and huddling together under the trees. There were even people sheltering on the bandstand, under the canopy.

The car turned into the forecourt of the Police Station in the Avenue Victoria, and Lecœur spoke a few words to the constable on duty. There were only one or two lights turned on in the entrance. It seemed a long time to Maigret before they reached Lecœur's office.

'In here. It's a bit spartan, but I didn't want to take you all the way to Clermont-Ferrand at this stage.'

He removed his hat, but did not venture to take off his jacket, which, like Lecœur's and Maigret's, was sopping wet about the shoulders. In contrast with the sudden drop in temperature outdoors, the room was very hot and stuffy.

'Take a seat.'

Maigret had retreated into his usual corner, and was watching the industrialist, under cover of filling his pipe. The man's face was absolutely impassive, as he looked from one police officer to the other, wondering, no doubt, why Maigret was not playing a more active role.

267

Lecœur, playing for time, pulled a memo pad and pencil towards him, and murmured, as though thinking aloud:

'Anything you say at this stage will be off the record. This is not an official interrogation.'

The man nodded assent.

'Your name is Louis Pélardeau, and you are an industrialist. You live in Paris, in the Boulevard Suchet.'

'That's right.'

'Married, I take it?'

'Yes.'

'Any children?'

After an appreciable pause, he said with an odd note of bitterness:

'No.'

'You are here for the cure?'

'Yes.'

'Is this your first visit to Vichy?'

'I've passed through it in the car. . . .'

'You've never come here with the specific intention of meeting any particular person?'

'No.'

Lecœur inserted a cigarette into his holder, and lit it. There followed an oppressive silence, then Lecœur said:

'You know, I presume, why I have brought you here?'

The man, his face still impassive, took time for thought. But Maigret could now see that his blank expression was not a sign of self-control, but rather of profound emotional shock.

He was completely numbed, and it was hard to tell whether he realized even where he was, as Lecœur's voice rang in his ears.

'I would rather not answer that. . . .'

'You came here of your own free will. . . .'

'Yes. . . .'

'You were not unprepared?'

The man turned to Maigret, as though appealing for help, and repeated wearily:

'I would rather not answer that. . . .'

Lecœur, aware that this was getting him nowhere, doodled on his pad before returning to the attack.

'Soon after your arrival in Vichy, you had an unexpected encounter with someone you had not seen for fifteen years. . . .'

The man's eyes were watering a little, but not with tears. It was perhaps due to the harsh glare of the single naked bulb, which provided all the lighting there was in this bare, normally unoccupied room.

'Was it your intention, when you went out with your wife tonight, to make a telephone call from a public box?'

After a moment's hesitation, the man nodded.

'In other words, your wife knows nothing?'

'About the telephone call?'

'If you like to put it that way.'

'No.'

'You mean that there are some matters regarding which she is not in your confidence?'

'You're absolutely right.'

'Nevertheless, you did go into a public call-box. . . .'

'She decided, at the last minute, to come with me. . . . I didn't want to put it off any longer. . . . I told her I'd left the key of our suite in the door, and that I thought I'd better let the hall porter know. . . .'

'Why was it that you didn't even finish dialling the number?'

'I had a feeling I was being watched. . . .'

'Did you see anyone?'

'I saw something move behind a tree. . . . Besides, by then I had realized that it was pointless. . . .'

'Why was that?'

He did not answer, but sat motionless, with his hands lying flat on his knees. They were plump, white, well-kept hands.

'Smoke, if you wish.'

'I don't smoke.'

'You don't mind if I do?'

'My wife smokes a lot . . . far too much. . . .'

'You suspected that the call might be taken by someone other than Francine Lange?'

Once again he did not answer, but neither did he deny it.

'You telephoned her last night, and told her that you would ring again to fix an appointment. . . . It's my belief that, when you went into that call-box this evening, you had already, in your own mind, fixed on a time and place.'

'I'm sorry, but I can't help you there. . . .'

He was having difficulty with his breathing, and wheezing slightly as he spoke.

'I assure you, it's not that I want to be obstructive. . . .'

'You would prefer to consult your lawyer first?'

He made a sweeping gesture with his right hand, as though to brush this suggestion aside.

'All the same, you will need a lawyer.'

'I'll do whatever the law requires of me.'

'You must understand, Monsieur Pélardeau, that, as from now, you are no longer a free man.'

Lecœur showed some delicacy in avoiding the word 'arrest', and Maigret was glad of it.

The man had made an impression on both of them. Here, in this tiny office with its dingy walls, sitting on a rough wooden chair, he seemed larger than life-size, and this impression of stature was enhanced by his astonishingly calm and dignified manner.

Both men had, in their time, questioned many hundreds of suspects. It took a lot to impress them, but this man was truly impressive.

'We could postpone this conversation until tomorrow, but, as I'm sure you'll agree, it would serve no useful purpose.'

This, the man seemed to be thinking, was the Superintendent's business, not his.

'What is your particular branch of industry?'

'Steel pressings.'

This was a subject on which he could talk freely, and he volunteered one or two particulars, just to show that he was willing to co-operate where he could.

'I inherited a small wire-drawing business near Le Havre from my father. Then gradually I was able to expand and build a plant at Rouen, and another in Strasbourg.'

'In other words, you run a very flourishing business?'

'Yes.'

He seemed almost to be apologizing for it.

'Your offices are in Paris, I take it?'

'Head office, yes. We have more up-to-date office buildings in Rouen and Strasbourg, but, for sentimental reasons, I've always kept the old head office in the Boulevard Voltaire.'

It was all past history to him. . . . This evening, in the space of time it took a liveried page-boy to deliver a written message, the greater part of his world had crumbled in ruins.

Probably because he was aware of this, he was willing to talk about it quite freely.

'Have you been married long?'

'Thirty years.'

'A woman of the name of Hélène Lange was at one time in your employment, was she not?'

'I'd rather not answer that.'

This was his unvarying response, whenever they stepped on dangerous ground.

'You do realize, don't you, Monsieur Pélardeau, that you're making things very difficult for me?'

'I'm sorry.'

'If it is your intention to deny the facts which I shall lay before you, I would rather you said so now.'

'How can I tell in advance what you are going to say?'

'Are you telling me that you are not guilty?'

'No. . . . In a sense, I am. . . .'

Lecœur and Maigret exchanged glances. He had made this terrible admission so simply and unaffectedly, without the slightest change of expression.

Maigret was thinking of the park with its great, spreading trees, its expanses of grass which, under the lamp standards, seemed too green to be true, its bandstand and garishly uniformed musicians.

In particular, he was thinking of the long, narrow face of Hélène Lange as he had seen it when, to him and his wife, she was merely the nameless woman they had christened 'the lady in lilac'.

271

'Did you know Mademoiselle Lange?'

He sat motionless, gasping as though he were going to choke. It was, in fact, an attack of asthma. He grew purple in the face. He took a handkerchief from his pocket, held it over his open mouth, and was soon doubled up with a fit of uncontrollable coughing.

Maigret was thankful not to be in his colleague's seat. Let someone else do the dirty work for once.

'I told you. . . .'

'Please take your time. . . .'

With eyes streaming, he fought to master the attack of coughing, but it persisted for several minutes.

When at last he straightened up, still red in the face, mopped his forehead and said: 'I'm very sorry . . .' the words were scarcely audible.

'I get these attacks several times a day. . . . Dr. Rian tells me that the cure will do me good. . . .'

He seemed suddenly struck with the irony of this remark.

'I should say, would have done me good. . . .'

They shared the same doctor, he and Maigret. Both had undressed in the same gleaming surgery, both had stretched out on the same couch, over which a white sheet was spread. . . .

'What was it you asked me?'

'Whether you knew Hélène Lange.'

'There's no point in denying it.'

'You hated her, didn't you?'

If it had been possible, Maigret would have signalled to his colleague that he was on the wrong track.

And indeed the man was staring at Lecœur in genuine amazement. When at last he spoke, this sixty-year-old man sounded as artless as a child.

'Why?' he whispered. 'Why should I have hated her?'

He turned to Maigret, as if appealing to him for support.

'Were you in love with her?'

His response was a puzzled frown, which surprised them both. Clearly the last two questions had thrown him off balance and, in some strange sense, changed everything.

'I don't quite see . . .' he stammered.

272

Then, once more, he looked from one to the other. At Maigret he looked hard and long.

It was as though they were somehow at cross-purposes.

'You used to go and see her at her flat in the Rue Notre-Dame-de-Lorette.'

'Yes,' in a tone of voice that implied, 'What of it?'

'I presume that it was you who paid her rent?'

He confirmed this with a slight nod.

'Was she your secretary?'

'She was a member of my staff.'

'Did your affair with her last long, several years?'

It was obvious that they were still at cross-purposes.

'I used to go and see her once or twice a week.'

'Did your wife know?'

'Obviously not.'

'She never found out?'

'Never.'

'Doesn't she know, even now?'

The poor man clearly felt that he was beating his head against a brick wall.

'Not even now. . . . All that has nothing to do with . . .'

Nothing to do with what? With the murder? With the telephone calls? They weren't speaking the same language, but neither realized it. No wonder they were baffled by their inability to get across to one another.

273

CHAPTER SEVEN

LECŒUR'S GLANCE fell on the telephone on his desk. He seemed about to lift the receiver, when he caught sight of a small white bell-push, and pressed that instead.

'Do you mind? . . . I don't know where this rings, or even if it's working. . . . We'll soon find out at any rate. . . . If anyone comes. . . .'

He was playing for time. They waited in silence, avoiding one another's eyes. Of the three men, Pélardeau was probably the most self-possessed, on the surface at least. Admittedly, as far as he was concerned, he had staked his all, and had nothing more to lose.

They heard at last, a long way off, the ringing sound of footsteps on an iron staircase, then on the linoleum of a corridor, drawing nearer, followed by a discreet knock on the door.

'Come in!'

It was a very young, well-scrubbed constable in uniform. In contrast to the three older men, he fairly radiated youthful vitality.

Lecœur, who felt something of an interloper in this place, said:

'I wonder if you could spare a moment?'

'Of course, sir. We were just passing the time playing cards.'

'We're going out for a moment. Be so good as to stay with Monsieur Pélardeau until we get back.'

'It'll be a pleasure, sir.'

The constable, having not the least idea of what it was all about, kept darting puzzled glances at the well-groomed visitor. He could not but be impressed.

A minute or two later, Lecœur and Maigret were standing in the doorway. The steps leading down to the forecourt were protected by an awning, but they could see a glittering curtain of rain in the darkness beyond.

'I was suffocating up there. . . . I thought you might be glad of a breath of fresh air too.'

The heavy storm clouds, streaked from time to time with lightning flashes, were now overhead, and the wind had dropped. The road was deserted, except for an occasional slow-moving car splashing through the puddles.

The head of the C.I.D. in Clermont-Ferrand, lighting a cigarette, watched the rain beating down on the metalled drive, and dripping from the trees in the grounds.

'I know I was making a hash of it, chief. I ought to have asked you to take over. . . .'

'He was at the end of his tether, numbed with shock. At first, there didn't seem any point in answering your questions. He was determined not to speak, whatever the cost. But, little by little, you won his confidence. . . . What more could I have done?'

'I thought. . . .'

'You succeeded, up to a point, in breaking down the barriers. . . . He was beginning to take an interest . . . to co-operate even. . . . Then something went wrong. . . . I don't understand it. It must have been something you said. . . .'

'What?'

'I don't know. . . . All I know is that it switched him off like a light. . . . I never took my eyes off his face, and at one point I caught a look of absolute astonishment and bewilderment. One would have to go back over every word that was said. . . . He had been so sure we knew more. . . .'

'More about what?'

Maigret sucked at his pipe in silence for a moment.

'Something that to him is patently obvious, but that we have missed. . . .'

'Maybe I should have had someone sitting in, taking a note of the interview. . . .'

'You wouldn't have got a word out of him. . . .'

'Are you sure you wouldn't prefer to take over from here, chief?'

'Not only would it be irregular, a point which his lawyer might well exploit at a later stage, but I shouldn't handle it any better than you. Quite possibly not so well.'

'I honestly don't know where I go from here. The worst of it is that, murderer though he is, I can't help feeling sorry for him. . . . I'm just not used to handling that sort of man. . . . He doesn't belong in the realm of crime. . . . When we came out of the hotel just now, I felt as though he had left a world in ruins behind him. . . .'

'So did he.'

'Do you really think so?'

'He refused to play on our sympathy, like a beggar in the streets. . . . He was determined to keep some semblance of dignity, whatever the cost. . . .'

'Will he break down in the end, I wonder . . . ?'

'He'll talk.'

'Tonight?'

'I shouldn't be surprised.'

'Should we carry on here or . . . ?'

Maigret opened his mouth as though about to speak, then, apparently thinking better of it, closed it again, and relit his pipe. At last he said evasively:

'Don't spring it on him all at once, but you might try leading up to the subject of Mesnil-le-Mont. You could, for instance, ask him if he'd ever been there?'

Lecœur couldn't make out whether he himself attached any great importance to this.

'Do you think the answer will be yes?'

'I couldn't say.'

'Why should he have gone there, and what possible bearing could it have on what happened here in Vichy?'

'It was just a thought,' replied Maigret apologetically. 'When one is adrift, one clutches at straws. . . .'

There was another very young constable on duty near the entrance, and, in his eyes, the two men standing talking on the stairs were persons of tremendous importance, who had reached the very pinnacle of eminence.

'I wouldn't say no to a glass of beer.'

There was a bar on the corner, but there was no possibility of getting to it in this downpour. As for Maigret, the very word 'beer' brought a wry smile to his lips. He had given his word to Rian, and he meant to keep it.

'We'd better go back.'

They found the constable leaning against the wall. He sprang smartly to attention, and stood motionless, while the prisoner looked from one to the other of the older men.

'Thanks, lad . . . you can go now.'

Lecœur returned to his seat, and began fidgeting with the memo pad, the pencil and the telephone.

'I wanted to give you a little time to think, Monsieur Pélardeau. I have no wish to harass you or tie you up in knots. For the present, I'm just feeling my way. . . . One tries to form a general picture, but sometimes one gets hold of the wrong end of the stick. . . .'

He was feeling his way, trying to strike the right note, like a musician tuning up before a concert. The man was watching him closely, but still betrayed no sign of emotion.

'You had been married some time, I take it, when you first met Hélène Lange?'

'I was over forty . . . no longer a young man. . . . I had been married fourteen years. . . .'

'Was it a love-match?'

'Love is a word that has different meanings at different stages of a man's life. . . .'

'At any rate, it wasn't a cold-blooded marriage of convenience?'

'No. . . . It was my own free choice. . . . And, in that connection, I have nothing to regret, except the misery I have brought upon my wife. . . . We're very good friends, and always have been. . . . No one could have been more understanding. . . .'

'Even on the subject of Hélène Lange?'

'I never told her. . . .'

'Why not?'

He looked from one to the other.

'It was something I just couldn't talk about. . . . I've never had much to do with women. . . . I've worked hard all my life, and I think perhaps, even in middle age, I was a bit naïve. . . .'

'Was it infatuation?'

'I don't know if that's the right word for it . . . Hélène was different from anyone I had ever known. . . . I was attracted by her, and yet somehow afraid of her. . . . She was so intense, I didn't know what I was doing. . . .'

'You became lovers?'

'Not at first . . . not for a very long time. . . .'

'You mean, she kept you dangling?'

'No, I was reluctant to. . . . You see, she had never had a lover. . . . But all this must seem very commonplace to you, I daresay. . . . I loved her . . . or rather, I thought I did. . . . She made no demands. . . . She seemed content to occupy a very small place in my life . . . just the few hours once or twice a week that you mentioned. . . .'

'Was there ever any question of divorce?'

'Never! Besides, in a different way, I still loved my wife. . . . I would never have agreed to leave her. . . .'

Poor man! He should have stuck to his office, his factories and his board meetings, where he knew his way about!

'Did she break it off?'

'Yes. . . .'

Lecœur and Maigret exchanged a brief glance.

'Tell me, Monsieur Pélardeau, did you go to Mesnil-le-Mont?'

His face took on an unhealthy, purple flush. With eyes lowered, he stammered: 'No.'

'But you knew she was there?'

'Not at the time. . . .'

'Was this after you had parted?'

'She had told me she never wanted to see me again.'

'Why was that?'

Once again, that look of utter bewilderment, as though he simply could not make out what was going on.

'She didn't want our child to. . . .'

This time, it was Lecœur whose eyes widened in amazement, while Maigret, apparently not in the least surprised, sat comfortably hunched up, like a contented cat.

'What are you talking about? What child?'

'Why, Hélène's . . . my son. . . .'

In spite of himself, a touch of pride crept into his voice, as he spoke of his son.

'Are you telling me that she had a child by you . . . ?'

'Yes . . . my son, Philippe. . . .'

Lecœur was seething.

'And she hoodwinked you into believing that. . . .'

But the man was shaking his head gently.

'There was no question of hoodwinking. . . . I have proof. . . .'

'What proof?'

'A copy of the birth certificate.'

'Signed by the Mayor of Mesnil-le-Mont?'

'Naturally.'

'And the woman named as the mother was Hélène Lange?'

'Of course.'

'And yet you never went to see this child, whom you believed to be your son?'

'Whom I believe to be my son . . . who is my son. . . . I didn't go because I didn't know where Hélène had hidden herself away to have the child. . . .'

'Why all the mystery?'

'Because she was determined that nothing should be done which might, at a later date—how can I put it?—place the child in an equivocal position. . . .'

'Wasn't that rather an old-fashioned view to take?'

'You could say so. . . . But Hélène was old-fashioned in some ways. . . . She had a strong sense of. . . .'

'See here, Monsieur Pélardeau, I think I'm beginning to understand, but for the moment, if you don't mind, we'll leave sentiment out of it. . . . Forgive me for putting it so bluntly, but facts are facts, and there's nothing either of us can do about them. . . .'

'I don't see what you're getting at. . . .'

His outward self-assurance was beginning to give way to a vague uneasiness.

'Did you know Francine Lange?'

'No.'

'You never met her in Paris?'

'No. Not in Paris or anywhere else.'

'Didn't you know Hélène had a sister?'

'Yes. She used to talk of a younger sister. . . . They were orphans. . . . Hélène left college so that her sister . . .'

Unable to contain himself any longer, Lecœur got to his feet. He remained standing. If there had been room for it, he would have worked off his fury by pacing up and down.

'Go on. . . . Go on. . . .'

He wiped his forehead with the back of his hand.

'So that her sister should have the education she deserved. . . .'

'The education she deserved, indeed! Don't hold it against me, Monsieur Pélardeau . . . but I'm going to have to cause you a great deal of pain. . . . I ought perhaps to have set about things differently, to have prepared you for the truth. . . .'

'What truth?'

'At fifteen, her sister was a hairdresser's assistant in La Rochelle. She was also, at that time, living with a taxi driver, and he was only the first of heaven knows how many men. . . .'

'She showed me her letters. . . .'

'Whose letters?'

'Francine's. She was at a well-known boarding school in Switzerland.'

'Did you actually go there and see for yourself?'

'No, of course not.'

'Did you keep her letters?'

'No, I just glanced through them.'

'And during the whole of that time, Francine was working as a manicurist in a hairdresser's in the Champs-Elysées! Don't you see, the whole thing, from beginning to end, was a sham? . . .'

The man was still putting up a fight. . . . But his self-control, though still remarkable, was beginning to crumble, and suddenly his mouth twisted in an expression so pitiable that Maigret and Lecœur could not bear to look at him.

'It's not possible,' he stammered.

'Regrettably, it's the truth.'

'But why?'

It was a last desperate bid to avert his fate. Let them say right out, here and now, that it wasn't true, that it was an ignoble police trick to undermine his resistance.

'I'm sorry, Monsieur Pélardeau. Until tonight, up to this very minute, I too never suspected the extent to which those two were in collusion. . . .'

He started to lower himself into his chair, but then sprang up again. He was still too overwrought to sit down.

'Did Hélène never raise the subject of marriage?'

'No. . . .'

This time, he sounded less confident.

'Even when she told you she was pregnant?'

'She didn't want to break up my home. . . .'

'In other words, you did discuss marriage. . . .'

'Not in the way you mean. . . . Only to explain why she was proposing to disappear. . . .'

'To commit suicide?'

'There was never any question of that. . . . But as the child would not be legitimate. . . .'

Lecœur sighed and, once more, exchanged glances with Maigret. Each knew what the other was thinking. Both, in imagination, were dwelling on the exchanges that must have taken place between Hélène Lange and her lover.

'You don't believe me. . . . I myself. . . .'

'You must try and face up to the truth. . . . Self-deception won't help you now. . . .'

'Can anything help me now?'

With a sweeping gesture, he indicated the walls of the little office, as though, to him, they were the walls of a prison cell.

'Let me finish. . . . I know it will sound mawkish to you, but she wanted to devote the rest of her life to bringing up our child, in the same way as she had brought up her sister.'

'And you were not to be allowed to see your child?'

'On what terms? How could she explain me to him?'

'You might have been an uncle . . . a friend. . . .'

'Hélène hated lying. . . .'

His voice had suddenly taken on a faintly ironic inflexion It was a hopeful sign.

'So she was determined that your son should never know that you were his father?'

'Later, when he came of age, she was going to tell him. . . .'

He added, in his strange, hoarse voice:

'He's fifteen now. . . .'

Lecœur and Maigret listened in painful silence.

'When I saw her in Vichy, I decided. . . .'

'Go on.'

'That I must see him, or at least find out where he was. . . .'

'And did you?'

He shook his head, and, this time, there were real tears in his eyes.

'No.'

'Did Hélène tell you where she was going to have the child?'

'In a village she knew. . . . She didn't tell me the name. . . . Then, two months later, she sent me a copy of the birth certificate. . . . The letter was posted in Marseilles. . . .'

'How much money did you give her before she left?'

'Does it matter?'

'It matters a great deal, as you will see.'

'Twenty thousand francs. . . . I sent thirty thousand more to her in Marseilles. . . . Naturally, it was my wish that, thereafter, she should have a regular allowance, to enable her to give our son the best of everything. . . .'

'Five thousand francs a month?'

'Yes. . . .'

'What reason did she give for wanting the money to be sent to a different town each time . . . ?'

'She was afraid I wouldn't have the will-power. . . .'

'Was that what she said?'

'Yes. . . . I had agreed, in the end, not to see the child until he came of age. . . .'

Lecœur's look plainly asked Maigret:

'What's to be done?'

But Maigret only blinked rapidly two or three times, and bit hard on the stem of his pipe.

CHAPTER EIGHT

LECŒUR was sitting down, having lowered himself very slowly into his seat. He turned to the man whose puckered face revealed all that he had just had to endure, and said, almost sorrowfully:

'I'm going to have to cause you still more pain, Monsieur Pélardeau.'

The man responded with an embittered smile, as though to say:

'Is that possible, do you think?'

'I feel for you, and indeed respect you as a man. . . . I'm not fabricating all this to trick you into making admissions which, anyway, would be superfluous. . . . What I have to tell you now, like everything I have told you so far, is strictly true, and no one is more sorry than I am that the truth should be so harsh. . . .'

A pause, to give his hearer time to prepare himself.

'You never had a son by Hélène Lange.'

He had expected a vehement denial, or at least a violent outburst of some sort, but he was met with a blank, expressionless stare, and silence. This was a broken man.

'Did you never have any suspicion?'

Pélardeau raised his head, shook it, and put his hand to his throat to indicate that, for the moment, he was unable to speak. He barely had time to get his handkerchief out of his pocket when he was racked by another attack of asthma, more violent than the first.

In the silence that followed, Maigret became aware that outside too it had grown silent. The thunder had ceased, and the rain was no longer thudding down.

'I'm sorry. . . .'

'You did have occasion to suspect the truth, didn't you?'

'Once. . . . Only once.'

'When?'

'Here . . . that night. . . .'

'When did you first see her?'

'Two days before. . . .'

'Did you follow her?'

'Yes, keeping out of sight . . . to find out where she lived. . . . I was waiting for her to come out with my son, or to see him come out alone. . . .'

'On Monday night, did you speak to her as she was going into the house?'

'No. . . . I saw the lodgers go out. . . . I knew she was in the park, listening to the music. . . . She always liked music. . . . I had no difficulty in opening the door. . . . The key of my hotel room fitted the lock. . . .'

'You searched through the drawers?'

'The first thing I noticed was that there was only a single bed. . . .'

'What about the photographs?'

'They were all of her. . . . Not one of anyone else. . . . I would have given anything to have found a photograph of a child. . . .'

'And letters?'

'Yes. . . . I couldn't understand it. . . . There was nothing. . . . Even if Philippe was away at boarding school, he must have. . . .'

'And she found you there when she got in?'

'Yes. . . . I begged her to tell me where our son was. . . . I remember asking her if he was dead . . . if there had been an accident.'

'And she wouldn't answer?'

'She took it all much more calmly than I did. She reminded me of our pact.'

'That she would give you your son when he reached the age of twenty-one?'

'Yes. . . . On condition that I should never make any attempt to see him before then.'

'Did she talk about him?'

'In great detail. . . . About when he cut his first teeth. . . . His childhood ailments. . . . The nurse she engaged to look after him when she herself was unwell. . . . Then school. . . . She gave me almost a day-by-day account of his life. . . .'

'But she never said where he was?'

'No. . . . She said that recently he had begun to take a great interest in medicine . . . that he wanted to become a doctor. . . .'

He looked straight at the Superintendent, without embarrassment.

'There was no such boy?'

'Yes, there was. . . . But he was not your son. . . .'

'You mean, there was another man?'

Lecœur shook his head.

'It was Francine Lange who gave birth to a son at Mesnil-le-Mont. . . . I confess that, until you told me so yourself, I had no idea that Hélène Lange had registered the child as her own. . . . The plan must have occurred to the two sisters when Francine Lange found she was pregnant. . . . If I know anything about Francine, her first thought must have been to get rid of it. . . . Her sister was more far-sighted. . . .'

'It came to me in a flash . . . as I told you. . . . That night, when I found that she was deaf to my entreaties, I used threats. . . . For fifteen years, I had looked forward with longing to the time when I should see this son of mine. . . . My wife and I have no children of our own. . . . When I knew that I was a father. . . . But what's the use?'

'You took her by the throat?'

'To frighten her. . . . To make her talk . . . I shouted at her . . . I demanded the truth . . . I never thought of the sister . . . but I feared that the child was dead, or crippled. . . .'

His hands slipped out of his lap and hung down limply, as though all the strength of that great, burly frame had drained away.

'I squeezed too hard. . . . I didn't realize. . . . If only she had shown the faintest spark of feeling! . . . But she didn't . . . not even of fear. . . .'

'When you read in the paper that her sister was in Vichy, it gave you fresh hope?'

285

'If the child was alive and Hélène was the only person who knew where he was, there was no one left to care for him. . . . I knew I must expect to be arrested at any time. . . . You must have found my fingerprints. . . .'

'Without knowing whose they were . . . though, in the end, we would have caught up with you. . . .'

'I had to know . . . to make provision. . . .'

'You worked your way, in alphabetical order, through the list of hotels. . . .'

'How did you know?'

It was childish, but Lecœur badly felt the need of a boost to his self-esteem.

'Each time you used a different call-box.'

'So you had tracked me down already?'

'Almost.'

'But what about Philippe?'

'Francine Lange's son was put out to foster-parents soon after birth—a family called Berteaux, small tenant farmers at Saint André-de-Lavion in the Vosges. . . . The sisters used your money to buy a hairdressing salon in La Rochelle. . . . Neither of them took the slightest interest in the child. . . . He lived with his foster-parents in the country until, at the age of two-and-a-half, he was drowned in a pond.'

'He's dead, then?'

'Yes. . . . But, as far as you were concerned, he had to be kept alive. All that about his childhood, his early schooling, his pranks, and his recent interest in medicine, was made up on the spur of the moment.'

'How monstrous!'

'Yes.'

'To think that any woman could. . . .'

He shook his head.

'It's not that I don't believe you . . . but somehow, my whole being revolts. . . .'

'It's not the first case of its kind in the history of crime. . . . I could tell you of others. . . .'

'No,' he begged. He sat hunched up, limp. There was nothing left for him to cling to.

'You were quite right just now, when you said that you didn't need a lawyer. . . . You have only to tell your story to a jury. . . .'

He put his head in his hands and sat there, very still.

'Your wife must be getting anxious. . . . In my opinion, it would be kinder to tell her the truth—otherwise she'll be imagining much worse things. . . .'

He raised a flushed face to Lecœur. He had probably forgotten her until then.

'What am I going to say to her?'

'Unfortunately, for the present, you won't have an opportunity of saying anything to her. . . . I am not at liberty to release you, even for a very short time. . . . You will have to accompany me to Clermont-Ferrand. But, unless the examining magistrate objects, which I'm certain he won't, your wife will be able to visit you there.'

Pélardeau, deeply disturbed on his wife's account, turned, in desperation, to Maigret:

'Couldn't you see to it?'

Maigret looked enquiringly at Lecœur, who shrugged as if to say that it was no concern of his.

'I'll do my best.'

'You'll have to be careful, because my wife has suffered from a weak heart for some years. . . . We're neither of us young any more. . . .'

Nor was Maigret. Tonight, he felt old. He couldn't wait to get back to his wife, and resume the humdrum routine of their daily life, walking through the streets of Vichy, sitting on the little yellow chairs in the park.

They went downstairs together.

'Do you want a lift, chief?'

'I'd rather walk.'

The streets were glistening. The black car, taking Lecœur and Pélardeau to Clermont-Ferrand, disappeared in the distance.

Maigret lit his pipe and, without thinking, put his hands in his pockets. It wasn't cold, but the temperature had dropped several degrees after the storm.

The shrubs on either side of the entrance to the Hôtel de la Bérézina were dripping.

'Here you are at last!' exclaimed Madame Maigret, getting out of bed to welcome him. 'I dreamt you were at the Quai des Orfèvres questioning a suspect, and having beer sent up to you every five minutes. . . .'

But, when she had had time to take a good look at him, her voice changed, and she murmured:

'It's over then?'

'Yes.'

'Who did it?'

'A very respectable man. He had charge of thousands of office and factory workers, but he never learnt much about the ways of the world.'

'I hope you'll be able to sleep late tomorrow morning.'

'I'm afraid not. . . . I've got to go and explain to his wife. . . .'

'Doesn't she know?'

'No.'

'Is she here in Vichy?'

'At the Hotel des Ambassadeurs.'

'What about him?'

'Within the next half-hour, he'll be behind bars in the cells at Clermont-Ferrand.'

She watched him closely as he undressed, but could not quite interpret his rather odd expression.

'How many years do you think he'll . . . ?'

Maigret always liked to have two or three puffs at his pipe before going to bed. He was filling it now. Without looking up, he said:

'He'll be acquitted, I hope.'

Epalinges
September 11, 1967